LP
LUCYS PEN
PUBLISHING

Library of Congress Control Number: 2025921045
ISBN: 978-8-9998788-09 (Paperback)
ISBN: 978-8-9998788-16 (eBook)

Published by **Lucys Pen Publishing LLC**
St. Louis, Missouri

Cover design by Nish Aigner
Interior design by Nish Aigner

For permissions, contact:
Lucys Pen Publishing LLC

info@lucyspen.com
www.LucysPen.com

Printed in the United States

Contents

Dedication — 1

Epigraph — 2

Preface — 3

About the author — 5

1. Mama Lucy — 7

2. The Knowing — 9

3. Mary Lou and the Dimes — 18

4. Freeman — 24

5. The House Her Father Built — 27

6. The Spirit of Talking — 31

7. The Womb is a Battlefield — 36

8. Manufactured Life — 40

9. What the Elders Saw — 44

10. The Question That Broke the Silence — 48

11. The Unraveling & The Visit — 51

12. The Wound That Talks Back — 55

13. The Porch, A Lady and a Girl　58

14. The Raven Who Named Herself　61

15. The Mirror Gate　64

16. The Four Keepers　68

17. The Storm Upstairs　73

18. The Release　77

19. A Voice of Her Own　80

20. The Root Woman of Rockwell Town　84

21. The Spirit of a Man　88

22. The Dream War　93

23. Basil for Basilisk　97

24. A Scent Not Yet Stirred　101

25. The Invitation　105

26. The Salt, The Rose, and the Whisper　108

27. Dressed in Knowing　111

28. The Club, the Craving, the Christ Flame　114

29. Holding the Flame　118

30. The Permission of Pleasure　122

31. The First Flame　125

32. The Knowing Brew　129

33. The Spirit in the Yellow Dress　133

34. Familiar Spirits Wear Family Faces 136

35. The Spirits That Never Left 139

36. The Waiting Child 143

37. His Heart Is Moving 147

38. The Alchemist's Gate 150

39. A Life Unbound 154

40. A Season of Sweeping 157

41. The Spirit at the Edge 160

42. The Woman I Was 164

43. The Wedding in the Garden 168

44. The Smoke and the Soak 172

45. The Velvet Club 176

46. The Body Speaks Back 179

47. The Return of Dalton 182

48. The Peach and the Poison 185

49. A Mirror in the Womb 189

50. The Threshold 192

51. Where Gods Lay Down Their Armor 200

52. The Sweet Return 205

53. The Tea After the Fire 208

54. The Petition 211

55. Mr. Charlie's Visit 215

56. The Steam and the Story 219

57. The Pine and the Proposal 223

58. Porchlight Communion 228

59. The Rooted Womb 231

60. The Hood and the Warning 235

61. The Milk and the Moon 239

62. The Council of Blood and Spirit 243

63. The Flame and the Flesh 247

64. The Steam Between Us 251

65. The Daughters of Her Spirit 254

66. The Smoke They Didn't Want 257

67. Smoke, Salt, and Story 261

68. What Was Stolen, What Remains 265

69. The Voices at the Market 269

70. Smoke, Blues, and Belonging 272

71. Perfume and Permission 275

72. The War in the Womb 279

73. She Who Catches Life 283

74. Turn the Child, Turn the Fear 286

75. The Right to Choose the Spirit 290

76. The Rope and the Return   296

77. The Snap of the Cord   303

78. What You Send, You Marry   306

79. No One is Above the Energy They Create   311

80. The Cost of Her Crown   314

81. Keep Your Power Clean   317

82. The Ring and the Roots   322

83. A Ring, A Reflection, A Name   325

84. The Induction of the Mother   329

85. The Gatekeeper's Dream   332

86. Spells for Sacred Love   336

87. The Women Who Came with Smoke   340

88. A Covenant of Flesh and Spirit   345

89. Bones Don't Lie   349

90. Her Freedom Papers   352

91. Sacred Union   356

92. The Breaking of Bonds   360

93. The Wrath of a Woman Scorned   364

94. Prayers That Don't Move Heaven   368

95. Freedom Papers   371

96. The Whirlwind   374

97.   The Birth of the Lightkeeper   379

98.   The Mother's Chain   385

99.   Visitors Bearing Light   391

100.   Maiden to Mother   395

Dedication

To the women who came before me, and the daughters who will come after. May this story be your bridge.

I hope I encourage you to harness, cultivate and nurse your gifts until they shine. Become one with them to unlock the God within you.

Did you get your key?

"Every generation waits for its healer. Every healer waits for the moment she can no longer hide."

— Nish Aigner

Preface

I did not write this book to entertain, I wrote it to remember.
When I look at the state of our world, I see what happens
when wisdom is silenced. When grandmothers are dismissed.
When crones are pushed aside and forgotten. In the absence of
their voices, our homes grow weaker, our morals shift, and our
communities lose their anchor.

Lucille: Maiden to Mother is the beginning of a trilogy that
seeks to restore what has been lost. This story is a song for
the women who endured, who carried fire in their hands and
healing in their words. It is a testimony to the way our grandmothers spoke life into us, even when the world tried to strip
it away.

I call this spiritual fiction because while the characters are imag-
ined, the truths within them are not. The skeleton key, the salt,
the bay leaves, the dimes , these are not just symbols in a story.
They are remnants of knowledge, pieces of a larger tapestry that
our ancestors wove to protect, to guide, and to sustain us.

This book is not perfect, but it is honest. It is my offering to the matriarchs, the mothers, the crones, the healers, who deserve to be remembered as beautiful, radiant, and sacred.

If you hear a voice in these pages that sounds like your grandmother, or if a sentence feels like something your spirit already knew, then I pray you hold it close. That is the gift of our lineage: wisdom does not die, it returns.

Thank you for walking with me into this story. May you find pieces of yourself in Lucille, and may you remember the light that has always been yours.

~ Nish Aigner

This book does not apologize for preaching. It stands as a sermon, a testimony, and a love letter to the wisdom of our grandmothers, the wisdom we cannot afford to lose.

About the author

Nish Aigner is a writer of spiritual fiction whose work bridges ancestral wisdom, women's voices, and the healing of generational bloodlines. Through her stories, she weaves the sacred and the everyday, inviting readers to step into a world where the past still speaks, and the future waits to be birthed.

Born with a gift for storytelling rooted in faith and resilience, Nish believes in the power of words to restore, empower, and guide. Her debut novel, *Lucille: Maiden to Mother*, is the first in a trilogy exploring transformation, legacy, and light.

When she is not writing, Nish is nurturing her vision through Lucys Pen Publishing, a company dedicated to lifting stories that carry depth, spirit, and truth. She is also a devoted mother, student of health and healing, and advocate for women and girls finding their voices.

Her mission is to remind women that their stories are keys, unlocking light for generations to come.

You can follow Nish's journey and future works through Lucys Pen Publishing on social media, or by visiting her online home at:

www.LucysPen.com

Chapter One

Mama Lucy

Mama Lucy didn't need to knock. When she arrived, doors unlocked themselves. Children ran to greet her with open arms, and grown folks straightened their posture as if the mere sight of her demanded better manners.

She was grace wrapped in wisdom, with silver curls pulled into a neat bun and eyes that had seen more than most dared to imagine.

Her home sat on the edge of a humble town in Mississippi, always scented with eucalyptus and sage, and very welcoming for pure spirits.

Folks came to her for all kinds of reasons, a fevered baby, a stubborn cough, a broken spirit, or a dream they couldn't make sense of.

Mama Lucy had something for all of it, some tea, a touch, a prayer, or a silence that said more than words ever could.

The church women said, "She was blessed," the old men said, "She was sharp," and the gossip at the corner store said, "She walked in the woods at night and talked to the moon".

The town talk was that she knew the name of every herb, and which ones could kill you slowly.

Some even swore they saw her speaking to a raven on her windowsill like it understood her. But no one ever said it too loud.

Because for all the mystery, one thing was true, Mama Lucy helped.

She healed what the hospitals couldn't, she soothed pain no preacher could touch, and she prayed in a way that made your bones settle.

So, whether she was a woman of God, a woman of science, or something in between no one dared to stop her.

You don't question the rain just because it falls quiet, you just thank the Lord it came.

Chapter Two

The Knowing

Long before she was Mama Lucy, she was just Lucille.

A quiet, sharp-eyed girl with knees always dusty from wandering where children weren't meant to roam.

Even then, she saw things.

Not ghosts in the storybook sense, but shadows that didn't belong to anyone, faces behind faces, and glimmers of light that would float around people like fireflies, some soft and golden, others flickering with a sickly green that made her stomach twist.

She called it "The Knowing", though she never spoke the words aloud.

At six, she could look at someone and tell when death had touched their shoulder.

At eight, she stopped shaking hands altogether.

Some folks' palms felt like ice, and others like they carried something twisted beneath the skin, something alive and watching.

She told her grandmother, Mary Lou, once. Just once.

They were shelling peas on the porch when Lucille paused and said, "Grandma, Miss Mabel's got something behind her eyes. Like a shadow."

Her grandmother's hand froze mid-shell, eyes going flat.

"You hush now, girl," she said low. "You don't speak on folks like that. You keep that kind of talk inside your head. *Or else.*"

Lucille knew what "or else" meant. Not in the way of bedtime warnings, but in the cold, final way of people being sent away in the middle of the night.

She'd heard stories of girls in other towns. Girls who "talked too much," or "saw too much." Girls who went missing. Or worse, girls who came back different.

So, she stopped talking about it. She didn't say anything to her family, not to her teachers, not even to herself.

But "The Knowing" never left.

It curled up in her bones, quiet and patient, waiting for the day she'd be old enough to use it without fear.

Until then, she watched.

And learned.

And when the woman down the road lost her baby, Lucille noticed the air in her house had turned heavy two days before.

When the neighbor boy came back from the city with wild eyes and shaking hands, she saw the smoke clinging to his clothes, even though no one else smelled a thing.

No one ever asked Lucille how she knew things. But some avoided her. Some crossed themselves when she passed. Others stared too long.

Lucille learned early that people fear what they can't name. But the spirits?

They never feared her. She hadn't planned to say anything. She never did.

But that Sunday, Lucille's chest felt tight the moment she walked into the church. The sanctuary smelled of perfume and sweat, the way it always did when everyone dressed in their best.

But the light, something was wrong with the light.

The sun streamed through the stained-glass windows, but over Deacon Harris, it bent. Dimmed. Like it didn't want to touch him.

Lucille watched from the back pew, her little white gloves tugged tight around her hands. She didn't speak. Just stared.

The air around him shimmered with something ugly. Not loud. Not visible to others. It pressed against him, crawling beneath his skin like ants.

Lucille tried to ignore it, gripping the hymnal so hard the pages curled.

But when the Deacon stood to speak, something whispered behind him, not with a voice, but a feeling.

He touches what he shouldn't. He hides what he breaks.

Lucille froze. Her breathing shallowed.

She didn't know what the words meant, not entirely. But she knew they were true.

Her hands started to sweat in her gloves.

She turned to her mother, sitting straight-backed and holy, nodding along with the sermon.

Lucille opened her mouth. And closed it again. Because how do you say the light refuses to touch him when you're nine years old?

How do you say *he's got something black curled up inside him like a snake* without them thinking you've lost your mind?

So, Lucille did the only thing she dared. She prayed. Not the kind of prayer they taught her at the altar, but the kind she whispered from her own bones.

God, make it stop. Not for me. For them. Make him stop. Let them see it.

The next week, Deacon Harris left town.

No announcement. No goodbye. Just gone.

Some said his wife found letters. Others said there was money missing.

But Lucille knew what she knew. And she never prayed the same way again.

Lucille first saw it on her sister when they were sitting at the dinner table. The candlelight flickered, catching her sister Claudine's face just right.

And there it was, perched on her shoulder like it belonged there, dark and hunched, with long fingers wrapped around her collarbone. It didn't have eyes, not in the way people do, but Lucille could feel it watching her.

Claudine was fourteen then. Pretty, sharp-tongued, and mean when no adults were looking.

That night, she slid her own slice of cornbread into her mouth and then, with a smooth movement, knocked Lucille's piece onto the floor.

"Oh no," Claudine said sweetly. "Butter fingers."

Lucille looked at the bread on the floor, then back at her sister, and the thing still sitting there, grinning without a mouth.

It was always there.

Sometimes it flickered, like heat above asphalt. Sometimes it loomed taller, darker, when Claudine whispered lies to their mother or pinched Lucille just under the tablecloth, where no one could see.

But Lucille knew that spirit fed on her sister's cruelty. Or maybe it caused it. She couldn't always tell which came first. She wanted to ask. To tell someone.

But how do you explain that your sister is mean because there's something else clinging to her?

So, she watched. And she learned. Some days the spirit was smaller, barely more than a haze.

On those days, Claudine would braid Lucille's hair without pulling or let her play with the red ribbon she kept in her drawer.

But other days,

Other days the spirit grew bold.

Its hands would press down Claudine's back like a puppeteer, and her voice would go sharp like broken glass.

"You think you special?"

Claudine snapped one morning, yanking Lucille's doll away and tossing it into the wash barrel.

"Always staring at people like you better than 'em. Like you know something."

Lucille said nothing.

Just stared at the spirit, which now looked right back at her, tilting its head as if it had been waiting for this moment.

She didn't cry. Not because it didn't hurt, but because she didn't want to feed the thing.

She had begun to learn that some spirits drink emotion, fear, sadness, anger. That's how they stick. That's how they grow. So she held herself still and prayed in her head: *God, don't let it get in me. Let her go. Please, let her go.*

That night, Lucille dreamed of fireflies. But not the glowing kind that danced in jars.

These were dim, gray, and heavy.

They clung to people in their dreams like damp cloth, whispering, squirming, feeding. And when she woke, she knew, people aren't always wicked on their own.

Sometimes, something rides them there.

The Dream of the Key

The dream came on a night when Claudine had been especially cruel.

Lucille had gone to bed with hunger curling in her stomach and her doll still damp from the wash barrel. She didn't pray like usual. She just closed her eyes and let the quiet take her.

But in her sleep, she was not in her room.

She stood in a field under a silver sky, where the moon hung low and wide like a watching eye.

The air shimmered with a strange calm, not peace exactly, but something holy.

Intentional.

Figures began to emerge from the mist, their faces shadowed but familiar.

Women.

One wore a long skirt and a headwrap knotted at the crown of her head.

When Lucille saw her, warmth spread over her scalp, like hands blessing her. A pressure eased behind her eyes, and she felt taller, steadier.

Another carried a satchel of herbs at her hip.

As she drew near, the air filled with the scent of bay and rosemary.

Lucille's chest opened, her breath deepened as though the woman had unlocked her lungs.

She felt a weight she hadn't realized she carried slide off her shoulders.

Then came an older woman, her back bent but her eyes bright as firelight.

Around her neck hung a long chain with a single, blackened skeleton key.

When Lucille looked at her, the ground beneath her feet steadied.

Her knees no longer wobbled, and she felt anchored, like stone was rising to hold her in place.

They didn't speak with mouths, but Lucille understood them anyway.

You are not the first to see what you see. You are not alone in this.

The woman with the satchel stepped forward and opened her palm.

In it sat a bay leaf, fresh and green, but pulsing with something more than life. She closed Lucille's hand around it.

Then the elder with the key lifted the chain and placed it in Lucille's palm.

It was cold at first, so cold it bit into her skin, but then it warmed, as if recognizing her.

A surge of energy ran through her arm, neither painful nor gentle, but alive.

This opens what the world cannot see.

This walks you through doors no man can build.

It is not passed by birth, but by calling.

Lucille's body trembled, not in fear, but in awe. Every hair on her arms stood on end.

Only women with spirits that reach for God can hold this. Not perfect women. Not proud ones. Petitioners. Those who kneel and ask.

Lucille wanted to speak, to thank them, but before she could, the women began to fade into mist. The last voice lingered:

Bay leaves protect. Salt seals. Keep both close.

She awoke with the key in her hand, its metal glinting gold in the real world. Not a dream. Heavy. Old. Cool to the touch.

Lucille didn't scream.

Didn't run to her parents.

She slipped the key under her pillow and stared at the ceiling until morning.

Later that week, when Claudine was in one of her moods, Lucille crushed a bay leaf and sprinkled salt across her doorframe.

Her sister wouldn't cross the threshold. She stood in the hall, confused, as though something unseen had pushed her back.

Lucille didn't smile, but she understood.

The gift of dreams was not imagination. It was an inheritance.

And the key, hidden beneath her pillow, wasn't just hers.

It was the door to a power that had been waiting generations to return.

Chapter Three

Mary Lou and the Dimes

Before she was Grandma Mary Lou with the house that smelled like peppermint and prayer, she was just Mary, a striking fourteen-year-old with skin like deep river clay, a sharp tongue, and a spirit the old men called "too grown for her age."

The women in her family whispered that "she had it."

The gift.

That kind of seeing that skips over eyes and gets straight to the spirit of a thing.

But Mary Lou didn't talk much about what she saw. Because, like Lucille would one day learn, the gift wasn't given for talking.

The ancestral women who visited her in dreams, women with firm jaws and unbraided hair, never moved their lips.

They spoke mind to mind.

Dimes, baby. Always keep three in your pocket.

One for the body, one for the mind, and one for the spirit.

They bend energy. Reflect it. Send it back.

So, Mary Lou did.

She slipped them into the corners of her dress pockets, cold and clinking like little promises.

The first time she carried them, the shadows that followed her on the way to school vanished.

She never questioned it again.

But Mary Lou had a pull toward danger. It lived in her blood like a second heartbeat.

While the other girls giggled at boys their age, Mary Lou's eyes wandered toward men who walked with the weight of years and secrets.

Men who had no business looking back, yet a few did.

Some older men avoided her, not because they were moral, but because they felt something when she looked at them.

Like her gaze peeled the flesh back and studied the spirit beneath.

She was too young to have that kind of knowing. Too aware.

But one man didn't avoid her. He met her eyes.

And she felt it. The same hunger she was still learning to name.

She met him one summer evening behind the old smokehouse on Willow Street.

She wasn't supposed to be out. But Mary Lou had learned how to move quietly.

Her parents didn't count their heads after supper. Not with eleven children under one roof. If you were smart and quick, you could slip into the dark and be back before the streetlamps blinked awake.

The man was older, at least twenty-five. Worked at the feed store, it always smelled like tobacco and sugarcane.

She had caught him watching her from the porch once. Just once. But it was enough.

That night, he smiled at her. Said her name soft. Let the silence between them thicken. And Mary Lou didn't feel scared.

Not at first. Until he stepped closer.

That's when she felt it. The spirit. Not behind him. Not beside him. But in him. Hot. Throbbing. Hungry.

It wasn't love, or even lust. It was something devouring. And the moment she saw it; she remembered the dimes.

She gripped them hard in her pocket, just as the spirit within the man reached outward. She could feel it trying to crawl into the space between them, coaxing her forward.

Use the coins, the ancestors whispered. *Seal the body, guard the spirit.*

Mary Lou didn't run. She stepped back, slowly and certain. Pulled one dime from her pocket and whispered over it, words she didn't even know she knew.

Then she tossed it to the ground between them. The air snapped. The man blinked. Frowned. Rubbed his eyes like waking from a fog.

"Thought you was somebody else," he muttered, backing away.

Mary Lou said nothing. Just turned and walked home. And that was the night she understood:

The gift wouldn't stop her from wanting things. But it would stop her from being destroyed by them.

Fire That Heals

Mary Lou learned to tame her hunger, but she never lost it.

She still felt the pull when a man with a deep voice walked by, or when the scent of musky cologne drifted through the air like perfume off a forbidden fruit.

But instead of letting it rule her, she studied it. Sat with it. Prayed over it.

Everything you feel has a use, the ancestors said.

Even the things you think are wrong.

By fifteen, Mary Lou had a new kind of awareness.

Her hips had grown fuller, her eyes steadier. Boys stopped teasing her. Men looked and looked away. And she learned that sometimes it wasn't her desire acting up, it was theirs, radiating from their spiritual bodies like steam.

She began to feel it in her palms. A heat, low and glowing, that built when she was near someone in pain, someone hurting or shameful, someone with too much want and nowhere to put it. Then came her test.

It was her cousin Jorelle.

Seventeen, sweet-faced, but shattered.

He'd just come back from a work stint up north, and something about him had changed. He wouldn't eat. Wouldn't speak much.

Kept himself in the shed behind the house, sweating through shirts and muttering in his sleep.

The family said he had nerves. Or that maybe he'd picked up something foul in the city.

But when Mary Lou got near him, she felt it clear as daylight.

A spirit of shame. Not just sitting on him, twined up in his belly. Knotted around his spine.

And it pulsed with the same heat she felt in herself when desire called, but his was twisted, backed up, burning inward.

She watched him for days. He couldn't look her in the eyes. Wouldn't take a plate from her hands.

One evening, she went to the shed alone. He didn't notice her at first.

Just sat there, shoulders hunched, eyes blank.

Mary Lou stood in the doorway and closed her eyes. She let the feeling rise, the warmth in her chest, the flutter in her stomach. The same sensation that used to lead her into trouble.

But this time, she didn't chase it. She let it fill her. And she prayed, not with words, but from within her body.

She stepped towards him and placed her hand on his back. I see it, she thought. And I don't fear it. The spirit flinched. She pressed harder, calling on the ancestral women. Let this be a fire that purifies. Not one that burns down. Jorelle stiffened, then groaned. A soft sound, like something leaving. His breath shook. He turned to her slowly, eyes wet, not with lust, not with fear but with relief. "Thank you," he whispered. "I didn't know how to let it go."

Mary Lou didn't speak. She just walked out into the night air, dimes warm in her pocket, the key of her future not yet forged, but waiting.

In that moment, she understood:

Desire wasn't her curse; it was her language. A way to read heat. To feel imbalance.

And, when wielded right, to heal what the world didn't know how to touch or handle with care.

Chapter Four

Freeman

By sixteen, Mary Lou's eyes had grown quieter, not dull but knowing.

She'd learned to walk with grace, to listen before speaking, and to hold her thoughts like pearls, shared only with the worthy.

She had dreams more often now, dreams full of symbols: water running backward, hands reaching through clay, mirrors that refused to reflect.

She didn't always understand them, but she always felt them.

That summer, while helping her aunt with a delivery down near Turner's Hill, she saw him again. Freeman.

She hadn't known his name when she was fourteen. Just the way the air changed around him. He had been taller than most boys, already with the posture of a man who carried something.

The first time they'd locked eyes, Mary Lou had felt heat, yes, but more than that; recognition. The kind that rattled the ribs.

Now, two years later, he was standing beside a wagon, tending to a horse with a calming whisper. His hands were dark and calloused, veins thick like vines, but there was stillness in him.

Like the kind you find just before a thunderstorm breaks open.

He looked up, and their eyes met again. But this time, he didn't look away.

Mary Lou's stomach twisted, not from nerves, but from a pull in her center. A gravitational shift. A knowing. She walked slowly, deliberately.

He waited.

"You don't remember me," she said, testing the waters.

"I remember your spirit," he said, without pause.

Later that evening, they sat under a sycamore tree. No one around. Just the wind, the hush of leaves, and the kind of silence that lets truth bloom.

Freeman told her his story, not all of it, just enough to explain why his presence felt like a soft flame.

His mother, Essie, had the sight. Everyone said so.

But she refused it, called it nonsense. Turned her back on dreams and buried her herbs in the yard.

Said prayer was enough, that "old ways" were a curse dressed up in ceremony.

But the spirits don't dissolve with denial. Energy can't be destroyed. If the gift isn't used, it must move.

Freeman was her only surviving child.

The others, three girls and a boy, never made it past the womb. His mother grieved, but deep down she knew: the gift she buried had no place to go.

So, it came to Freeman. Not gradually, not gently.

"All of it hit me after she passed," he said, eyes fixed on the horizon.

"At thirteen, I woke up with a ringing in my ears that didn't stop for days. I started dreaming other people's dreams. Started seeing things before they happened. Folks thought I was cursed. But I wasn't."

He turned to her, voice quiet.

"I was full. Overfull. With a gift that was never meant for me but came anyway." Mary Lou stared.

The air buzzed.

They were both bound by legacy, but from opposite ends:

She, shaped by women who poured into her. He, shaped by a woman who poured nothing, leaving room for everything.

And still, they understood each other, not just the heat, not just the hunger.

But the burden.

That night, Mary Lou dreamed again.

She stood in a field, like before. The ancestral women watched from a distance, saying nothing. But this time, one held out a second key.

And she placed it in Freeman's hand; the metal looked polished like it had been waiting for generations to return.

Chapter Five

The House Her Father
Built

Lucille's father built their home with the help of his family and it was beautiful.

It sat at the edge of Jasper Lane, half shielded by pines, with ivy that kissed the front steps and a wraparound porch that looked like it was made for prayer and lemonade.

From the outside, it looked modest, ordinary even. A nice house for a quiet family.

But what folks didn't know, couldn't know, was that the bones of that house held more than just memories. It held secrets, best wishes, and barriers.

It held Lucille's protection.

Her father, Dr. Eli Green, was a man of few words and deliberate action. One of the few wealthy black men in town who earned his fortune with calloused hands and a scalpel's charm.

His medical practice served the whole county, black, white, or otherwise, and his patients trusted him in the way people trusted rivers: steadily, intuitively.

But Eli Green was also a careful man. He'd seen envy twist neighbors into enemies. Seen how smiles could hide curses, and he'd married a woman who knew these dangers better than anyone.

Lucille's mother, Hattie, wasn't just beautiful, she was cautious.

Raised by Mary Lou herself, Hattie had learned that unguarded blessings often became targets. So, when the money started flowing, she told her husband plainly:

"We may be well off, Eli. But we will never throw it in anyone's faces. Not here."

And they didn't, no fancy cars, no pearls at church and no big speeches at the town meetings. The Green family lived well for a black physician in those times and always gave back to the community. They were adamant that if they didn't flaunt their wealth the evil eye would never come knocking.

But Lucille?

Lucille saw what couldn't be seen.

Even before she knew how to name them, she felt the eyes on the house. Not physical ones but spiritual ones, probing. watching, creeping toward the windows like fog.

At twelve, she began sweeping the porch with saltwater and cedar, just like Mary Lou had taught her.

At thirteen, she buried a jar of bay leaves, red clay, and blessed dimes beneath the front step, north side first.

By fifteen, she was walking the entire property line barefoot, whispering prayers passed down through her bloodline, reinforced by dreams that told her where the cracks in the spirit wall were forming.

The spirits didn't just test people.

They tested homes.

They tested boundaries.

Lucille's specialty wasn't healing like her grandmother's. It wasn't spirit walking like her great aunt.

Lucille was a builder, a sealer, a binder. And the house her father built became her first true altar.

Behind the wainscoting, she placed herbs wrapped in linen. Inside the baseboards, she hid palm ash and whispered scriptures.

At each window, she affixed tiny protection sigils written in oil only she could see under candlelight. In the center of the home, under a loose floorboard, she placed the skeleton key, wrapped in white cloth, bound with three knots.

Let no spirit pass who does not carry peace.

Let no harm rest where this house breathes.

Let the legacy of protection live longer than the walls.

Most people walked in and just felt safe, but they couldn't name why. Dogs never barked inside the house and babies always stopped crying. Sick folks often felt better just sitting on the porch.

No dark presence ever lingered there for too long, because Lucille had sealed it in blood, salt, and prayer. She knew a protected house must be protected daily.

Energy didn't sleep.

Envy didn't expire.

And spirits? Spirits always tested the foundations.

Chapter Six

The Spirit of Talking

Lucille's mother, Hattie Green, was not a healer. She didn't mix herbs or dream of keys. She didn't see spirits hovering behind people's eyes or whispering from shadows like her daughter did.

But she had a gift, she could talk. No, not just talk, she could move people with her voice. She often calmed storms, started them, and changed the course of a room with a sigh and a sentence.

And she knew her power well.

When she was still Hattie Louise Mayweather, she used that tongue to pull the brightest man in town into her orbit, or so people think.

Dr. Eli Green, quiet and brilliant, with hands that saved lives and ears that listened when Hattie spoke. Others had tried to catch his attention even though he had a fiancé.

But Hattie? She spoke, and he believed, or so he thought he did.

"You're going to marry me one day," she told him when she was twenty years old, bold and charming working in the university library.

"You think so?" he asked.

"I know so," she smiled. "Because I said it. And when I say something, it stays said."

He laughed, and within a year, he made her Hattie Green. But the gift of talking doesn't come without rules.

Mary Lou told her once, when she was a girl: *The tongue is a blade, baby. It can cut rope or cut throats. What you say, moves energy, so don't play with what's holy.*

But Hattie never liked to be told what to do and used her gift when it suited her: To guide/control her husband and children.

And too often, gossip.

She didn't always mean to start trouble. But her words carried weight. And once they were released, they traveled far.

She'd mention a woman's husband "staying too late at the juke joint" in the church kitchen and by the next week, that marriage was cold.

She'd remark about someone's child "looking a little pale lately" and sickness would follow, whether by fear or by force.

She said too much, too loosely.

Mary Lou watched her daughter use a gift meant to bless and bind as a tool for commentary. Not evil but wasteful.

When Lucille was thirteen, Mary Lou sat down on the back porch. Hattie was hanging linens inside, humming sweet and sharp. Mary Lou didn't raise her voice, didn't scold. She just looked Lucille in the eye and said:

"Your mama has a gift. The spirit of talking, strong in her bones but she used it sideways. Turned honey into noise, that's why she never got her key."

Lucille blinked. "She never?"

"No key," Mary Lou said, folding her hands. "Because keys don't pass to the careless, you don't get them for being gifted. You get them for being faithful."

Lucille said nothing, but something in her spirit locked in place that day. A quiet promise, she would not let her gifts fall sideways. She would not be remembered for whispers when she was born for walls and warfare.

Years later, she would still hear her mother's voice drifting through the house:

"You know what I heard about that woman down the road,"

Lucille would smile kindly but, in her heart, she kept her own tongue tied tight when the spirit said so. She knew the power in speaking and the cost of misusing it.

That night, after the talk on the porch with Mary Lou, Lucille couldn't sleep. The house was still, the kind of quiet that made the floorboards feel like they were listening.

Moonlight painted the walls silver. The ceiling fan turned in soft circles, but her thoughts moved faster than wind. *No key*, Mary Lou had said, because she turned honey into noise.

Lucille rolled over in bed, staring at the soft silhouette of her doorframe. She understood what grandma meant.

She knew her mother's gift had power. She'd watched it work on her father all her life.

The way one word from Hattie Green could settle him like a warm cloth. Could push him to build, buy, believe. And yet, she never used it on Claudine.

Lucille felt the old pain rise.

The pinches under the dinner table.

The time Claudine took the last piece of chicken just to watch her go without.

The moments she whispered, "You're nothing special," with that calm, cruel voice right before hugging her in front of their parents.

Lucille had learned early to hide bruises and blessings alike. But her mother had eyes and a mouth that could change tides.

So why had she said nothing?

Why hadn't she used her gift of speech to speak up?

Why hadn't she called Claudine into stillness like she did Daddy?

A tear slid down Lucille's cheek before she could stop it. Not because she was sad but because she was angry. Underneath that anger sat a quieter emotion, lucidity.

Mama had the power. She just chose where to use it.

Lucille sat up in bed and swung her feet to the floor. The wood was cold beneath her toes. She crept over to the window and looked out over the yard, the trees, the grass, the house she covered in spells and prayers.

She had used everything in her to protect this home. To protect people, even when they didn't deserve it.

And her mother? She protected an image, peace, but not her child.

That night, Lucille didn't dream of spirits. She didn't hear voices; she just sat in the dark with the truth:

Some people are gifted. But not everyone is brave.

Chapter Seven

The Womb is a Battlefield

Lucille had tried for years to read her mother.

Not just her face or her tone, but her spirit. The energy behind her words. The currents beneath the surface, but every time she reached, she found silence.

Not emptiness, blockage. A thick, intentional veil. It wasn't until her 16th birthday that she finally asked Mary Lou outright:

"Why can't I read her?"

Mary Lou was quiet for a long moment, sipping chicory from her mug, eyes focused on the trees outside. Then she said, without turning her head:

"Because when she was pregnant with you, she cursed what you were."

Lucille's breath caught. "What I was?" Mary Lou turned slowly, eyes steady.

"You weren't just a baby. You were a return. A spirit long gone, called back through the bloodline. Powerful. Whole. Made of light so fierce it scared her."

The vision had come to Hattie in her second trimester. She was folding linens, hands dry and her ankles swollen, when the world around her faded. She stood in a clearing, windless, still.

Then a woman appeared.

Not just any woman, an ancestor. Barefoot, dark-skinned, eyes ancient and kind. She didn't speak through her mouth. She spoke into Hattie's mind:

I'm coming back through you. The child in your womb is me. I've waited a long time to return. You will bring me forth.

Hattie stumbled backward, mouth open, heart racing. Because she felt it, not a threat, but a reckoning.

She had seen Claudine's spirit in the womb too. Playful, petty, loud, but manageable.

Lucille was different. Her energy filled the room. It didn't kick; it glowed.

And Hattie felt small. She smiled during the day. Wore maternity dresses in soft pastels. Let women at church touch her belly and guess the baby's name. But at night? She'd curl into herself and whisper curses into the dark.

"I didn't ask for this. You will not rule me."

"You think your light makes you better? You will not take my place."

Sometimes she cried after. Sometimes she didn't. Sometimes she pressed her hands to her belly and begged the spirit to go back where it came from.

But Lucille stayed. Wrapped in a womb full of confusion, envy, and inherited pain.

Loved by a father. Overshadowed by a sister. Resisted by a mother.

And yet, she came into the world quiet, eyes wide, spirit still blazing.

The curses lingered, stitched into the air long after Hattie whispered them.

That was years ago, but the echoes still lived inside Lucille.

Back in the present

Lucille stood alone in her kitchen, one hand on her chest. She had felt her mother's blockage before, but now she understood why:

Curses had been stitched into her very name. Not by witches, but by the woman who birthed her.

And still Lucille forgave her.

Because she now knew something else: Mary Lou hadn't always been "the blessed woman" either.

In her younger years Mary Lou wore short skirts and threw sharp words.

She had years where she flirted with fire and refused to pray.

She, too, cursed what she didn't understand.

And still, the ancestors waited. They waited for her to rise into her calling.

Just like they waited for Hattie.

Just like they had once waited for Lucille. But Lucille? She didn't make them wait long.

She walked into her purpose, even as the woman who birthed her tried to hold her back with silence.

Because blood might carry a gift, but the spirit chooses who gets the key.

And Lucille had been chosen twice:

Once by the ancestors. And once by herself.

Chapter Eight

Manufactured Life

No one would ever call Hattie Green a failure. She was elegant, well-spoken, and always appeared in control. She had a doctor for a husband, two daughters, a clean home, and neatly pressed clothes.

She brought pies to church and hosted Sunday dinners with just the right amount of charm.

But Hattie knew the truth: She had built nothing herself.

Everything she had, her home, her name, her social grace was tied to Dr. Eli Green. And that had always been the plan.

Not a marriage of passion, but of strategy. He had the mind; she had the mouth.

With her gift of speech, she kept things in order, especially him.

Hattie never followed her true life's calling. She felt it tugging at her when she was sixteen. She could deeply feel the urge to counsel, to speak life in souls, to mediate, to teach, but unfortunately, she silenced it.

She learned quickly that her voice could make people do things.

Say yes. Say sorry. Say "I do."

So instead of lifting people, she bent them, and for a while, it worked.

She whispered her way into status, into influence, into security. But her gifts were rooted in manipulation, not mission and that kind of power always ages bitter.

She would wake some nights, sweating, heart racing with visions half-formed in her mind.

A garden overran.

A tongue that grew thorns.

A baby born glowing in the dark.

She always pushed those dreams away. Hattie refused to believe that anything pure could come through her.

Not with what she'd done.

She had secrets, real ones. The kind no one in church would suspect.

The rituals she performed in private. The things she buried under the porch. The jars she kept hidden in her vanity drawer.

How do you keep a man like Dr. Eli Green?

You don't love him. You bind him.

Hattie never believed in full submission. She believed in soft power.

She made herself necessary, not adored.

One mistake she made was thinking that nobody could see it until Lucille was born and forced her to look in the mirror.

From the moment she held her daughter, she felt the difference.

Lucille didn't cry. Didn't fuss. She just watched. As if she knew things.

Hattie felt exposed every time the baby stared up at her with those still, ancient eyes.

"She knows," Hattie would think.

She came back with eyes that don't forgive.

Claudine had been easier, high-pitched, loud, pretty but most of all manageable.

But Lucille?

Lucille had power without trying. She didn't scheme. She didn't bend. She simply was.

Lucille made Hattie rage in ways she couldn't explain. She masked it well, too well, as that was her specialty. Hattie smiled at church, bragged about her daughter's intelligence. Braided her hair tight, even kissed her goodnight.

But inside?

She hated that little girl's light, because it reminded her of what she gave up.

Lucille didn't need a man.

Didn't hide her spirit. Didn't whisper to survive. She walked in truth and every time she did, Hattie's own spirit recoiled.

She would never say it out loud. Not even to herself. But in the corners of her heart, Hattie envied Lucille's strength.

Her courage to walk alone. Her refusal to beg for love or permission. Lucille was becoming everything Hattie could've been, if she'd followed her gift instead of using it as a weapon.

Now, whenever Lucille enters the room, Hattie straightens just a little.

Her voice gets sweeter. Her eyes get sharper. Not out of love. Out of defense. Because deep down, she knows:

Lucille is the woman she never had the bravery to become.

The skeleton key never came for Hattie; her heart was too spiteful.

So, it waited for the child she tried to silence.

Chapter Nine

What the Elders Saw

The house gleamed. Candles floated in crystal holders. Laughter rolled like music between the hallways.

Polished shoes clacked against the hardwood, and jazz wrapped around the guests like velvet.

It was the kind of evening Hattie Green lived for.

A ballroom-style gathering inside the Green family home, filled with well-to-do Black doctors, lawyers, professors, and entrepreneurs.

Folk who had pulled themselves up through the grit of history and dressed now in silk and satin to prove it.

Everyone was someone. Everyone had a story to tell.

And Hattie was in her glory, at least, she was supposed to be.

Her dress shimmered gold. Her hair was pinned high and tight. Her lipstick, a deep plum, matched the pearls on her ears.

She walked into the room like a queen receiving guests in her court. And yet... She couldn't take her eyes off Lucille.

Lucille didn't sparkle. She glowed. She wasn't loud. She didn't beg for attention. But her presence pulled people in, especially the elderly.

Women in long robes, beads at their waists. Men with greying beards and eyes that had seen both war and spirit.

People who had built legacies and carried lineages on their backs. They were the type who didn't waste words.

But they kept drifting towards Lucille.

One elder, Mother Alma, a retired midwife and dream-seer, took Lucille's hand with a look of recognition.

"You have hands like a vessel," she said softly. "You carry peace."

Lucille nodded, humbly.

Another woman, Sister Gertie, leaned in and whispered something that made Lucille smile, then touch her chest with gratitude.

Even Elder Malcolm, a quiet man known for laying hands in back rooms and pulling sickness from bone, said:

"She got a spirit that stays open. Unlocked. That's rare."

Hattie heard all of it. Every. Single. Word.

She smiled through it. Clapped politely. Took slow, careful sips from her glass of chilled elderflower wine.

But inside? She burned.

Because she remembered being Lucille's age, craving that same recognition, especially from the elders.

She remembered walking into rooms like this, wearing her best dress, hoping for a nod, a blessing, a moment of seeing.

But they never came to her. And now she understood why.

They had seen something on her back then: pettiness. Performance. Control.

They saw through the softness of her voice and the shine of her shoes.

They saw that she used her gift to shape rooms, not to serve them. So, they smiled at her out of respect.

But they loved Lucille out of truth.

Hattie excused herself quietly. Slipped down the hallway and into the kitchen, where the music couldn't reach. She gripped the edge of the sink, knuckles tight, and stared out the window into the darkness.

"She doesn't even try," she hissed.

"She just.......... exists."

"And they give her what I worked for."

Her reflection in the window blurred, moonlight casting pale light across her face.

For a moment, her envy rose so strongly it choked her.

She wanted to walk back into that room, take Lucille by the hand, and say something to knock her down a notch. But she didn't.

Because one thing Hattie had learned was this:

You can't curse what was anointed before birth.

You can talk about it. Work around it. Try to outshine it. But that kind of light?

It doesn't dim.

It reveals.

And tonight, Lucille had been revealed not as a guest in her own house, but as the true center of spiritual gravity.

And Hattie? She was just... standing in it.

Burning in the light she once carried and never claimed.

Chapter Ten

The Question That Broke
the Silence

The house had emptied. Music faded. Footsteps dwindled. The last of the candles flickered out.

But the tension remained. Lucille stood in the hallway, barefoot now, her dress soft against her skin.

Her spirit felt heavy, not from exhaustion, but from everything left unsaid.

She hadn't missed the glances. The way her mother's jaw tightened when the elders spoke to her. The cold smiles. The distant compliments.

The way Hattie floated through the party like she was hosting a performance, not a celebration.

Lucille felt it deep in her bones. The shift. The resentment. The rage.

And she was tired of pretending it wasn't there.

She found her mother in the sitting room, still dressed in gold.

Her lipstick smudged, her untouched drink sweating on the side table.

Hattie didn't look up as Lucille entered. Lucille stood in the doorway for a moment before speaking.

"Why don't you like me?"

The words dropped like a stone in a still lake.

No fluff.

No filter.

Hattie blinked but didn't move. Lucille stepped closer.

"You smile in public. You speak like we're fine. But I feel it. I've always felt it. Since I was little."

Hattie finally looked up, eyes sharp. "Don't start with me tonight, Lucille."

"No," Lucille said, voice rising. "I am starting. I need to hear it. Because I've twisted myself into knots for years trying to earn warmth from you that never came. And I want to know why."

Hattie stood now, spine stiff, chin high.

"You think I don't love you?"

Lucille's voice cracked. "Love and like are not the same, Mama."

"You're my daughter."

"But you don't like me."

Silence stretched, Hattie's hand tightening on the armrest, her jaw clenching. Then Hattie exhaled slowly, her voice low and tight.

"You remind me of everything I gave up. That's why."

Lucille blinked. Hattie continued, barely above a whisper.

"You walk through life like you owe no one anything. You use your gift without apology. People see you. They love you for who you are."

She paused. "I had to craft everything I became. I had to make people love me. Make them stay. Make them listen. And still, I was never enough." Her lips trembled just once.

"And then you come along, with your visions and your peace. And you didn't even have to try. That's what burns me."

Lucille's breath caught. She wanted to scream. Cry. Run. But she didn't. She stepped forward and said:

"I didn't ask to be born full, Mama. I didn't come here to compete with you. I came through to you because you were the vessel chosen. And I've spent my life honoring you, your house, your name, your silence."

Lucille's eyes welled, but her voice didn't shake.

"But I won't shrink anymore to make you feel better."

Hattie said nothing. Just stood, frozen in gold, suddenly looking older than she ever had. Lucille turned to leave but paused in the doorway.

"You didn't like the light in me, Mama. But it came from the same place yours did. You just, turned yours sideways."

Then she left. Not with rage, with release.

Truth doesn't heal on command. But it always unlocks something. And tonight, it unlocked Lucille.

Chapter Eleven

The Unraveling & The Visit

Shattered in Gold

The house was still. The kind of still that only follows when something sacred has been broken.

The party had ended. The guests were gone.

Lucille's footsteps had long since faded down the hallway and Hattie stood alone in the sitting room, trembling. Her fists were clenched. Her lips were drawn tight in a line.

And then, without warning, she threw the wine glass.

It shattered against the fireplace, crimson droplets streaking the cream wall like blood. Her chest heaved, the silence around her no longer felt elegant, it felt like judgment. She yanked the earrings from her lobes and let them clatter to the ground. Her mascara ran in crooked lines down her face. Her lipstick, once perfectly drawn, now smeared in the corners like a mask halfway torn. She gripped the edge of the vanity. The same one where she hid her jars, her powders, her private little manipulations.

"I gave everything for this life," she whispered. *"Why wasn't that enough?"* Her voice cracked. "Why wasn't I enough?" She saw her reflection in the mirror, but it didn't look like her.

It looked like a woman pretending to be a queen, dressed in golden threads that were never hers to wear honestly. She sank to the floor, sobbing. Not from weakness, but from the truth catching up to her.

Because Lucille's words still rang in her ears:

"You didn't like the light in me, Mama... But it came from the same place yours did."

And at that moment, Hattie knew: She had been given the same fire. But she chose to use it to warm herself.

Lucille let it light the whole room.

And that difference? That truth?

Shattered her more than the glass ever could.

In the Spirit: The Three Who Walk Between

Meanwhile, Lucille sat at the edge of her bed, barefoot, legs folded, her hands still shaking, not from fear, but from release. She stared at the moonlight on her floor. It moved like water, soft and fluid.

She felt hollowed out.

But then... she felt something else. The air shifted.

The scent of lavender, ash, and cedar drifted into the room, familiar, yet impossible to place. And when she looked up...They were there.

Three women in hooded robes, standing in the corner of her bedroom like shadows born of moonlight. They did not speak with mouths. They never did. Their voices moved like a breeze inside her spirit.

You did what she could not. You spoke truth with love. You did not curse her. You called her forward. That is the difference between judgment and alignment.

Lucille's eyes welled with tears, but she didn't cry. She felt... held.

The center woman, tall, robed in dark indigo stepped forward and lifted her hand. Inside it was a small, circular charm, etched with a spiral and a flame.

The fire within you has not burned you. It has refined you. This is not the end of the grief. But it is the beginning of your full inheritance.

The charm floated toward Lucille's hand and settled in her palm, warm and alive.

The second woman, robed in crimson, added:

You carry the ache of many women. But you are also the balm. And balm-bearers are always visited.

The third woman in gray stepped close, her voice the softest:

Let her weep. Let her break. But do not take her breaking into yourself. Let the key stay yours.

Then, just like fog lifting with the morning sun, they were gone. But the scent remained.

The warmth stayed in her hand.

And Lucille lay back on her bed not in defeat, but in peace.

Because some spirits come to fight and others come to affirm.

And tonight?

The ones who walked between had done both.

Chapter Twelve

The Wound That Talks
Back

Hattie never mentioned the glass. She swept it up before sunrise. Wiped the wall clean. Applied fresh makeup. Made breakfast like it was any other morning.

When Lucille walked into the kitchen, Hattie smiled, tight-lipped and hollow.

"Sleep well?" she asked, as if nothing had happened.

Lucille said nothing. Because she understood now: Hattie didn't apologize. She rewrote. Within a day, Hattie was on the phone with her cousins in Georgia.

"I try to do right by everyone," she said softly, just loud enough for Lucille to overhear.

"But sometimes your own children... they grow cold. Forget who held them. Who protected them."

She went on and on about her sacrifices.

About how ungrateful Lucille had become.

How distant.

How judgmental.

"I gave her everything I had," Hattie said. "And it's never enough."

Lucille stood in the hallway, eyes closed, jaw clenched.

Not because the words hurt. Because they were familiar.

She had heard them from Claudine a hundred times. Claudine had perfected the art of re-centering.

Any time she caused pain, she became the one who was wounded.

"Did you Break Lucille's toy?

"I didn't mean to, she's too sensitive."

"Are you lying about something?

"She's always been jealous of me. That's why she's watching so hard."

Even when they were children, Claudine always knew how to spin the room around her like a tornado, always the eye, calm, pitiful, innocent.

And Lucille had swallowed it for years. Until she learned to name it:

Narrative manipulation. The curse of the unaccountable spirit.

It didn't hit. It didn't scream. It just... rewrote.

It bent light and made mirrors reflect the wrong face.

Lucille stepped outside, the air was warm and smelled like a storm was on the way.

She sat on the porch, her charm from the elders tucked beneath her shirt.

And she whispered, not to anyone, but to the spirit realm that was always listening.

"Let this stop with me."

"Let me hold no pain that isn't mine."

"Let me no longer carry the chaos they create."

She wasn't angry anymore, just gained a clearer picture.

Because pity parties built on denial weren't healing, they were prisons.

And she wasn't going to visit those prisons anymore.

Chapter Thirteen

The Porch, A Lady and a Girl

Her name was Jalena Mae, seventeen, loud and beautiful. She was angry for reasons she didn't know how to name.

She came to Lucille's porch because her grandmother made her. Her grandmother always loved how Lucille carried herself as a young lady coming of age.

"She doesn't listen to nobody," the old woman said, her voice tight with shame and weariness. "But maybe she'll listen to you."

Lucille didn't promise anything. She just said, "Let her come."

Jalena Mae showed up in cut-off shorts, arms crossed, chewing her gum like it was a threat.

She sat without a hello. Lucille offered her a glass of sweet tea, Jalena Mae refused.

"You gone be one of them 'lay hands' women?" she asked.

Lucille smiled. "No. I'm gone be one of them listen with my bones women."

Jalena Mae rolled her eyes, but something shifted, almost imperceptibly.

Not a surrender, but interest.

Lucille didn't ask questions. Didn't prod, she just sat quietly and waited.

The silence stretched like soft cotton between them, and finally, Jalena Mae spoke.

"People say I'm too much. Too loud. Too mean." She paused. "I just don't like people thinking they can tell me who to be."

Lucille nodded. "Sounds like you've had to protect yourself too long."

She flinched, not visibly, but spiritually.

Lucille felt it, the presence riding her. Familiar, not possession, but attachment.

It was the spirit of projection and pity, the same one that lingered in Hattie's house. The same whisperer that clung to Claudine.

It fed off wounded girls who never got to be girls, only defenders, manipulators, or masks.

Lucille reached into her basket and pulled out a small pouch, white cloth filled with clove, lemon balm, and blessed water.

She held it out. "Put this under your pillow for seven nights," she said. "It won't change your life. But it'll soften what's wrapped around you."

Jalena Mae took it without saying a word. She didn't say thank you. But when she got up to leave, she turned back.

"You different."

Lucille smiled, slow and warm.

"So are you. That's the whole point."

Nightfall

That night, as the moon rose, Lucille sat by her window and prayed.

Not just for Jalena Mae, but for every girl forced to inherit someone else's fight.

Every woman shaped by mothers too proud to soften. Every child born with a light they were punished for.

"Let me be what I needed," she whispered. "Let me love the reflections I used to hate."

And just like that, the air shifted, another lock inside her spirit turned.

And somewhere in the distance, a bell rang, a sound only the gifted could hear.

Chapter Fourteen

The Raven Who Named
Herself

The bell rang just after midnight.

Lucille drifted into half-sleep, the way spiritually sensitive women often do, never fully gone, always listening between worlds. It wasn't a bell from the church. Not from the wind chimes.

This one rang inside her bones. It was low, hollow and final.

She sat up straight, sweat beading at the base of her neck.

The room was still, the moon hung fat and golden over the treetops.

And then, she heard the caw. Deep, measured and near.

Lucille rose, walked barefoot to the window and opened it without hesitation.

There, perched on the iron railing of her front porch, was a raven.

Black as ink, its feathers shimmered with the faint blue of twilight.

Larger than any she'd ever seen. Then it tilted its head.

Watched her.

You heard the bell, she thought.

The raven didn't speak with words. But Lucille understood her anyway.

You've crossed into another phase, the voice said. But it wasn't in her ears, it embedded into her spirit.

Your work is no longer bound on earth, but now also in the places between.

Lucille stepped outside slowly, the air was thick, fragrant with sage and cedar smoke from her earlier prayer.

The raven didn't flinch; she stared at Lucille with a kind of intelligence that wasn't animal but ancestral.

What's your name? Lucille thought softly, almost afraid of the answer.

The raven blinked once. *I don't have one. But you may call me Sophie.*

Lucille's heart stirred.

The name didn't come from her head but rose up from deep within her belly.

A name spoken by her blood before her tongue.

Sophie, she repeated. *You came because of Jalena Mae?*

The raven turned to the left, toward the trees.

She was the key that opened next door. But this is not about her. This is about you. You are ready for more.

Lucille looked to the sky, unsure if she was dreaming. But everything around her felt more real than waking life.

The porch boards under her feet.

The cool air on her face.

The raven's eyes, holding too much memory to belong to just a bird.

Sophie cawed once more.

Protection has many layers, she said.

You've sealed your house and you've guarded your spirit. Now you must learn to travel.

There are threads between worlds. Gates that need watching. Spirits who seek more than mischief.

And you, Lucille, are a gatekeeper.

Lucille didn't speak. She only nodded, her eyes wet, her heartbeat steady as if she had always known this moment would come.

And deep in the trees, wind stirred the leaves like whispers from unseen mouths.

The ancestors were watching, and now, she was not alone.

Sophie lifted into the air once, then circled her head and perched on the porch rail again where she would remain, a sentinel.

Lucille whispered: "Let's get to work."

The night listened to their spiritual connection, and all the bells of the land rang.

The veil had opened, and the real work was only just beginning.

Chapter Fifteen

The Mirror Gate

The house was silent when the "Knowing" struck her chest like thunder.

Lucille was in her study, sifting through old bundles of dried herbs, when the weight settled between her ribs. Not fear. Not urgency.

Summoning.

She turned slowly toward the arched mirror on the far wall, an old, antique thing that had belonged to Mary Lou's mother, and hers before that.

The frame was carved with grapes, doves, and wild roses, but the glass itself had always been cloudy, as if it never reflected the present quite right. The carvings weren't decoration but were prayers in wood, pressed by hands generations old.

Lucille had dusted it, prayed near it, lit candles before it.

But tonight?

Tonight, it hummed low and subtle but real.

And then she felt it.

|*The key*|

She moved without question, walked to her altar chest, and unwrapped the bundle hidden beneath the floorboard.

There it laid, blackened with age, yet still warm like she was gifted today. When she touched it, the blackness fell away as if it was being activated again.

The skeleton key.

Sophie fluttered onto the windowsill, watching without blinking.

It is time, child of the line, she said, her voice a soft echo in Lucille's spirit.

Lucille stood in front of the mirror and held the key close to her chest.

The mirror remained still, opaque.

Waiting.

She breathed deeply to the soul of her back.

Then stepped forward, inserting the key into a barely visible groove in the side of the frame, one she had never noticed before.

It clicked.

Once.

Twice.

Then the mirror shifted, the glass rippled, slow and silver, like a pond kissed by wind.

It no longer reflected her face; it showed a path.

Stone. Archways. Firelight.

And the air smelled of jasmine, ash, and memory.

Lucille looked at Sophie.

You sure you're ready for this? The raven asked, not mocking, but sincere.

Lucille nodded once.

"I've been ready since before I was born."

She stepped through the mirror.

Not walking, crossing.

Her body felt weightless but grounded. Every part of her was aware. Her spirit moved first, and her flesh obeyed.

Sophie followed, her wings brushing the veil like silk.

They emerged into a hallowed corridor, lined with ancient stone and lit by floating orbs of warm gold.

And then, the women of her bloodline began to appear.

Not ghosts, but echoes, ancestors as embodied memories.

Each stood beneath their own arch, dressed in the garments of their time.

The first woman stepped forward. Dark skin, eyes bright as stars, mouth unmoving.

Yet Lucille heard her voice like thunder wrapped in velvet.

Welcome, granddaughter of the line. We have been waiting. You are the first in three generations to enter of your own choosing. And the last was not ready.

Lucille's chest tightened. Awe pressed into her ribs like hands.

Another woman emerged beneath the next arch. She wore a crown of woven reeds.

When Lucille looked at her, she felt a rush of cool air sweep over her face, like river water.

Then came a woman holding a staff carved with moon symbols. The staff glowed faintly, and Lucille's palms grew hot, as though they were mirroring its power.

A third ancestor stepped forward, copper bands circling her neck. Her eyes were sharp, unflinching, and Lucille felt pressure behind her own eyes, like truth demanding to be seen.

Then came another, hands broad, palms lined from years of catching babies as a midwife. She carried the scent of rosemary and blood. At her presence, Lucille's knees went weak, as if remembering a pain, she had never lived but inherited.

Generations of chosen women.

And every single one of them looked at Lucille with something between pride and recognition.

Sophie perched at the edge of the veil, her feathers pulsing with light.

We're only at the beginning, she said.

And Lucille believed her.

Because she was no longer a woman of protection alone.

She was a traveler. A bloodline bearer.

And a bridge between what is seen and what never dies.

Chapter Sixteen

The Four Keepers

The air in the ancestral realm shimmered like heat rising from sacred ground.

Lucille stood at the center of a circular stone floor, etched with ancient symbols, spirals, eyes, waves, fire marks.

Above her, the sky was neither day nor night, but a soft, glowing in-between. Around her, the great women of her bloodline stood in silence.

Watching.

Waiting.

And then, they emerged.

The three hooded mothers, robed in indigo, crimson, and gray, stepped forward from the light beyond the archway.

They circled Lucille like stars orbiting a center. Their hoods cast no shadows. Their presence felt like memory turned into sound.

You carry the bones of many women, the indigo-robed mother spoke first. *But without mastery of the elements, your gift will remain limited.*

The crimson robed mother stepped closer.

Protection without balance breeds pride. Healing without fire breeds passivity. Sight without grounding opens you to madness.

Lucille stood still, hands open. "I'm ready," she whispered.

The gray-robed mother lifted her head slightly. *Then let us begin.*

The First Element: Earth

The indigo mother extended her hand and touched the stone floor.

Immediately, vines sprouted between the cracks, thick and alive, twining around Lucille's ankles, not to bind, but to root..

Earth is your foundation, the mother said. *It is your blood. Your name. The stories buried in your bones. Without it, your power has no place to return to.*

Lucille closed her eyes. She could feel it, the weight of all the women who came before her.

The feel of red clay. The warmth of bay leaves. The dimes in her pocket as a child.

She breathed deep, and the vines retracted, leaving footprints glowing in the stone.

Her calves tingled, as if soil were filling her veins.

The Second Element: Air

The gray robed mother stepped forward.

She blew a soft breath across Lucille's forehead, and suddenly wind surrounded them, spiraling with whispers. Voices from the past. Some in English. Some in languages older than time.

Air is the word before it's spoken. The warning before it arrives. The thought passed from dream to dream.

Lucille raised her hand slowly and the wind responded.

She moved her fingers like she was playing a harp made of sky.

The voices brushed her earlobes like cool breath.

The whispers became clearer: guidance. truth. intuition.

When the winds shift, you must listen, the mother said. *And when they scream, you must hold your tongue.*

Lucille bowed her head. She understood.

The Third Element: Fire

Then the crimson robed mother stepped forward.

She extended her hand, and fire rose around the edge of the circle, not destructive, but pure.

Lucille felt the heat, but it didn't burn. It called out.

Fire is not rage, the mother said. *It is precision, movement and action.*

It is the moment you said, "Why don't you like me?" It is the part of you that refuses to stay silent.

Lucille stepped toward the flame. The fire bowed to her.

You have the gift of the torch, the mother said. *You walk ahead so others may see. But remember, fire must be fed with purpose, or it consumes its bearer.*

Lucille whispered: "I will feed it with truth."

<u>The Fourth Element: Water</u>

The three mothers stood in unison and stepped back. A pause.

Lucille waited for another to arrive.

None did.

Then she heard it, a ripple behind her.

She turned. And saw herself.

Another Lucille, cloaked in blue, eyes glowing, feet bare.

The version of her that carried grief and compassion like sacred oils.

The part of her that had not yet been named.

Water is memory, the spirit Lucille said. *It is the tears you did not shed. The forgiveness you gave without being asked. The way your spirit flows around anger instead of sinking into it.*

Lucille's eyes filled with tears. She stepped toward herself, and they merged. A wave coursed through her chest, cleansing as it went.

In that moment, she understood, Water cannot be taught, only remembered.

The stone beneath her feet pulsed with life.

The air around her lifted her breath like wings.

The fire circled in a soft dance.

And water, her own body, rose in harmony.

The three hooded mothers spoke together for the first time:

Now you are not just gifted.

You are balanced.

A daughter of all four.

Lucille stood taller, the key now glowing at her side.

Sophie cawed once, proud and still.

Lucille breathed in, then out. Her spirit stood steady, balanced. She lifted her chin. "I'm ready for the work."

Chapter Seventeen

The Storm Upstairs

The smell of fried fish and cornbread still lingered in the walls.

It was Sunday, and the family had gathered again like they always did.

On the surface, it looked like any other visit, plates scraped clean, iced tea sweating on coasters, Claudine's laugh ringing too loud in the hallway.

But Lucille felt it.

The shift. The spirit. The storm.

It had been bubbling since the moment Claudine came in smiling too wide, praising too quick, touching things she had no business touching.

Lucille had learned long ago that Claudine's sweetness was a signal. It came just before she turned sour.

By the time the dishes were cleared, the words had already started.

It began small.

"Why you always so serious, Lucille? You act like you know everything just cause you pray and play with plants."

Lucille didn't bite.

She never did, not right away.

But Claudine's spirit wasn't looking for silence. It was looking for fuel.

"You think you better than me cause you got your little herb pouches and fancy candle spells?"

"Say what you wanna say, Claudine."

"I am saying it. You walk around like you was chosen. Like the ancestors are just dancing around your head."

Lucille stood still in the hallway. She wasn't angry. Not this time.

Just... disappointed.

Because Claudine hadn't changed. She still carried the blame shaped victimhood she'd inherited from their mother. Still rewriting the world to avoid looking in a mirror.

And speaking of mirrors, Hattie dried the same plate three times, humming louder with every word, as if noise could erase the truth. Pretending not to hear.

Lucille took a step forward. "You jealous, Claudine?"

The words came with a calm, measured carefully not to insult.

But to name.

Claudine's eyes flared. "Jealous? Of you?"

"Yes," Lucille said. "Because I stopped needing approval a long time ago. And you still can't breathe unless someone's clapping for you."

"Girl, you got some nerve."

"No, you got some shadow."

The hallway went quiet, even the floorboards seemed to hold their breath.

Claudine stepped closer, her voice dropping.

"You don't know what it's like to be compared your whole life. To be told you're pretty but Lucille's wise. You got the prayers. You got the praise. I got told to shut up and smile."

Lucille's face softened for a moment. Then sharpened again.

"You were loved, Claudine. You were held. Mama just didn't love me the same and you used that to your advantage."

The kitchen faucet turned on. Hattie had finally decided to make noise. But still no words.

Lucille shook her head.

"You think I'm the enemy. But I've spent my whole life protecting the house you slept in. Sealing the doors. Cleansing the air. Praying over a sister who bit me beneath the table and smiled in front of guests."

Claudine's mouth opened, then closed. Because somewhere inside, she remembered.

Lucille stepped back, voice low but clear.

"This ain't about power, Claudine. It's about peace. And you keep trying to pull me into war."

And then she turned to the kitchen. Looked straight at Hattie's back.

"And you… heard all of it. Like always."

The faucet turned off.

A long pause.

And Hattie, without turning around, said: "I don't get in y'all's mess."

Lucille laughed once. Dry. Hollow.

"But you made it." Then she walked upstairs.

And for the first time, Lucille didn't feel guilty for not fixing the chaos.

She learned peace wasn't a gift someone handed you.

It was a gate you built yourself, and she was finally guarding hers.

Chapter Eighteen

The Release

Lucille's bedroom was dim, lit only by a single beeswax candle.

The flame danced gently, casting soft shadows on the walls, shadows that didn't threaten, just witnessed.

She sat at the foot of her bed, cross-legged, wrapped in her softest white shawl. The air smelled of cloves and cedar.

Sophie perched silently on the windowsill, her presence steady, watching.

In Lucille's left hand, a dried bay leaf, veined and strong.

In her right, the skeleton key, still warm from the mirror, still humming from ancestral use.

And before her, an open journal.

On the page, written in her own careful, steady hand, Psalm 91: He that dwelleth in the secret place of the most High shall abide under the shadow of the Almighty...

She read it softly.

Once.

Then again, louder.

And then, a third time, this time with her whole spirit behind it.

Each word fell like water on fire. Not to soothe, but to extinguish what didn't belong to her anymore.

When the final line left her lips, she closed the journal. Held the bay leaf over her heart and held the key to her throat.

"Release my mother and my sister," she whispered, voice firm and slow. "From my love. From my covering. From my protection. They are no longer my responsibility.

I have carried what they refused to hold.

I prayed when they cursed.

I loved where they resented.

And I return them now to the hands of their own spirit guides."

The bay leaf grew warm. The key pulsed once in her palm, then it stilled.

"Let them walk their own road, Spirit," she said.

"Even if it means they stumble. Even if it means they fall. They are not mine to catch."

She placed the bay leaf into the flame of the candle. The smoke curled upward, carrying her words into the unseen. The scent rose sweet, earthy, final.

The key in her palm cooled, no longer humming, as though it, too, had been released. Its work finished for now.

Lucille didn't cry. She exhaled, the breath long and shaking, like it had been waiting years to leave her body.

And with that breath came a sense of unburdening so complete, her shoulders dropped, her chest opened, and her hands unclenched for the first time in years.

Sophie let out one soft caw. *You've returned what was never yours to keep,* the raven said in her mind.

Lucille nodded. "Let the gate close."

And in the spiritual world just beyond her walls, a door shut quietly.

No slam. No drama.

Just an ending that sounded like peace.

Chapter Nineteen

A Voice of Her Own

Lucille had always been lovely. But at eighteen, she stepped into something beyond beauty, a kind of grace that made rooms pause.

Not because of her hair or her skin or her figure, though all were striking.

But because she walked with certainty.

She didn't declare herself.

She didn't explain.

She simply was.

Most people noticed, but not her mother.

Lucille had tried, more than once, to talk to Hattie about her future.

She'd bring it up casually while folding laundry or setting the table.

"Mama, I think I want to study botany."

"Hmph. You want to play in dirt for a living?"

"Or I'd like to open an apothecary one day. Maybe a healing space."

"You need to find a husband first, Lucille. All that plant talk won't keep a roof over your head."

So, Lucille stopped asking.

Stopped sharing.

And quietly began to plan without permission.

One afternoon, she found her father in the study.

Dr. Eli Green, always surrounded by books and quiet, always calm. His study always smelled of tobacco, ink, and French leather. You knew you were in the company of a manly man.

She stood in the doorway, tall in her soft blue dress, braids pinned up, hands clasped gently in front of her.

"Daddy?"

He looked up, glasses resting at the edge of his nose.

"Yes, baby?"

"I want to go to school," she said. "For botany."

He blinked and took a slow sip of his coffee.

"You've always had a gift for growing things."

She nodded.

He studied her face for a moment, longer than he usually did.

"If you're sure, we'll make it happen."

No grand speech.

No conditions.

Just support.

Lucille should've felt joy. Instead, she felt something else rising from her belly, a question she'd never dared to ask before.

She stepped inside the room, voice soft, a lump in her throat, a tremor in her chest, "Daddy... why didn't you ever take up for me?"

He looked up, startled. "What do you mean?"

"When Claudine would lie, or when Mama would ignore me. When I'd come to dinner with tears in my eyes and pretend, I was fine, you knew. You saw it. So why didn't you ever say anything?"

Silence.

Then he removed his glasses. Set them on the desk.

"I thought keeping the peace was the same as protecting you."

Lucille's heart broke a little at the words, not because they were cruel, but because they were honest.

She thought of her own definition of peace, not silence, not pretending, but truth. He hadn't known the difference.

"It wasn't," she whispered, "You protected the house. But not the daughter inside it."

Her father's eyes welled, and for the first time in her life, she saw regret on his face.

"I didn't know how to stand up to your mother," he admitted. "She was the force. I was the stillness."

Lucille stepped forward. "I needed the force and the stillness."

He reached for her hand. Held it gently.

"I know, baby. I know now."

That was the closest she ever got to an apology from either of her parents. And it was enough.

Not because it healed everything, but because she was already healing herself.

And the woman she was becoming didn't wait for permission to grow.

She straightened her shoulders, smoothed the front of her dress, and lifted her chin, not for anyone else, but for herself.

Chapter Twenty

The Root Woman of
Rockwell Town

Lucille first saw the house on a rain-washed Tuesday and It stood tall at the edge of Mississippi's Rockwell Town.

A quiet place two towns over where people still hung wind chimes in trees and trusted signs in dreams. The house was green, but not with paint, it was green with ivy.

The whole front of it swallowed in vines and moss, as if the land itself had decided to hold it in a constant embrace.

A hand-painted wooden sign hung from a curved iron post:

Mama June's Root & Remedy

Below that:

Tinctures. Tonics. Tea. Truth.

Lucille's heart started to beat faster as she stepped onto the porch.

The woman who opened the door had hair like a thundercloud, piled high and streaked silver and black.

Her skin was the color of old mahogany.

Her eyes were golden brown with flecks that moved like flames.

She wore a thick house dress and bare feet, with a sprig of rosemary tucked behind one ear.

"You must be the girl with the questions," she said, before Lucille could speak.

Lucille blinked.

"I.........yes ma'am. I read your notice. You were looking for help?"

"Help," the woman nodded. "And somebody to pour life into. One always follows the other."

Lucille held out her hand. "Lucille Green."

"June," the woman said. "Most just call me Mama June."

The next morning, Lucille returned with one suitcase, a journal, and a small sachet of dried bay leaves.

Mama June handed her a skeleton key, not like the one passed by Lucille's ancestors, but a practical one, rusted and real.

"Your room is upstairs. You pay what you can, and you sweep what you see. No gossip, no wasted water. And don't ask what's in the locked cabinets unless something starts glowing."

Lucille smiled wide for the first time in days. This wasn't a school. It was a sanctuary.

Days turned into weeks.

Lucille worked in the shop, arranging jars, grinding roots, learning the names of leaves and the temperature of oils.

She learned to listen to how a plant speaks when crushed.

She swept the floors clockwise every evening with a broom bound in twine and hawthorn.

Each sweep seemed to pull more than dust from the floor.

The house grew lighter, calmer, like it was breathing with her.

She watched as townsfolk came for more than tinctures.

Some left crying.

Some left laughing.

Some left with bundles wrapped in black cloth.

But all of them left lighter.

One evening, just as dusk settled, Mama June poured two cups of hot nettle tea and sat across from Lucille in the garden.

"You're not here for plants," she said softly.

Lucille looked up. "No?"

"No," June said. "You're here because Spirit needed to take you out of the house where you were being drained."

She leaned closer.

"You're not just gifted, child. You're bound to something ancient. And that means your training needs earth, hands, and silence. Not desks."

Lucille felt her throat tighten.

Mama June wasn't guessing. She was reading.

"You see things, don't you?" June said.

"Yes."

"Dream in full color. Know when someone's lying before they speak. Feel the dead before you smell them?"

Lucille nodded, barely breathing.

"Then let me teach you what they won't teach in schools. Let me show you what only root women pass down. Not spells but alignments. Not power, but balance."

Lucille reached for her tea with steady hands. "Yes, ma'am. I'm ready."

From that moment, the lessons began.

Mama June didn't give lectures. She gave tasks. Challenges. Riddles. Rituals.

For the first time in her life, she felt seen by someone who wasn't surprised by her light.

And more than that, someone ready to teach her how to protect it.

Chapter Twenty-One

The Spirit of a Man

It was near closing when Beatrice Langley walked in.

She was a woman Lucille had seen in passing, always dressed in silk blouses, always quiet, always followed too closely by a man who rarely spoke but always stared.

Today, she came in alone.

But not truly alone.

Lucille saw it the moment the door opened.

The air shifted. The candle flames in the apothecary bent sideways. The dried lavender above the counter twitched.

And standing just behind Beatrice, almost fused to her back like a shadow made of tar, was a man's spirit.

Broad. Sunken-eyed. And twisted with the scent of mold, rust, and rage.

Lucille blinked slowly but didn't look away.

She didn't want him to know she could see him.

Beatrice's voice trembled. "I just came for something to help me sleep."

Her hands shook slightly as she reached for a jar of valerian.

Lucille looked to the left, where Mama June stood grinding rosemary at the back table.

Without looking up, June spoke calmly: "That woman's not alone."

Lucille swallowed hard. "I know," she said softly.

Mama June set the pestle down and wiped her hands on her apron. "Describe it."

Lucille stepped closer to Beatrice, then spoke with her eyes fixed just over the woman's shoulder.

"A man. Big. Skin looks rotted. He's gripping her like a coat she can't take off. His hands sit on her chest, right where the heart chakra lies."

"Dead?"

"Yes. But feeding."

Mama June nodded.

"She thinks she loves him?"

"She did. But now he's using that love to hold her in place."

Above them, Sophie rustled her wings once, a warning, as if she too smelled the rot unraveling.

June stepped closer now, her movements slow and deliberate. "Miss Beatrice, you trust us?"

Beatrice looked between the two women, clearly unsure why the air felt thick, and her skin felt hot.

"I... I think so. Why?"

Lucille spoke gently. "Because something's clinging to you, Miss Beatrice. Something that used to be a man. But it's not love anymore. It's control."

Beatrice's eyes filled with tears instantly. Not confusion, recognition. "I can't breathe at night. I wake up and feel like something's pressing me down."

"It is," June said, already moving to light a small white candle. "And we gon' unstick it."

The Ritual

They sat Beatrice in the center of the room, where the floors formed a natural spiral in the grain.

Lucille placed a bowl of salt water at her feet.

Mama June lit charcoal, crushed dragon's blood resin, and added bay and rue.

The room filled with smoke making the unseen uncomfortable.

Lucille looked at the spirit now clearly.

His mouth twisted into a smile but there was panic behind it. He was starting to feel them.

Mama June circled the room, whispering verses she didn't read from any book.

Lucille stayed still in front of Beatrice, holding her hands, speaking softly, "You don't belong to him anymore.

He can't live in your love.

Return him to the dirt.

Return him to the dark.

What was never sacred must not stay."

The spirit started to pull back, first one arm, then the other. He fought. Growled.

Smoke curled around him like rope.

Beatrice began to shake. Her eyes fluttered. "I'm scared."

Lucille leaned in, her third eye pulsing. "Don't be. That fear ain't yours. It's his. Let him feel it."

At that, Beatrice let out a sound, half sob, half scream.

And the spirit peeled away, dislodged by the power of two women. One who could see and one who could make the spirit feel unwelcome in the body it clung to.

With a loud hiss, the bowl of salt water cracked.

The spirit collapsed inward and vanished, sucked into the floor like smoke drawn into a bottle.

As the spirit vanished, Lucille felt the skeleton key in her pocket warm faintly, as though acknowledging the gate had been shut properly.

Silence.

Then stillness.

Beatrice exhaled like she hadn't done it in years. She slumped forward into Lucille's arms, sobbing softly. Her chest rose fully for the first time, a breath that sounded almost foreign in her own body.

And Lucille whispered, "You're free, baby. You're free now."

After Beatrice left with balm, instructions, and a little black bag of protective herbs, Lucille sat on the floor in silence.

Mama June brought her tea and sat beside her. "You saw him clearly," she said.

Lucille nodded. "He tried to look like love."

"They usually do."

The candle flickered. Sophie cawed once from the rafters above.

Lucille looked into the flame and whispered:

"I'm ready for the next one."

Mama June smiled. "That was just the beginning."

Chapter Twenty-Two

The Dream War

Lucille fell asleep with the window open, the scent of basil and pine drifting in from the herb garden below.

Sophie slept at the foot of the bed, wings tucked, but her feathers twitched, she knew something stirred.

Lucille had saged herself before bed, burned palo santo, and whispered her usual prayers.

But some spirits are persistent.

Some don't need the front door.

They slip in through the cracks in dreams.

The Dream

Lucille found herself sitting in an old subway car, metallic, humming, flickering overhead lights.

She knew immediately it wasn't real because she hadn't taken a train since childhood.

But there she was, alone in a car that felt too long. The windows were black, as if the train wasn't going anywhere.

And then...

He boarded followed by a dark bird shadow whose eyes glowed like faint gold.

The spirit and Sophie.

The same spirit that had clung to Beatrice's back like rot.

But now he wore a face. Handsome. Smiling. Polished.

"You're stronger than the other one," he said, sliding into the seat across from her. "But strong girls get tired too."

Lucille didn't respond. She just stared, waiting.

The spirit leaned in. "All that light... must be exhausting to hold up."

Then, the subway lights cut out.

When they flickered back on, Lucille was no longer in her dress.

She stood in the center of the car wearing a fitted midnight black ninja suit, soft leather and woven linen stitched with golden thread.

On her back were two swords. The hilts carved from bones and set with a bright green basil emblem, glowing faintly.

She reached over her shoulder and drew them both.

The spirit smirked. "What's this? A little fantasy?"

"No," Lucille said calmly. "A warning."

The train began to shake. Not from motion, but from resistance.

The spirit lunged, his form shifting. Sophie's croak rang sharp, splitting the dark like a bell.

His face melted, bones cracking, jaw distorting into something grotesque and inhuman.

Lucille moved fast.

One slash, then two.

The basil blades sizzled where they cut, burning through shadow and illusion.

The spirit screamed, not in pain, but in fear.

"I fed off her for years," it hissed. "You think a dream will stop me?"

"It's not a dream," Lucille said, eyes glowing now. "It's a boundary."

She raised the swords over her head and brought them down in an X across his chest.

The spirit exploded into dust.

The subway doors burst open, and golden light spilled in like floodwater.

The metallic screech of the train faded as Lucille began to wake up.

The Wake

Lucille woke up before dawn, heart steady, breath calm. The skeleton key started pulsating on top of her altar.

Sophie stood at the windowsill, wings open, eyes sharp. *He tried you.*

"He lost." Lucille rose, walked to her altar, and lit a single candle.

She placed two basil leaves on her altar and lit them on fire in her cauldron.

"You may knock," she whispered into the air. "But you may not enter."

Outside, the wind rustled the herbs gently, it was a quiet nod from the spirit realm.

Chapter Twenty-Three

Basil for Basilisk

The sun had just begun to touch the edge of the ivy-covered shop when Lucille entered the front room.

Mama June was still in the back garden talking to the lemon balm, so Lucille decided to clean the counters and rearrange the drying herbs.

While dusting the shelf beneath the register, her hand bumped a thick, worn book.

The cover was cracked, and the corners were curled like dry leaves.

Stamped faintly across the front in fading gold: Antidotes

She pulled it out carefully and opened it at random.

The page it landed on stopped her breath.

In dark green ink, written with the steadiness of someone ancient and certain:

"Basil for Basilisk"

Beneath it, a sketched drawing of a serpent with six black eyes, dragon wings, and fangs leaking venom into the soul of a woman asleep.

In the windowsill of the shop, Sophie rustled her wings once, as though she too recognized the name written in green ink.

Lucille whispered the words aloud.

"Basil is the only known plant that can burn through the venom of the Basilisk, a serpent spirit that binds through dreams, illusions, and sexual entrapment. Most victims never know they've been taken, only that their will, joy, and voice have been drained."

She stepped back slowly, heart thudding.

The skeleton key on her altar, even from the next room, warmed faintly, a quiet acknowledgment of her boundary spoken aloud.

That's what he was.

The spirit in my dream.

The one who grinned at her in the subway before turning into a twisted shadow.

Lucille's dream swords hadn't been symbolic.

They'd been medicine.

Just then, the front door creaked open.

Mama June entered, wiping dirt from her hands, carrying a basket of marigolds.

She raised an eyebrow at Lucille holding the book. "Ah. So the book called you."

Lucille turned to her. "The dream... last night. The spirit wasn't just a bad man; it was a basilisk. A serpent. I fought him in my dream with two swords marked with basil leaves."

Mama June stopped in her tracks. "You saw the swords?"

Lucille nodded. "Felt them in my hands. Knew what to do."

Mama June set the basket down and sighed, folding her arms. "That spirit wasn't just a parasite, baby. He was a predator."

She walked to the counter and opened the book to another page.

Showed Lucille a diagram of energy points along the human body, with notes scribbled in old handwriting:

"Glamour magic enters through desire. It blinds the third eye, silences the throat, binds the root."

"Beatrice never stood a chance," June said.

"Because she let him in willingly. With her heart, and her body."

Lucille frowned. "But she didn't know he wasn't human."

"That's the trick," June said. "Glamour spirits don't show up in smoke and red eyes. They show up in Cologne. In deep voices. In the man who listens so well, touches so soft."

She leaned in, eyes sharp now. "And if your spirit ain't awake when your body says yes, you can end up bound in a bed with something that don't belong on this side of the veil."

Lucille felt a chill crawl across her skin.

June continued. "Sex isn't just with body, child, it's a ritual, it's an active portal. It's agreement and some folks don't sleep with you to love you; they sleep with you to enter you. To feed, to hide, to rule."

Lucille swallowed hard. "Beatrice's spirit was breaking because she gave consent in ignorance."

June nodded solemnly. "She didn't know how to vet spirits or men. That serpent used her softness against her."

Lucille looked back at the page.

The sketch of the basilisk hissed without moving.

She touched the basil emblem softly and whispered, "Not me. Never again."

Mama June smiled, half-grim. "And now you know why we pray before we entertain. Why we sage the sheets. It is why we fast after heartbreak. You're not just protecting your body, Lucille, you're protecting your name, your light, your bloodline."

Chapter Twenty-Four

A Scent Not Yet Stirred

It was hot that day.

Not just summer-hot but spirit-heavy. The kind of heat that made jasmine open early and bees buzz a little slower.

Lucille had just finished placing fresh rosemary bundles in the windows when the bell above the shop door rang.

She turned, wiping her hands on her apron.

And in walked a man whose presence cracked the air open like thunder on dry ground.

He was tall, with skin the color of sweet cream and cane syrup.

High yella, with freckles on the bridge of his nose and a gold hoop in his left ear.

His hair was braided and hung low behind him.

His eyes? That peculiar, ancient gray that sometimes showed up in Geechie blood, stormy, unreadable, unforgettable.

He walked with a slight limp. And when he spoke, it was molasses dipped in smoke.

"Afternoon, ma'am. I was told y'all carry healing salves, somethin' strong for deep wounds. I took a bad fall off my horse down in St. Landry."

Lucille nodded, trying to keep her voice even. "You'll want the plantain and comfrey rub. I make it myself."

"You the medicine woman here?"

"I'm a student," she said. "But I know my roots."

"I bet you do," he said, eyes dipping low and then rising respectfully.

Sophie started to rustle her feathers as if she was dancing for Lucille.

Behind the curtain, Mama June stiffened.

She didn't come out. She didn't need to. She sniffed the air like a hunting dog.

No male imprint on Lucille. Not yet.

Still untouched. Still pure in scent and spirit.

But that tension?

It was rising fast.

Mama June reached for her peppermint oil and dabbed it behind her ears, just in case things needed cooling.

Lucille returned with a jar of thick, dark salve wrapped in muslin.

As she handed it to Adolphis, their fingers touched.

Only for a moment. But it was enough.

The air shifted again.

The candle behind the counter flickered hard.

Adolphis cleared his throat, but his eyes were softer now. Curious.

"What's your name?"

"Lucille."

"Lucille," he repeated, like it tasted good.

He tucked the jar in his satchel and tipped his hat.

"Reckon I'll be back soon. If the horse throws me again, or not."

Lucille smiled without meaning to. "We'll be here."

When the door closed, Lucille stood still, pretending to adjust a jar.

"You alright?" came Mama June's voice from the back.

"Of course," Lucille called back.

June appeared, drying her hands with a dish towel, her brow lifted. "Uh huh. And the river don't flood."

Lucille turned slowly. "You knew?"

June walked past her, sniffed the air dramatically.

"Please. Ain't no man ever touched you, not even in a dream. But that one, whew, your whole spirit leaned forward when he walked in."

Lucille blushed, deeply. "I didn't mean to..."

"You ain't gotta mean to, baby, chemistry don't ask for permission. But don't let that soft voice and pretty eyes blind you, a man like that ain't just flesh, baby. Sometimes Spirit sends temptation to see if you can read past pretty."

She touched Lucille's shoulder gently. "Some men carry more than charm. Some carry attachments.

Before you let one near your altar, you better read his soul."

Lucille nodded. "I will."

Mama June smiled, slow and knowing. "Mmhm. Just don't read it with your eyes closed."

That night, Lucille stood at her window, straightening her shoulders, looking out at the moon.

The wind was cool and for the first time, she whispered a prayer not for healing or protection, but for discernment.

"Spirit, if he's mine, show me. If he's not, shut the door before I open my heart."

And somewhere far off, a raven flew under the moonlight, wings slicing through truth.

Chapter Twenty-Five

The Invitation

The nights had become heavier since he left. Lucille couldn't sleep as deeply. Her hands fidgeted more when she grounded herbs.

Even Sophie tilted her head at her now, watching her with suspicion, or maybe concern.

But it wasn't worry that stirred in Lucille. It was hunger.

Not just for touch.

For becoming.

She was nearly twenty. Still untouched, not by fear, not by trauma, but by choice.

Still, lately, that choice felt like a waiting room.

And Adolphis Buckner had stepped into it with heat in his bones.

Lucille tried not to think about the way her stomach flipped when he looked at her.

The way her palms warmed when she thought about what his skin might feel like.

She tried to bury it in tinctures and prayer.

But every time she closed her eyes, she saw that slow smile, that gold hoop, the scent of something clean but wild.

It was almost two weeks to the day when the bell above the shop door rang again.

Lucille was restocking valerian root and nearly dropped the whole jar when she turned and saw him.

"Adolphis."

Walking straighter now. Back wrapped in linen but no longer stiff.

His face lit up the second he saw her. "Well now," he said, voice honeyed.

"Didn't think I'd be lucky enough to find you behind the counter again."

Lucille blinked slowly, then smiled, trying not to look too eager. "You're healing well."

"Thanks to y'all. That salve's the real deal."

She handed him a small bottle of lavender oil as a gift.

"For the scars. They'll fade faster."

He took it gently, letting their fingers touch for a moment longer than necessary.

"I was wondering something, Miss Lucille."

"Yes?"

He shifted slightly. "Would you... be open to dinner?"

Lucille froze, just a second, but not from fear.

It was confirmation that this wasn't just her imagination.

It wasn't just hunger in her bones; it was reciprocated.

She smiled, lips barely parting. "I think I would."

He grinned, his eyes flickering with that same stormy softness.

"I know a little place near the water, in the next town over, its Quiet. Great southern food, soul music so I just need you to pick the day my lady."

"I reckon I could be convinced."

"Done."

He tipped his hat again. "See you soon, Lucille."

The moment the door closed behind him, Mama June appeared from the back room like a ghost.

She didn't speak, just stared.

Lucille avoided her gaze and walked toward the back counter. "Don't say a word."

June didn't until Lucille disappeared up the stairs.

She then, picked up her tea and said softly, "Don't forget your spiritual glasses when you get dressed for dinner."

Lucille lay on her bed and exhaled, half laugh, half prayer.

Because she was already wondering, would this be the start of a love story, or a test?

Either way, she was going.

She got up and looked out the window, Sophie flew to the windowsill.

Somebody has the yearning to become a woman, Sophie said.

Chapter Twenty-Six

The Salt, The Rose, and
the Whisper

Lucille poured the last of the rose oil into the steaming bath. The scent bloomed around her like a soft cloud, floral, thick, and heady.

A few drops of vanilla for sweetness.

Epsom salt for cleansing.

She eased into the tub with a slow exhale, her body disappearing beneath the water like a prayer being answered.

The candles flickered low.

The windows were open just enough to let in the sound of crickets.

The water touched her collarbones, and her skin sighed in relief.

She closed her eyes, not to sleep, but to just to be.

But the moment her mind loosened its grip on the room, they came.

The Realm of the Mothers

She found herself not in the bath, but standing in an open field of silver mist.

Barefoot and clothed in white linen that glowed from within.

There were no stars, only light.

And before her stood the Three Hooded Mothers, their backs to her, facing the horizon.

One turned.

Then another.

The last didn't move.

Child, the first one said, voice like wind through pines.

You are bathing for a man, the second one added, with no judgment, only truth.

Lucille bowed her head slightly. "He stirs me," she whispered.

The third mother finally turned, slowly, then her hood fell back.

It was Mary Lou, Lucille's grandmother in her younger, wilder form.

Her eyes burned brightly.

Then let him stir you, she said. *But do not let him root you.*

Lucille stepped forward. "What do you mean?"

We don't see him with you in the seasons ahead, said the first.

He doesn't die, said the second.

He just... doesn't stay.

Mary Lou spoke last. *He's a spark, Lucille. Not the fire.*

Lucille's heart trembled. "But I feel something. It doesn't feel wrong."

It isn't, said Mary Lou.

He's not innocent, but he's not guilty either.

He's a messenger, a transition point.

A key that doesn't open forever but opens the next.

Lucille blinked slowly. "Will I give myself to him?"

The second mother tilted her head. *That is your choice.*

But if you do, added the first, *do not give him your future. Only give him what was meant to move.*

The mist began to rise, curling around Lucille's legs, soft and cool.

Mary Lou stepped forward, touching her forehead gently. *Feel everything,* she said.

But remember not everything you feel is meant to last.

Lucille nodded, tears filling her eyes.

Then, she woke up.

The Wake

Back in the bath, the water had cooled, and the candles were nearly out.

Lucille sat up slowly, her hand moving to her chest.

The rose scent was still thick.

But now, she felt precision beneath it. Not sorrow or fear just... understanding.

She stepped out, wrapped herself in her softest towel, and whispered, "He's not mine to keep. He's mine to meet."

Chapter Twenty-Seven

Dressed in Knowing

Lucille stood in front of the full-length mirror in her room, lit by the golden hue of late evening light.

She had taken her time soaking in oils of jasmine, rose, and sweet orange.

She had polished every inch of her brown skin until it glowed.

She painted her nails the color of ripe pomegranate, deep, rich red.

Her hair was rolled and curled, falling in soft waves over her shoulders, a single red rose pinned above her ear.

Her lips matched her nails, and her dress was a warm cinnamon hue. It laid softly against her skin and it was cut just low enough to offer a soft glimpse of the woman she had become.

There was a hint of cleavage announcing her arrival into the realm of the masculine.

She smelled like heaven itself, earthy, floral, unforgettable.

She didn't smile in the mirror, but she nodded and said "I'm ready."

Sophie peeping in and enjoying the glow on Lucille, *Beautiful woman*, and cawed.

Before she could reach the door, Mama June called from the hallway. "Lucille."

Lucille turned, breath caught, like a girl caught sneaking out.

Mama June stepped into the doorway, arms folded.

Her expression was unreadable, part approval, part concern. "You look like a prayer about to be answered," she said.

Lucille smiled, her heart thudding. "It's just dinner."

"Ain't nothin' ever just when you're walking into it like that."

They sat down together on the edge of Lucille's bed, the soft rustle of fabric between them.

June took her hand gently.

"I know the energy moving in you. The kundalini rising. The aches at the base of your spine, like something sacred and trapped. That's not just desire. That's life waiting for direction."

Lucille nodded slowly. "I feel it. Like I've been holding it forever."

"You have," June whispered. "But baby, let me tell you somethin' plain. The masculine... it can wake you. But it can also write on you. And sometimes, it don't write with ink, it writes with life."

Lucille's eyes welled. "You think I'm not ready?"

"No," June said. "I think you are. But I also think you need to know something before you open your gates."

She leaned closely. "He is not the father of your children."

Lucille blinked. "How do you know?"

"Because I smelled it the first day he walked in. He's not made for legacy. He's made for activation. He's a bridge, not a destination."

She let that sit.

Then added gently: "So don't confuse awakening for forever."

Lucille squeezed her hand. "I won't."

June reached into her apron and handed Lucille a small sachet of mugwort, bay, and motherwort, tied with red string.

"Keep this on you for clarity, not for blocking. You don't need to run from desire. Just make sure you're walking with your whole spirit, not just your body."

Lucille tucked the sachet into her purse, kissed Mama June on the cheek, and whispered: "Thank you for raising my mind before my womb."

June laughed softly. "That's what I'm here for."

As Lucille stepped out into the warm evening air, the scent of her skin lingered in the doorway like a promise.

The wind whispered through the trees, and Sophie the raven circled once overhead, cawing softly.

Tonight wasn't about losing anything. It was about stepping into her own power.

And she was ready.

Chapter Twenty-Eight

The Club, the Craving, the Christ Flame

The jazz club sat low in the corner of the next town over. No sign out front, just a green awning and a single red light above the door.

Sophie's croak echoed faintly in her mind, reminding her she wasn't stepping into this moment alone.

Inside, it was velvet and mahogany. Everything warm and mystical.

A trio played in the corner, sax, upright bass, brushed snare pulling golden notes from the air like threads of silk.

Lucille stepped in and time slowed, heads turned, but Adolphis stood.

The moment he saw her, his breath caught.

His lips parted, but no words came.

She moved like a rose in bloom. Hair curled to perfection, rose tucked high.

The scent of her skin, rose oil, jasmine, and something ancient. Red lips. Cinnamon dress.

Cleavage like scripture.

"Damn," he whispered as she approached. "You didn't come to dinner, Lucille. You came to change my whole damn life."

She laughed softly, kissed his cheek, and sat. "You clean up nice yourself, Buckner."

He was wearing a black linen shirt, open at the neck, a silver chain peeking out.

Skin golden under the lights. Eyes soft, searching.

They ordered wine. A red so dark it looked like blood in the candlelight.

The saxophone cried gently as Lucille sipped and met his gaze.

"I dreamed of you," Adolphis said suddenly. "Before I met you."

Lucille raised a brow. "Did you?"

"Didn't know it was you at the time. Just saw a woman... covered in light and fire, walking through water."

Lucille smiled gently.

"Sounds like she was walking between worlds."

"She was. And when I saw you the first time, I felt it in my bones. Not lust, not even love. Just... recognition."

Lucille's stomach tightened in a way that felt like both danger and destiny. "You speak like you feel things deep."

"I do. Always have. That's why I move slow with women.

But you…" he paused, voice lower, rougher, "you got that fire that don't burn. That Christ heat."

She blinked. "Christ heat?"

He leaned in, eyes flickering. "Yeah. Not religion, but consciousness. The holy kind. The kind that don't ask you to be small to be chosen.

The kind that says, 'Let me meet you where your soul is sitting upright."

Lucille sipped her wine slowly. "That's what you're craving?"

"Craving it like air," he said. "With you."

The band played a slower number. He stood and extended his hand.

"Come dance with me, Lucille."

She hesitated only for a breath and then rose.

They moved slowly on the small floor, surrounded by other swaying bodies and shadowed candlelight.

Adolphis placed his hand at the small of her back.

Not low. Not possessive. Just there, present, grounding her.

Lucille let her head rest near his collarbone. And for a moment, just a moment, the world faded.

It wasn't about sex. It wasn't about a future. It was about Christ consciousness rising in them both.

Two flames, flickering in rhythm, heating the space between their ribs.

He kissed her hand as the song ended.

"Whatever this is," he whispered, "I wanna honor it, even if it don't last."

Lucille met his gaze, calm and with certainty. "Then let's dance it fully, while it's ours."

In her mind, Lucille silently repeated her prayer "If he's mine, show me. If not, shut the door."

Chapter Twenty-Nine

Holding the Flame

As the weeks passed. Lucille had begun to measure time by the sound of Adolphis' boots on the wood floors of the shop. He showed up most days now. Sometimes he just wanted to say hello. Sometimes with fresh peaches from a nearby stand.

Once with a small bouquet of sage and yellow roses. "Not try-na rush nothin'," he said, handing them to her. "Just like bringing beauty to beauty."

He started helping Mama June unload shipments of herbs, even though June gave him side-eyes the entire time.

"He's good muscle," she whispered to Lucille, "but remember so was Delilah before she revealed the secret about Samson's hair."

Lucille only smiled. But she felt it too, the weight of attention. The way Adolphis watched her hands when she prepared tea. The way he looked at her lips when she spoke slowly.

The way his fingers sometimes lingered at the small of her back when no one was watching. They went out often now.

Dinners. Evening walks. Quiet conversations by the river.

He listened. He laughed. He didn't push. But the fire between them?

It was there, always there. It wrapped itself around them like a second atmosphere.

Lucille had stopped denying it. Her dreams were warmer and thoughts more vivid.

She had started wearing red more often, oils with muskier undertones.

She even changed her sheets, twice, just from the tension in her skin when she lay down.

And yet... She was still a virgin.

Not because she lacked desire, but because something deep inside her still whispered:

"Be careful what doors you open with your body, some spirits ride in through pleasure like thieves through an open window."

And Adolphis felt it. He never said the words, but sometimes his hands shook when he touched her waist.

Sometimes his voice cracked when he said goodnight. Sometimes, when he leaned close, she could hear the restraint in his breath.

One night, they sat on the back porch of the shop. The moon was full, and the crickets played their steady song.

Sophie tilted her head from the porch rail, her golden eye catching the moonlight, as if to say, name your fire carefully.

He brushed a curl from her face. "You know I want you."

Lucille nodded. "I know."

"You feel it too?"

"Every time I breathe."

He kissed her neck softly. Paused. "Then what's stopping you?"

Lucille looked out into the trees. "The fire scares me. Not yours. Mine."

He rested his forehead against hers. "That's the part I'm tryna reach."

She pulled back, not harsh, just gentle. "I know. But you can't rush a flame that was born sacred.

It'll burn wrong if it's pushed."

He sat back. Frustrated, maybe. But not angry. "I'm not tryna break you, Lucille. I just wanna help you feel the whole of yourself. Make you feel like a woman."

She looked him dead in the eyes. "I already feel like a woman, Adolphis. What I don't feel yet... is safe enough to burn."

He nodded slowly. Then stood. "I can wait," he said. "But don't wait so long you lose what's real just because you feared what could be."

Then he kissed her hand.

And left.

Sophie cawed once, low and steady, as though blessing the choice.

She sat in silence for a bit after he left, holding her own flame steady. She touched the sachet Mama June had given her, steady as Sophie's gaze, and whispered inwardly,

"I will burn when I choose, not when I'm asked."

Chapter Thirty

The Permission of
Pleasure

Lucille didn't sleep that night. The moonlight kept her up, pouring through the open window like it was watching her. She sat at the edge of her bed, journal open, pen idle.

Sophie, the raven, watched from the bookshelf, head tilted. Lucille had written the same sentence four times: "Desire isn't sin... but is it safe?" She closed the journal softly and made her way to the kitchen.

Mama June was already there, as if she'd been waiting. No apron. No oil. No work in her hands. Just a candle lit low, and a cup of tea she'd already made for Lucille.

"Come sit, baby," she said without turning.

Lucille sat obediently. June placed the tea in front of her, then leaned her elbows on the table, eyes steady and warm.

"You scared you gon' go to hell for feelin' what you feel?"

Lucille didn't answer, but her face did.

June nodded slowly. "I remember that fear. I carried it like a Bible in my chest. Took me years to figure out I wasn't holy because I denied myself. I was holy because I knew when to say yes with my whole soul."

Lucille whispered, "But I was raised to think it's wrong... to want. Especially before marriage." Sophie shifted on the shelf, her wings extended, giving Lucille authorization to fly.

"Wrong?" June chuckled. "Then explain why your body lights up like a lamp when that man so much as breathes your name?"

Lucille looked down, ashamed. June reached over and lifted her chin.

"Look at me. Your body don't lie, and God didn't make it by accident. You think the Creator put all them nerves between your thighs just so you could feel guilt every time they wake up?"

Lucille swallowed, tears brimming. "I don't want to lose control."

"Then learn how to ride it," June said, voice firm now. "You ain't meant to be controlled by it or to suppress it. You're meant to honor it, baby. Learn it, guide it, and know when you're opening a door versus unlocking a damn portal."

She sipped her own tea, then added, "A man like Adolphis, he ain't here to tame you. He's here to witness your becoming. But if you shame your body every time it reaches, you gon' confuse discipline with denial."

As Mama June spoke, Lucille felt the skeleton key warm faintly on her altar upstairs, not in warning, but in permission. Lucille was starting to notice the skeleton key is connected to her in more ways than one.

Lucille wiped her eyes. "So, it's not wrong to... explore?"

June leaned back in her chair and said softly: "It's not wrong to feel joy in your own skin. It's not wrong to want someone to help you expand spiritually, emotionally, and physically. What's wrong is when you let other people's fears write your map." She touched her chest. "You've got a compass in here. And you've got women behind you that burned quietly their whole lives because they were told pleasure made them dirty."

She stood now, circled the table, and hugged Lucille from behind. "You are not dirty. You are divine, and when the time comes, when your yes feels like a blessing, not a bargain, let it be full. Let it be sacred and let it be yours."

Lucille wept in her arms, tears not just of fear, but of release.

And in that kitchen, wrapped in the arms of a woman who had long since stopped apologizing for her softness, Lucille felt her body come home to itself.

Chapter Thirty-One

The First Flame

The next day began like any other. Lucille watered the herbs. She pressed rose petals into oil. She sat with Mama June for tea. But something had shifted. The tension that once wrapped itself around her chest like wire had melted. There was peace in her eyes.

Not because she had decided, but because the decision had made space for her.

Adolphis arrived in the late afternoon. He knocked gently, and when she opened the door, he took one step back, not because she startled him, but because she stunned him.

She wasn't dressed up. No red lips. No fancy gown. Just a linen wrap dress, soft curls down her back, and bare feet on the porch floor. But her energy was different. Open. Present. Unafraid.

"You alright?" he asked.

Lucille smiled. "I am."

"You look..."

"Ready," she finished.

They didn't speak much, words felt too small for what was happening between them.

They walked through the garden. The scent of basil, rose, and rain hung low in the air.

When he reached for her hand, she didn't flinch. When he kissed her, she didn't tremble. She leaned in.

And when she led him to her room, she did not ask permission.

She offered presence.

The Union

The room smelled of frankincense and orange blossom.

Sophie, sensing the moment, flew to the window and stood guard.

Candles lit the corners of the room. The shadows they cast danced slowly on the walls.

Lucille removed her dress like she was peeling back a layer of history. Adolphis kissed each shoulder like he'd been given a sacred map.

They didn't rush.

Their eyes stayed locked as fingers moved, as breath deepened. The first touch was not about hunger.

It was about remembrance. Two old souls meeting again beneath new skin.

He placed his hand on her womb before anything else. "You sure?" he whispered.

"I've never been surer of anything in my life."

When he entered her, it was with breath, slow, deep, trembling at first.

Lucille exhaled, and the whole room seemed to exhale with her. She didn't cry.

She didn't shake. She opened.

And together, they moved, not in thrusts, but in waves. In rhythm with the ancestors who watched silently from behind the veil.

His hands stayed on her waist. Her fingers in his hair. Their foreheads pressed together like a prayer.

There was soft moaning and heavy rhythmic breathing from the two souls mixing not only in the physical, but in the spiritual as well.

Just a heat that built from the root and rose, chakra by chakra, until their breath synced like one instrument.

"I feel... everything," he whispered.

"You're supposed to," she replied.

"It's never been like this."

"It's never been me," she said.

And when they climaxed, it wasn't a burst. It was a rising.

A golden light in the belly. A soft quake in the bones. A holy hum in the chest that echoed long after the movement stopped.

They lay still afterward. Skin against skin.

The sweat between them glowed under the candlelight. The skeleton key pulsing matching Lucille's heartbeat.

Lucille felt no shame. No worry. No wondering what would come next.

Because in that moment, she was whole.

And he? He was speechless. But his spirit bowed to Lucille's.

Mama Junes words repeating in Lucille's mind, "Don't confuse awakening for forever."

Chapter Thirty-Two

The Knowing Brew

The morning light touched the curtains softly. Lucille stirred beneath the sheets, her skin still humming from the night before.

Adolphis lay beside her, breathing slowly, his hand resting across her hip.

But her eyes were open. Not in regret. Not in confusion.

But in the knowing.

She rose gently, pulled on her robe, and stepped out into the quiet hallway.

The house felt different. Not heavier.

Just... more aware.

The smell of herbs drifted from the kitchen. Not cooking herbs, but womb herbs.

Lucille entered and found Mama June already there, standing at the stove, stirring something thick and fragrant in a small pot.

No words passed between them at first.

Just glances.

Just a soft exchange of breath.

Mama June looked up, eyes steady, and said without turning, "So... how was your first full moon?" Lucille blushed but didn't hide. "Beautiful."

June nodded. "Mmmmmm, I felt it, the walls told me." She poured the mixture into a mug and set it on the table. "Here. Drink this."

Lucille sat, wrapped her hands around the warm ceramic. "What is it?"

"Mugwort, raspberry leaf, nettle, cinnamon bark. It'll cool the fire, clear the gate, and tell your womb to hold its peace."

Lucille sipped slowly, Sophie fluttered her wings softly, signaling the cleansing has taken root.

Lucille's eyes closing for a moment, "You still don't think he's the father of my children?"

June shook her head gently. "No. Your spirit told me weeks ago. The ancestors whispered it again this morning. He was meant to stir you, not seed you."

Lucille exhaled, long and soft. "I don't want to bring life through the wrong doorway."

"Then honor that," June said. "A womb is not just for babies, it's for purpose, for legacy. You don't owe anyone access just because they touched your soul. Some souls are only meant to pass through.

Not stay."

Lucille took another sip, eyes steady now. "It didn't feel wrong. It felt... sacred."

"It was," June said. "But sacred don't always mean forever. Sometimes sacred just means complete."

She reached over and touched Lucille's hand. "You did what you needed to do. Now you need to do the rest. Cleanse. Close. Give thanks and keep walking."

And Lucille did just that.

After her tea, she bathed in fresh rosemary and moonwater. The steam rose around her like a spirit, curling and dissolving into the ceiling beams, carrying her relief upward.

Mama June knocks softly and said through the door, "Every woman in our line gave birth, some to children, some to visions, some to whole communities. Don't you ever think creation only comes through pain and labor."

Lucille let out a tear with a sigh of relief, she knew that she didn't do the wrong thing.

While drying off she lit a white candle and wrote a thank-you letter to her body.

She burned lavender and whispered to the ancestors,

"I honored your warning. But I also honored my womanhood. Thank you for trusting me."

She thanked her body for its patience, for carrying her fire without letting it consume her, for holding her until she was ready.

She closed her eyes to seal the letter, no longer questioning. Not in regret, not in confusion but in the knowing.

The skeleton key lit up in a faint rainbow-colored shadow that bounced to the floor and wall.

The candle flickered once, casting a long shadow across the floor.

Lucille then hears the voice of Mary Lou;

The gate is closed, child, but the path ahead is still being written.

Chapter Thirty-Three

The Spirit in the Yellow
Dress

Lucille was only eight years old the first time she saw the spirit ride someone right in front of her.

It was a Saturday afternoon.

Hattie was throwing a small backyard gathering, a garden party for her church friends.

Peach cobbler, deviled eggs, little cakes in paper cups.

Everyone wore florals and smiles like masks.

Lucille had been helping set the table when Loretta showed up. She arrived in a bright yellow dress, hips swinging, a perfume cloud trailing her like smoke from a candle that won't go out.

Hattie clapped and hugged her, loud and laughing.

But Lucille froze, because something was moving behind Loretta's eyes. Something dark and slick, like an oil slick with teeth. A spirit with long fingers and taker energy.

It wasn't looking at Hattie. It was looking toward the house at the room where Lucille's father kept his books and sat quietly on Sundays.

When Loretta smiled, that spirit grinned through her teeth. Lucille felt her stomach twist. She gripped the edge of the table and whispered under her breath:

"She don't belong here."

Later that afternoon, while the women gossiped under the mimosa tree and sipped on sweet tea, Lucille slipped into the kitchen and tugged at her mother's apron.

"Mama..."

"Hmm?"

"Miss Loretta got a spirit on her. A takin' one. I think she want Daddy."

Hattie's whole body stiffened for a half second then she turned, eyes sharp. "You don't say things like that."

"But Mama...."

"No. I don't want to hear none of that spooky mess right now. That woman is my friend. You just don't like how she laughs. Now go outside and stay in a child's place."

Lucille stood there for a beat too long, lower lip trembling. "But I can see it."

"You see too much," Hattie snapped, now flustered and red-cheeked.

She poked her fingers into Lucille's chest and said, "And it's gonna make people stop liking you if you keep talkin' that way."

Lucille came back out of the room, and that was the first time she learned, sometimes the truth makes you lonely.

And sometimes, mothers don't protect you... because they're protecting the wrong people.

A week later, Lucille overheard her father arguing with Hattie about boundaries.

She didn't know what it meant back then.

But the energy said enough, and she never saw Loretta again after that month.

But the spirit?

It winked at Lucille through the window the day Loretta drove away.

Chapter Thirty-Four

Familiar Spirits Wear
Family Faces

By the time Lucille was ten, she had stopped trying to convince people of what she saw. She just started watching. It was around then she learned one of the most important truths of her life, "The best way to learn spirits... is to study your own family." Because some spirits don't knock on the door and simply come in.

They're born in the blood.

They ride behind last names.

They speak in tone and pattern.

They show up in generational cycles, not always to destroy, sometimes just to repeat.

Lucille first noticed it in her Aunt Genevan. She was funny, loud, and could light up a room. But every time a man gave her attention, she shrunk.

Apologized.

Got clumsy.

Numbed herself.

Lucille once saw a spirit sitting on Aunt Genevan's shoulder, rocking and whispering in her ear. It had no face, just a silhouette of memory. One day Lucille asked Mary Lou about it.

"Why she got a spirit of shame on her?"

Mary Lou, always one to tell the truth, lit her pipe and said, "Cause her mama had it, and her mama's mama did too. That spirit knows our line."

Lucille blinked. "So, it's been in the family?"

"Longer than we have."

She watched her cousin David next. He was always angry, always ready to fight. Not mean, just... tight, like his spirit had no space to breathe. One afternoon, while he helped her fix a tire, Lucille saw a small black dog-shaped spirit following him. It didn't bark. It just growled under its breath, keeping pace with every step. She watched it for weeks.

Until one day, David broke down crying after punching a hole in a shed wall.

That night, Lucille asked Mary Lou again. "What's following David?"

"Spirit of abandonment," she said without hesitation.

"His daddy left, and so did his daddy's daddy. The spirit don't leave 'cause it's familiar. It thinks it belong."

Lucille felt her chest ache. "So... some spirits don't even know they hurtin' us?"

"Exactly," Mary Lou said. "Familiar spirits ain't always evil. They're unhealed and they need recognition. You can't cast out what you keep feeding through silence and tradition."

From then on, Lucille started journaling every spirit she saw around her family. Aunt Thelma's fear spirit, who made her clean obsessively and fear open windows. Uncle Ray's lust spirit, who made him disappear every time a new pretty face smiled at him. Her own sister Claudine's jealousy spirit, which sat on her chest like a cat when she slept. And sometimes, even Hattie's gossip spirit, which looked like a sharp-beaked bird always whispering nonsense in her ear.

Lucille began understanding, not every generational curse is loud. Some just dress up as personality. Some sit quietly and pass through birthdays, inheritances, and baby showers.

And most folks never question them, because they wear the face of someone we love.

But Lucille did.

And that's when she started becoming a true seer.

Chapter Thirty-Five

The Spirits That Never
Left

The bell over the shop door jingled.

Lucille looked up from the drying lavender bundles just as Angelina came in, slow and hesitant, like the weight of her memories followed two steps behind.

She was dressed in worn jeans and a faded sweatshirt, sleeves tugged low over her wrists even though the day was warm.

Sophie eyes started to glow a golden color immediately after seeing Angelina.

Mama June stepped from the back room, wiped her hands on a cloth, and gave a single nod. "You ready, baby?"

Angelina didn't answer right away. She just stood there, eyes glossy, hands shaking just enough to notice. "I... I just need something to help me stop," she whispered. "I keep drinkin'. Every time I think I'm done, I ain't."

June stepped closer. "You ain't drinkin' liquor, Angelina, you drinkin' pain that ain't been named yet. The spirits you takin' in, they ain't from the bottle. I'll go gather what we need and you calm and guide that spirit into the waters to brine em'."

Lucille moved gently to Angelinas side. She didn't ask questions. Didn't push. She just reached out and took her hand, guiding her toward the back room.

The Story Behind the Spirits

As Mama June prepared the water, Lucille sat with Angelina. They lit a single white candle.

The room smelled of chamomile, lemon balm, and vetiver.

Angelina stared into the flame, and the words began to tumble like an old dam breaking open. "I was fourteen the first time he touched me, he was older. Said I was beautiful. Said it was love.

I didn't know better."

Lucille closed her eyes softly, listening.

"Got me pregnant! My family lost their minds and took me to Alabama. Said I had to 'clean it up and nobody could ever know." Her hands began to shake harder. "After that, I just... stopped bein' somebody."

Mama June re-entered, quiet as shadow. She set down a bowl of salts, black salt, Epsom, and ground rue.

"You still in there, Angelina," she said. "They tried to bury you, but baby, you ain't dead. You just need a resurrection."

The Salt Bath

The tub in the back room was already steaming. Mama June sprinkled in lavender, mugwort, lemon peel, and fresh rosemary.

Lucille anointed Angelina's forehead with frankincense oil, whispering softly:

"You are not dirty. You are not ruined. You are not to blame."

Angelina undressed with trembling hands. She stepped into the water like it might reject her but it didn't. It welcomed her.

Lucille and June stayed nearby, eyes turned respectfully, but holding sacred space.

Angelina sank deep into the warmth, she cried. First softly, then fully.

She cried for the baby, for the girl she was, for the bruises and for the silence. And as the tears hit the water, the spirits began to lift.

Not just the ones from the bottle, but the ones that had clung to her skin like shame.

The bath turned darker, not with dirt, but with grief being drawn out.

The skeleton key began to rattle as if it was guiding the spirits away from the house.

Aftercare

When she emerged, wrapped in a thick white towel, she looked lighter. Not healed just yet, but... seen.

And that was the beginning.

Mama June handed her a bundle of wild yam root, rose petals, and calendula. "Steep this every day for seven days. Drink it while speakin' life over yourself. No apologies. Just truth."

Lucille added a small jar of salt to the bag. "For your next bath. Whenever the spirits try to come back."

Angelina looked at them both, eyes shining. "You think I can really stop?"

Mama June stepped closer. "You already did, baby. The moment you walked through that door."

Chapter Thirty-Six

The Waiting Child

The bell above the shop door rang low.

It was early morning, the kind where the sun still yawns and the air is thick with dew.

Lucille was restocking calendula when Lila Miller stepped inside, petite, quiet, but with tension in her step like her bones were tired of carrying questions without receiving answers.

She looked around shyly before approaching the counter.

"Hi, I... I'm looking for something to help my womb. I've had three miscarriages in the last two years, and my doctor says it's just bad luck. But I feel like my body's missing something. Maybe iron or magnesium... I don't know."

Lucille stepped forward, ready to offer care, but as soon as she reached for Lila's hand to read her pulse... She froze.

Something was already with her. Not attached like a parasite. Not heavy like grief.

But... hovering.

A small presence, feminine, ancient, and insistent. Nestled in the lower part of Lila's womb space, not physical... but there. Like a child waiting in a room just behind the veil.

Lucille blinked, her breath caught for a second. "Lila..." she said gently, "when did you first feel like something was trying to come through you?"

Lila looked confused.

"I... I guess after my first miscarriage. I started dreaming about a little girl. Curly hair. Bright eyes.

Sometimes she talks to me. But it's just a dream, right?"

Lucille shook her head slowly.

"That's not a dream; that's a spirit child. She's not gone; she's been waiting too long. She's stuck between worlds because no one helped her cross."

Lila's eyes filled with tears. "Are you saying... I'm keeping her here?"

"No," Lucille said, stepping from behind the counter. "I'm saying she's waiting for something that hasn't been healed yet. She chose you, Lila. But not just your body, your spirit. And right now, your spirit is grieving more than your womb."

The Ceremony of Release

Mama June appeared silently from the back, holding a cloth bundle of blue lotus, motherwort, and angelica root.

"She ain't tryin' to haunt you," June said. "She's just lost and she's hungry for light."

They drew the curtains. Lit the white candles. Lila lay down on the anointing table, and Lucille placed her hands gently over her belly.

She whispered to the spirit-child:

"You are known. You are loved. You are not forgotten."

She anointed Lila's lower abdomen with mugwort oil, then began the ancient womb song passed down from her maternal line, a low hum that vibrated deep through her palms and into Lila's womb space.

Lila began to cry. Not in panic. In recognition.

Mama June burned cypress and lavender, speaking words to guide the child spirit toward the light.

"You came through the wrong door, baby. Go back now. When the time is true, you'll return."

The room grew still. The candle flame flickered once, then stilled completely. Sophie flew around the house letting out a caw.

Lucille opened her eyes. The presence was gone. Not banished. Not erased.

Just... released.

The skeleton key pulsated making waves as if it was dancing the babies spirit back to the heavens.

Aftercare

Lila sat up slowly, wiping her eyes. "I feel... empty."

"That's not emptiness," Lucille said softly.

"That's space for healing. For timing. For return, if it's meant."

Mama June handed her a tea blend wrapped in soft muslin. "Take this for seven days. Speak blessings over your womb. Not wishes, blessings. And if that child spirit is yours to carry one day, she'll come back through the front door, not the shadow."

Lila hugged them both before she left, lighter than when she entered.

That night Lucille lit a candle in her room for all the children between worlds.

Not to summon them, but to let her know she had been seen.

Mama June let Adolphis in without even warning Lucille, she knew her soul would need to be held tonight after this spiritual lesson.

Lucille made love to him like she was trying to conceive a child that very night.

All the stars were shining bright and Sophies silhouette crossing the full moon back and forth as the sparks of love filled the air.

Chapter Thirty-Seven

His Heart Is Moving

They'd just finished another slow, steamy session where breath led the rhythm and their skin sang in soft gasps. Adolphis rolled off her, chest rising, eyes to the ceiling. Lucille turned to her side, still warm, still glowing, but something felt different.

Not his touch. Not the way he held her. But his energy. It was already folding in on itself. She lay still, trying not to feel it, trying not to listen too deeply. But then it came.

That familiar whisper in the back of her mind, wrapped in ancient rhythm, *His heart is moving.*

Her stomach dropped. She blinked at the ceiling and slowly exhaled. Not gone... but going. Adolphis got up, pulled on his shirt, and stood near the window. She sat up quietly, sheet wrapped around her, watching his shoulders.

"You leaving?" she asked.

He turned halfway. "Got offered a big job. Masonry work. Tennessee. Good money. Good people." He avoided eye contact.

Lucille nodded slowly. "How long you known?"

"A few weeks." That hurt more than the news itself.

Sophie was planted on Lucille's windowsill outside but immediately flew away, as she knew what was about to happen.

"And you didn't think to say anything?"

He shrugged, that same shrug men use when they want to soften a blow they know they're responsible for. "Didn't wanna mess this up. Didn't wanna say goodbye before I had to."

Lucille stood, the sheet falling slightly, her posture tall and bare and unapologetically woman. "You already said it. Just without words." She didn't cry. She didn't curse.

She just walked to her altar and lit a single white candle. "I dreamed of you before you came," she said softly. "And I saw the exit before you knew you were walkin' toward it."

Adolphis looked at her now, full of some sorrow that couldn't undo anything. "I didn't come here to hurt you."

"But you did," she said, voice steady. "And I'm strong enough to feel it without folding."

He crossed the room, touched her waist. "Lucille…"

"Don't," she said, firm. "If you love me, don't make this harder by pretending you're staying."

He stepped back. The candle flame flickered. And the room felt heavier now, not from grief, but from the weight of a chapter closing itself. He hugged her from behind tightly and said "I'm so sorry Lucille but I have to take this job, it's my chance at making real money."

Lucille stayed silent and all the elders' words rang true, *He's not the father of your children.* They kissed passionately and began to make love again. Multiple times, like they knew they would never see each other again.

Later that night, after he left, Lucille sat alone on the edge of her bed after bathing. She held the skeleton key in one hand, a bay leaf in the other. She whispered a prayer:

"Thank you for what he unlocked. Now let me lock the door he walked through."

She burned the leaf. Let the smoke rise. Let the ache root itself in wisdom, not sorrow. And as the flame died down, so did the fire between them, not extinguished, just transformed.

Lucille was officially a woman now and she knew it.

Chapter Thirty-Eight

The Alchemist's Gate

The house was still.

The wound of Adolphis's absence had become a quiet drumbeat in Lucille's chest.

She didn't cry.

Not because she didn't hurt, but because she had learned what to do with the ache.

That night, while journaling beside her altar, a sudden gust of wind blew through the window. The candle flickered violently. Sophie tilted her head and let out a single low caw.

Lucille stood up slowly. "They're calling me back."

She took the skeleton key from her pouch, walked to the arched mirror in her room, the one no one else could see reflections in.

She turned the key.

The mirror rippled like water touched by spirit.

And she stepped through.

The Temple of Transmutation

The spirit realm was dusky, warm, full of golden light pulsing like breath.

The three hooded mothers stood in a circle of stone, each robe a different hue, obsidian, amethyst, and deep crimson.

They didn't speak with mouths. Their thoughts poured into her mind like scripture.

You are no longer a watcher. You are now a wielder. What you feel, you can now bend. What you carry, you can now break and reshape. We will teach you the stages of alchemy.

One of the mothers stepped forward and laid out seven stones, each etched with a symbol glowing faintly.

They began to chant, not in a language of this world, but in a rhythm that stirred the elements inside of Lucille.

The Ritual of the Seven Stages

1. Calcination: Burning Away the Ego

A small flame appeared above Lucille's open palm.

Old memories flickered through the fire, Hattie's silence, Claudine's cruelty, Adolphis leaving.

She saw each, breathed deep, and whispered, "I release the lie that I am unworthy."

The flame dimmed.

2. Dissolution: The Breaking Down

Water poured over her from nowhere, washing off the soot.

Lucille knelt as the water pooled, showing her reflection.

She saw herself as she truly was, scarred, holy, beautiful, imperfect.

"This is who I've always been. Not broken, just unrefined."

3. Separation: Choosing What to Keep

The mothers held out two hands, one full of stones, the other feathers.

Lucille reached for both, placed the feather in her heart, the stone in her belly.

"I keep the softness and the weight that makes me grounded."

4. Conjunction: Merging Spirit and Flesh

A vine sprouted from her feet, curling up her body, wrapping her arms.

It didn't trap her, it rooted her. She began to glow.

She felt her sexuality, spirituality, and intellect merge, not compete.

"I am not divided. I am divine in all directions."

5. Fermentation: The Birth of the Sacred Self

A golden moth landed on her shoulder.

It turned to light and entered her chest.

She inhaled deeply and saw herself at 30... 40... 80.

She saw herself as a leader of women, a teacher of balance. She smiled.

"So this is who I'm becoming."

6. Distillation: The Rise of Pure Truth

Steam swirled around her, extracting only what was eternal.

Every false belief, about love, control, needing permission drifted away like fog.

"I am not too much. I am not too late. I am not made for small places."

7. Coagulation: The Final Stage: The Gold Within

Her feet touched the stone circle. The symbols on the ground glowed.

Lucille stood tall. Her eyes shimmered with gold.

Her hair floated slightly from her shoulders.

Her voice rang out, not as echo, but as command:

"I am the flame that refines. I am the water that remembers. I am the stone that cannot be moved."

The hooded mothers bowed their heads.

And Lucille... became the alchemist.

She stepped back through the mirror, barefoot, glowing faintly. Sophie cawed once.

And Lucille, for the first time, felt no fear about what would come next.

Chapter Thirty-Nine

A Life Unbound

The evening came with soft thunder, the kind that rolled low and far off, more like a memory than a warning.

Lucille and Mama June sat outside the shop, tea steaming in clay cups. The herbs were bundled and hanging to dry.

Sophie rested on the railing, watching the wind shift. Lucille rocked gently in her chair; eyes fixed on the horizon.

"Mama June... you ever had children?"

June sipped her tea, didn't answer right away. Instead, she smiled a small, knowing smile.

"No, baby. I didn't."

Lucille turned toward her, curious. Not judgmental, just open.

"Why not? If you don't mind me askin'."

June set her cup down, folded her hands across her lap. "Because I didn't want to be tied to a man in that way."

Lucille blinked. "Tied?"

June looked at her square in the eyes.

"There are bonds, and there are bindings. A child is a beautiful thing, sacred. But it comes with soul cords, deep ones. Once you let a man give you a child, you are bound to his energy, even if he gone. Even if he's trash. And I knew myself too well."

She leaned back in the chair, the wood creaking softly. "I'm a feeler, Lucille. I don't just love, I absorb. I don't just hear, I sense. And baby, I didn't want no man to sit in my spirit like a tenant who don't pay rent."

Lucille laughed, but not to mock. It was the kind of laugh you give when something makes painful sense.

June continued:

"I've made great love in my life. The kind that sings between the bones. But I understood something early, love is temporary without manipulation and ultimatums. And I ain't never been one to beg."

She paused and added gently:

"So, I loved fully, but I didn't hold. And I never let one stay long enough to dim my sight or drown my gifts."

Lucille was quiet now, sitting with the weight of June's words. "Don't you ever get lonely?"

June looked up toward the darkening sky. "Sometimes. But I'd rather be lonely in truth, than partnered in illusion."

She turned back to Lucille. "This life chose me, same way yours chose you. Not everyone's meant to mother through the body. Some of us mother through spirit, through touch, through teaching. I got daughters, Lucille. I just didn't give birth to them. You one of 'em."

Lucille felt her eyes sting, but she didn't cry. She just reached out and held Mama June's hand, warm and calloused and steady.

"I'm grateful you didn't settle. Otherwise, I'd have never found you."

June smiled again, this time with a softness Lucille would carry forever.

"And I'd have never had you to teach."

Chapter Forty

A Season of Sweeping

The summer came thick and humming, sweet with honeysuckle, heavy with heat. But inside Mama June's shop, it was the season of cleansing.

Not just herbs or baths this time, the bones of the building, the doorways, the corners, the air.

"Everything living got memory," Mama June told her, "And baby, so does space."

Cinnamon & Water

Lucille had just finished organizing jars of burdock root when Mama June handed her a rusted tin bucket filled with steaming water.

She dropped a bundle of cinnamon sticks, crushed clove, a pinch of salt and red pepper into the water and stirred it with a wooden spoon that looked older than the shop itself.

"This here's sweet fire. We mop the floor with it every Thursday. Cinnamon don't just smell good, it clears stagnant love, broken promises, and any spirits too bitter to let go."

Lucille dipped the mop and began to move in long, intentional strokes.

"Mop from the back of the shop to the front, always toward the door. Push the mess out, don't trap it inside."

As she moved, Lucille felt something shift, not in the room, but in her chest.

Old tension. Words she hadn't spoken. Memories she didn't know were stuck inside her skin.

Mama June smiled knowingly. "See, it ain't just the floor we clearing."

Rice in the Windowsills

Later that week, just after twilight, Mama June called her to the window with a bowl of uncooked rice.

"Hags like to ride people at night. Especially when they are jealous or bitter. They come in like wind, through cracks, through sleep, through pain. Rice in the windowsills confuses 'em."

Lucille raised a brow. "Why?"

"Too many choices. They gotta count it. By the time they done, sun already rising."

Lucille poured rice gently into each windowsill, whispering Psalm 121 under her breath, as June had taught her.

"You don't just protect with force, Lucille. Sometimes, you protect with wisdom and trickery. That's the magic of the old women."

Creolin and Pine

One morning, the air felt off. Lucille could sense it before she entered the front door. A heaviness. Not evil, just uninvited.

Mama June was already boiling a pot near the stove, pine needles, turpentine, and the sharp, tarry scent of Creolin rising into the air.

"Some spirits need more than prayer. They need pressure."

She poured the mixture into a metal bowl, grabbed a rag, and handed another to Lucille.

"We gonna wipe down every doorknob, threshold, and mirror. Creolin don't just clean, it commands."

Lucille gagged a little at the smell.

June laughed. "That's how you know it's working."

Together they scrubbed the shop down, humming old spirituals as they worked. When they were done, June stood at the door and said loudly:

"Ain't nothin' welcome here but peace, purpose, and protection. If you can't help, you can't enter."

The air shifted.

Lucille could feel it.

And Sophie, perched by the mirror, flapped once and settled.

That night, Lucille wrote in her journal:

"Protection isn't just defense, it's maintenance. A life must be swept the way a floor is swept.

Regularly, prayerfully, and with purpose."

Chapter Forty-One

The Spirit at the Edge

It started with the mirrors.

Three of them, one in the front room, one near the apothecary shelf, and one above the basin. They all began to hum. Not audibly, but with vibration.

Lucille felt it in her throat before she saw anything.

Mama June had just finished anointing the door with lemon oil when she paused.

Her head tilted slightly. Her eyes narrowed. "You feel that?"

Lucille nodded slowly. "Been feelin' it since last night. But now it's louder."

They stepped out onto the porch. The trees were still.

The sky thick and low, as if something heavy pressed down from above.

Then Lucille's eye twitched. She turned just fast enough to miss it.

A flash in the corner of her sight.

Red.

Purple.

Moving like a shadow that remembered how to dance.

The First Glimpse

That night, Lucille lit a candle by the window. Sophie began cawing low and rhythmic, not in fear, but in warning.

Lucille looked out toward the trees behind the shop. There it was.

A figure, not solid, not fully smoke, weaving through the tree trunks like a memory trying to break back into the present. It didn't step. It glided.

Its aura pulsed in deep red, rage, blood, revenge and soft purple, the color of bitter royalty and broken spiritual lineage.

Lucille's mouth dried, "Mama June...."

"I know," she said from behind her, already holding the creolin and a bowl of ash.

"It's not a stranger," June added, eyes narrowed. "It's a familiar. And it ain't here for the shop. It's here for you."

It Speaks

The next afternoon, while sweeping the back corridor, Lucille paused at the rear screen door.

She saw it again, closer this time. Right on the edge of the garden where the rosemary grew.

And then,

Lucille…

She froze.

The voice was dry and thick, like gravel soaked in molasses. It didn't echo. It just landed, heavy and personal.

Lucille, I'm coming for you…because of Mary Lou.

Lucille's hand clenched the broom so tight the handle cracked.

"You ain't got permission to speak my name," she whispered through clenched teeth.

Your grandmother bound me. Trapped me in the veil. And you, you're the blood that walked back through the door she locked.

Lucille slammed the door shut.

The Gathering

That night, she and Mama June built a small altar by the fire pit out back.

"He's old," June said. "One of the ones Mary Lou banished from a client. But if he stuck to the family bloodline…he's been waitin, circlin'. Lookin' for weakness."

Lucille didn't flinch. "He won't find it here."

June handed her a purple candle, a pouch of graveyard dirt, and a mirror painted with sigils of silence and return.

"He wants your fear. Don't give it to him. Stand in your bloodline. Call Mary Lou if you must."

Lucille nodded, calm now. Her hand never shook as she poured salt in a wide circle and lit the candle inside it.

As the flame rose, so did the wind. The figure stood now just beyond the circle, form flickering between man and mist. But he could not pass. Lucille lifted the mirror.

"In the name of the women who bore me, in the name of the keys I carry, return to your shadow. You have no claim."

The figure screamed, not loud, but sharp enough to cut air. Then vanished, like water evaporating off stone.

Sophie flapped once.

The candle stilled. Mama June exhaled deeply.

"It's always the old ones who wait the longest. But you held your ground."

Lucille didn't smile. "Let him come again. I know who I am now."

The altar flame snapped high, throwing shadows against the trees.

And in that moment, Mary Lou's voice rose from the fire, steady as ever,

Child don't mistake rage for weakness. It is the hammer that forges your will. Use it, don't wear it.

Lucille closed her eyes, spine straightening, the fire no longer wild, but harnessed. She opened them again, golden flecks dancing in her gaze.

She also remembered the first lesson of alchemy, **calcination:** burn away the ego, refine the dross.

This fire wasn't there to consume her. It was here to temper her. She breathed it in, let it roll through her veins, and whispered, *"I am the flame that refines."*

Chapter Forty-Two

The Woman I Was

Lucille sat in meditation at her altar, the mirror covered in a deep red cloth, the skeleton key held in one palm, bay leaf in the other. Sophie perched behind her. The candle flickered.

She whispered the call. "Mary Lou... grandmother... I need you." The mirror shimmered, and the veil opened like breath. Lucille stepped through.

Beyond the Veil

Mary Lou stood in a white linen dress, her silver hair wrapped, her eyes blazing like warm coals. Her presence was soft, but her power rumbled underneath, ancient and knowing.

She was waiting, as if she knew Lucille would come. Mary Lou said, *You saw him, didn't you?*

Lucille nodded. "He said you bound him... after taking a married man who belonged to a wicked bloodline."

Mary Lou closed her eyes and exhaled slowly. *That was the last man I ever took without discernment.*

Lucille swallowed. "Tell me everything. I need to understand why he's still coming for me."

The Wild Woman

Mary Lou walked slowly through the spiritual field, barefoot, regal, unashamed.

I had your fire, Lucille. That deep, knowing, root-burning heat. It could pull men without a word. Could make 'em dream about me without ever touching their skin.

Lucille listened, wide-eyed, as Mary Lou continued.

But I was reckless. I was young and knew I was powerful, knew I was... craved. So I played.

She paused, voice lower now.

I didn't just take single men. I took married men too. Even when I knew better. Even when I felt the chill in my bones that said, she's watching.

The Bloodline of the Witch

One man... he was different. His wife was from a dark line, Old Carolina witches. They didn't pray; they plotted. She wasn't in love with him. He was just hers. A trophy. A possession. And when I touched him, she sent something ancient after me.

Lucille felt the air shift even in the spirit world. Shadows passed through the grass like ghosts retracing old steps.

It found me in my sleep. Bit at my womb, tried to twist my soul. Made my mirror crack and my hips ache. Made every man I kissed after that turn to dust in my spirit.

Lucille whispered, "What did you do?"

The Binding

I ran to a church, not for forgiveness. For protection. The preacher's wife had the gift, she helped me trap it in a mirrored box behind the altar. And that day, I knew, no more games.

I fasted. I cleansed.

I took back every word and whisper I ever sent to the wrong man.

She turned and looked Lucille square in the eye.

That was when I earned my skeleton key. I didn't get it at 18 like you. I got it when I stopped playing with sacred things like they were toys.

The Warning

Mary Lou stepped closer, placing her hand over Lucille's womb.

You got the same fire, baby. But you don't have to burn the way I did. You already learned that sex is sacred. But now you must know who you share it with determines what spirits enter your house.

Lucille whispered, "Is he still bound?"

Yes. But your blood woke him. You walk like I did. You carry pieces of that moment with you. And that's why he's after you now.

Lucille took a breath. "So how do I send him back fully, how did he even get unbound enough to come to the shop?"

Mary Lou smiled, fierce and proud. Not with fear. Not with guilt, but with truth.

You call him by name. You tell him the debt is closed. You tell him, I am not my grandmother's shame. I am her evolution. Spirits can project into spaces they smell blood even if they are bound. That's why your mind should always be protected Lucille. Keeping spirit at bay isn't a small feat.

Lucille reached for her grandmother's hand. "I won't carry your karma. But I'll carry your wisdom."

Mary Lou leaned in, kissed Lucille's forehead. *That's all I ever wanted.*

Lucille stepped back through the mirror. The shop was still. The red cloth fell over the mirror again.

And outside, in the distance, the air hissed, like something slipping away in defeat.

Sophie laned in front of the front door of the shop, flew in a circle around the haint ceiling and blue glass bottles. Then flew off towards the moon.

Chapter Forty-Three

The Wedding in the
Garden

The sun hung hot and still over the garden behind the house Lucille hadn't entered in years.

It was beautiful, no doubt, white chairs in rows, magnolia blooms, and soft jazz spilling from the live bland.

But the air buzzed wrong.

"There's too much smiling goin' on," Mama June muttered as she adjusted her wide-brim hat. "That kind of happiness don't come without help."

Lucille scanned the yard, polka-dot dress fluttering around her knees, curls pinned just right. But her eyes stayed sharp.

She wasn't here for show. She came because Claudine invited her.

And brought Mama June because intuition demanded back-up.

Spirits in the Soil

As soon as Lucille stepped onto the grass, she felt it tugging at her ankles. The energy of things buried like old fights, slammed doors and cries that echoed through the wallpaper.

Childhood memories clenched her gut.

Sophie cawed once from a nearby pecan tree.

Lucille whispered: "I feel it too, girl."

June tapped her cane softly against the dirt and looked toward the altar being set up.

"That ain't love sittin' on that man," she murmured. "That's binding work."

Lucille turned, narrowing her eyes at the groom. Tall, handsome. Shoulders too straight and eyes a little... vacant.

And then she saw them.

Red-rope roots, stained with Claudine's blood, crawling from her into him. They wrapped his waist. Coiled around his spine. Claudine stood proud next to him glowing, but not from joy.

From control.

Hattie's Hollow Performance

Inside the house, Hattie floated from room to room in glitter and pearls, putting on a performance Lucille had seen a thousand times growing up.

"Oh Lucille, you came! Look at you, baby, so grown! You always were the quiet one."

Lucille nodded. She was still quiet but watching and on alert.

Hattie's smile twitched but didn't falter.

Mama June walked by and caught a whiff of something sharp, copper, clove, and scorched rose petals. She leaned in toward Lucille.

"She tried to cover it. But that's Claudine's blood I'm smellin'. Fresh work. Done maybe a week ago."

Lucille clenched her jaw. She looked at Claudine across the room, laughing too loud, her new ring flashing. There was triumph in her eyes, but not peace.

The Military Man

Back outside, as the ceremony was about to begin, a man approached Lucille near the lemonade table. He was tall, skin kissed by sun, hair sharp, Air Force clean. Polished, but not stiff.

"You don't look like you from around here," he said with a smile.

Lucille tilted her head. "I'm from here. Just don't carry it like luggage no more."

He laughed, eyes lingering, not with lust, but with curiosity. "That a fact? Well... this is gonna sound forward, but... you look like someone with stories."

Lucille sipped her lemonade. "You wouldn't believe half of 'em."

"Try me."

Sophie cawed again, circling above, as if amused.

The Ceremony Begins

As the vows were spoken, Lucille watched the veil shimmer over the groom's eyes. She saw spirits crouching at the corners of the altar. One holding a bowl of Claudine's hair. Another scribbling names in ash.

Lucille knew what it meant. This marriage was sealed with more than paper. It would hold, for now, but not without cost.

As the crowd applauded and Claudine beamed, Lucille leaned to Mama June.

"You think she knows what she's done?"

"She knows. She just doesn't care. Not yet."

Lucille looked back at the officer, who gave her a nod.

And in that moment, she understood, she came to witness a wedding.

But she'd also come to see what her own power would never be used for.

Chapter Forty-Four

The Smoke and the Soak

The moon was waning, pulling gently on the tides of every-thing within. Back at the shop, the air felt heavier than usual, like laughter had been used to cover up too much pain at Claudine's wedding.

The kind of spiritual grime that clung to the soul, even after you smiled through it. Mama June walked in first, removed her hat, and untied her headwrap slowly.

"We brought somethin' back from that house," she said. "And it ain't no leftovers."

Lucille nodded, unzipping her polka dot dress and kicking off her shoes. "I feel it all over me. In my scalp. Behind my knees. Under my ribs."

Mama June already had the copper tubs pulled out, one for each of them, set near the back door under the moonlight that spilled through the curtain. She dropped handfuls of Epsom salt into the water with purpose, followed by bay leaves and dried rose petals that floated like spells. The sound of the salt hitting the bottom of the tubs sounded like tiny little prayers cracking open.

"This right here," she said as she reached into a jar, "is for undoing."

Sacred Smoke

Mama June struck a match and lit a hand-rolled joint, the scent herbal and earthy, with a faint note of clove. She took a long draw, holding it like a prayer before releasing it into the air. Then she pulled out another one from her velvet pouch and handed it to Lucille. "First time?"

Lucille hesitated. "Yeah. I always been scared to lose control."

Mama June winked. "We don't lose it. We share it for a while. With the Earth.

With the ancestors.

With the part of us that remembers peace."

Lucille lit it. Coughed once. Then relaxed as her body began to hum.

Soaking & Speaking

Both women eased into their tubs, robes off, heads wrapped in soft cloth, skin gleaming in candlelight.

Lucille leaned her head back. "I needed this. The house... the way Claudine had those roots tangled around that man...It made my stomach flip."

Mama June took another puff, blew it toward the window. "That girl walkin' around with the same spell her mama used. Problem is, she don't know what price Hattie paid for it."

Lucille exhaled slowly, the warm water lifting weight from her bones. "Why would a woman chain a man like that?"

"'Cause she don't believe he'd stay otherwise. 'Cause she's scared of real love and scared of being left. Root work without soul work is just... fear with seasoning."

The Prayer

The two sat in silence for a moment as the moon crept higher. Then Mama June spoke in a tongue Lucille didn't recognize soft, ancient, maybe Yoruba, maybe something older.

Lucille whispered Psalm 91 under her breath, her bay leaf floating in the water like a tiny shield. The smoke curled around them, wrapping the room in a veil.

"Any spirit," June said, "any memory, any root that don't belong to us be gone.

Back to the dust.

Back to the wind.

We are washed.

We are covered.

We are free."

Lucille repeated it softly, the smoke finally calming her heart.

As the water cooled, both women sat with clarity, not answers, not conclusions, just space to breathe.

Lucille looked over at June. "You think she's gonna be okay?"

Mama June shrugged. "She'll either learn the hard way...Or not at all. But you, you just let that girl's story remind you of what you ain't never gotta do."

Lucille smiled, lifted her joint again, and let the smoke rise like an offering.

Sophie flew through the smoke with open wings and out the window with a beautiful flowing glow. She carried both of the exhaled smoke to the Gods of the sky.

Chapter Forty-Five
The Velvet Club

Lucille lay on her side, her skin warm and sweet from rose oil, her breath slow and full.

The candle still flickered at the edge of her vision, casting long shadows across the room.

The bath had melted away her tension, but the smoke of Mary Jane had unlocked something else. Something deeper.

Something burning.

Her hips shifted slightly under the sheet. Her belly pulsed low, like it held ancient rhythm. She felt a pull. A call. A memory. Her eyes fluttered shut...

The Dream: Velvet, Smoke, and Fire

Lucille opened her eyes to find herself standing in a dimly lit club draped in velvet, the air thick with cigar smoke and slow jazz humming like a heartbeat. The scent of whiskey, cologne, clove, and womanhood hung heavy.

Women moved in elegant, sensual patterns, hips swaying slowly, not for men's pleasure, but as ritual. Their movements were prayers in motion.

They wore silk, gold jewelry, and anklets that chimed softly as they walked barefoot across polished wood floors.

The men watched in reverence, not hunger.

They were dressed in dark suits, eyes heavy with recognition, not desire, but honor.

"This," Lucille realized, "is a temple."

And she was part of it.

The Seductress

Lucille looked down and found herself in a deep red gown with a slit up to the thigh and shoulders bare.

A glass of something sweet and dark in one hand. Bangles on her wrist.

Her hips moved before her mind did, pulling her into the circle of women.

"This is who I used to be," she whispered, "A seductress. But not the kind they warned me about."

No.

This was the old way. The original dance.

Where women used rhythm and gaze and scent and touch to unlock life force from the masculine. To call it forward, not just for sex, but for vision.

For creation.

For healing.

A woman passed her, pressing a rose to her lips.

"We are the portals," she said, "Men don't make life… they only awaken it. We deliver it."

Sacred Fire

Lucille felt the heat return to her belly. Her womb hummed. Her breath deepened.

The fire wasn't shameful here. It was sacred and it didn't ask for permission.

It moved with God, not against Him.

"Your fire is not the enemy," said a voice behind her.

She turned.

A man with gold eyes, not threatening but wise, stood with a crown of cedar on his head.

"You only need to master it. Not fear it."

The Awakening

The music swelled.

Lucille danced with her sisters, women of past lives, ancestors, teachers, midwives of sensuality and spirit.

And as the drums rose, so did the light.

Lucille woke up suddenly, back in her room.

Chest rising. Thighs are still trembling.

The candle was out.

Sophie stared at her from the windowsill, eyes unblinking.

Lucille whispered into the dark: "I'm not afraid of the fire anymore."

Chapter Forty-Six

The Body Speaks Back

The morning sunlight slanted through the shop's windows, catching dust in a golden haze. The energy was still soft from the bath the night before, and Lucille sat at the counter with a glass of lemon water, her journal beside her, untouched.

She was staring off. Thinking. Feeling.

Mama June came in from the back, robe tied loose, headwrap freshly knotted, skin glowing as if she'd slept under the stars.

"You quiet," she said, eyeing Lucille. "But not the peaceful kind."

Lucille bit her lip and looked up. "I still feel it. The… fire. Even after all that cleansing. After the smoke, and the bath, and the dream. It's still there."

June chuckled, deep and smooth. "Course it is, baby. You alive, ain't you?"

She poured herself a mug of tea and leaned on the counter beside Lucille.

"You think 'cause I'm older I don't feel it too?" she asked, raising an eyebrow.

Lucille smiled shyly. "I don't know... I guess I figured it cools down after a while."

Mama June sipped her tea, eyes steady. "It don't cool. You just learn how to carry it.

Like coals under your ribs, keeps you warm. Don't mean you gotta burn the house down."

<u>Wisdom of the Body</u>

She leaned closer. "Let me tell you something. I still feel the fire. I honor it. Sometimes, I handle it myself. And when I do, I do it with love, not shame."

Lucille blinked.

Mama June continued. "It ain't about needing a man to put it out. Ain't about denying it neither. It's about getting close enough to your own body...To speak to it, and let it speak back."

Lucille sat still, soaking it in.

"You can admire a fine man, God knows I still do, but don't go handing over your temple key just 'cause your thighs hum. Learn your rhythm. What you like. What makes you sing inside, not just moan."

Learning to listen, Lucille ran her hand along the spine of her journal. "I don't think I've ever asked my body what it likes. I've only ever worried what someone else might want."

Mama June tapped the counter gently. "Then that's your homework. Ask. Your body's been talking your whole life, through cramps, goosebumps, tears, even hunger. But you gotta listen with kindness, not rules."

She smiled, slow and knowing.

"You take care of you first. Then if somebody worthy comes along, you'll know the difference between hunger and connection. Between needing a body... and choosing a soul."

Lucille nodded slowly, the truth landing in her like warm honey.

She wasn't broken.

She was burning.

And the fire was hers to hold, not hide.

Chapter Forty-Seven

The Return of Dalton

The bell over the door chimed just after noon.

Lucille glanced up from behind the apothecary counter, jotting notes from a new herb blend she'd been experimenting with.

Her curls were loosely pinned, bay leaf tucked behind one ear, lips glossed in the color of cinnamon bark.

Sophie saddled in Mama Junes old rocking chair, following Daltons every move.

He stepped in like the wind brought him, tall, composed, skin sun-warmed and uniform crisp even in civilian clothes.

"You're a hard woman to find," he said, with a crooked smile.

Lucille blinked, heart still steady. "That so?"

"Mhm. Your sister Claudine said she didn't know where you were located. Which... I found odd."

Lucille's smile didn't move, but her eyes did. "She been sayin' that since we were kids."

He stepped closer, not arrogantly, but like a man who respected space and still owned his stride.

"I came by the house one day to drop something off for your parents," Dalton continued.

"I asked about you. She said you were 'somewhere off being strange."

Lucille gave a soft laugh. "That sounds like Claudine."

He watched her, his gaze thoughtful but not invasive.

"You have a way about you," he said. "Like… you don't demand attention. But you receive it anyway."

Lucille tilted her head, brushing a bay leaf into her notebook. Lucille swore she smelled Claudine's perfume, faint and bitter, though the woman was nowhere near.

"And what does a man like you do with that kind of woman?"

"Worship her a little," he said simply. "Cater to her. Not out of weakness. Out of respect."

A Jealous Sister's Shadow

Lucille could feel the old energy, Claudine's jealousy, floating at the edges of the moment.

Growing up, Claudine didn't want men to love her. She wanted them to chase her, then blame them for not being what she needed.

Lucille, on the other hand, didn't chase or entertain. She just was.

And that difference created wounds between them that never quite healed.

"Claudine always hated when people saw me clearly," Lucille said, voice soft. "Especially the ones she wanted to ignore her the least."

Dalton nodded slowly. "I didn't ignore her. But she wasn't you." He slid a small box onto the counter, a compass pendant with a bronze chain.

"Found this in a little shop on base. Reminded me of you. Something about direction, knowing where true North is."

Lucille held it, fingers tracing the symbol. The skeleton key lighting up the altar in a fiery red from the heat Lucille was conjuring up.

The pendant felt warm, and Lucille saw it starting to glow a faint red. She quickly closed her hands so Dalton couldn't see it.

Then, without hesitation, she met his eyes. "You got plans this weekend?"

Dalton smiled. "I do now."

Lucille said yes not from pressure or curiosity, but from full ownership of her feminine power.

She was no longer afraid of love. No longer afraid of being seen and no longer interested in hiding to make others comfortable.

This wasn't hunger.

This was conjunction, the merging of fire and form.

Love didn't own her anymore. She owned it.

Chapter Forty-Eight

The Peach and the Poison

The sun was gentle that morning, the kind that warmed without burning.

The local farmers market buzzed with chatter, tambourines, and the sweet scent of basil and baked bread.

Lucille wore a linen skirt, off-the-shoulder top, and her favorite beaded sandals.

Her curls were wrapped loosely in a scarf that danced every time she laughed.

Dalton walked beside her, tall, composed, soft-spoken.

He carried her canvas tote with ease, stopping every few feet to guide her toward something new, fresh okra, summer squash, red honey apples.

"You ever tasted a Georgia peach like this?" he asked, holding one up with reverence.

Lucille smiled. "I grew up on 'em."

He peeled the skin back slightly, sliced off a bite with his pocket knife, and gently fed it to her.

She let the juice drip down her lips. "Mm. Still sweet."

Dalton laughed. "Ain't sweeter than you."

Claudine was watching across the lot, behind a crate of tomatoes. Sophie spotted her and poached in a tree above.

She hadn't meant to run into them. She was picking up some catering herbs for a dinner party.

But the moment she saw Dalton's hand on Lucille's lower back, guiding her with care, not ownership, not force, she froze.

And then she saw him bend slightly to whisper in Lucille's ear. Lucille threw her head back in full laughter, unguarded, unconcerned with eyes.

Dalton picked a bunch of sunflowers from a bucket, paid the vendor, and handed them to her like it was second nature.

Claudine's stomach twisted. "Why him?" she hissed under her breath. "Why does she always get the men who... see her?"

The envy rooting inside of her back home, Claudine stormed into her bedroom and opened her altar drawer.

She yanked out the pouch of red string, rose thorns, and a small satchel with her husband's hair, gathered quietly over the last month.

She laid out her binding jar, already stained with wax from previous work.

"You gonna love me," she muttered. "You gonna hold me like that. You gonna look at me like I'm air."

She lit her black candle and whispered a chant, not from her heart, but from her wounds. She added more roots.

She cut her palm and let fresh blood fall into the jar. "This time, you'll feel me."

That was the hardheadedness in Claudine Mama June could smell on her for ages. It was an ancient bloodline curse on some women.

The Backfire

That night, her husband came home late. He barely greeted her. He took one look at her and said, "Why you look so... tense? Every time I walk in the house it feels like pressure."

He went straight to the den and fell asleep on the couch with the TV on.

Claudine stood in the hallway, chest tight, the smell of burnt roses and blood still clinging to her clothes. She went back to the altar.

The candle had gone out.

The wax had melted sideways dripping onto the floor.

The string inside the jar had unraveled completely. And the water she'd added?

Turned black. Sophie Started flying around the shop outside as if she knew the spell didn't work.

She fell to her knees. She wasn't in love. She was in control.

And even her roots knew the difference.

Claudine didn't truly love him; he was just useful for her image and imagination. She didn't even like him at all, not one bit.

The Shop

Lucille had taken a bath and was using her dusting powder when she heard Mary Lou's voice, *true love cannot be bound.*

She felt the energy off immediately and remembered she heard Sophie flying uncontrollably outside. Her stomach curled and then released three times. "Someone's trying to cast something and its close."

Sophie let out three loud croaks to confirm what Lucille was feeling.

Your sisters messing with dark arts.

Chapter Forty-Nine

A Mirror in the Womb

The morning after the root work backfired, Claudine sat at the edge of her bed, staring at nothing. Her fingers trembled slightly as she rubbed her stomach.

She hadn't told anyone yet, not even her husband.

The test had turned pink three days ago. And instead of joy, she felt a tight, low fear.

Sophie slipped in through the windowsill and flew below her altar.

<u>Flashbacks of Silence.</u>

As she brushed her hair at the vanity, she suddenly remembered Daddy, always coming home in silence.

His suit still crisp, scent of cologne and metal and ink. He'd hang his coat on the door, kiss Hattie on the cheek like it was a habit, not a hello, then disappear into his study.

"He's working," Hattie used to say. "He's a man with responsibility."

Claudine used to believe it. But now, now she realized.

He never smiled at Hattie the way Dalton smiled at Lucille. Never reached for her hand in public. Never looked like he remembered he loved her.

A Daughter of Image, Claudine sat up, tightening her robe. "I built my life to match Mama's," she whispered aloud.

She wore pearls. She threw the garden parties. She made sure her husband was respectable and clean-cut.

But never once had he kissed her forehead with softness. Never once had he stopped what he was doing to look her in the eye just to say, "You good?"

And now, she was pregnant. "What kind of love is this child going to witness?" she wondered. "Another performance? Another quiet war behind closed doors?"

The Crumbling

She walked to her altar. Not to do work. Just to sit. To be still.

The candle from the day before had turned black at the base.

The water in the jar remained dark and cloudy. Her stomach turned. Her hand brushed across her belly.

"I wanted to be chosen," she whispered. "But I never learned how to choose me."

Tears slipped down her cheeks silently.

She wasn't angry with Lucille.

She was ashamed.

Because while Lucille lived fully, Claudine had performed expertly but never been fully loved.

Lucille's Skelton key begin to flash a faint black and gray hue, which startled her. She felt something dying in Claudine.

Chapter Fifty

The Threshold

The bell above the shop door never rang. But Mama June still knew.

She stood behind the counter, wiping out a clay bowl when her left ear buzzed, a low warning. She turned slowly, peeked through the floral curtain by the window.

There it was.

A silver sedan, idling across the street.

Claudine.

Sitting still as stone, lip stick fresh but haunted.

Sophie fluttered onto the porch railing, feathers ruffling, her head cocked toward the car. She let out three sharp caws, a signal Lucille had once written in her seer's journal,

"When Sophie croaks in threes, something is crossing the line between silence and truth."

Claudine glanced over at Sophie and rolled her eyes. She's never trusted that *weird bird.*

Mama June narrowed her eyes. "Mmm," she murmured, "she waiting like shame got her on a leash." She placed the bowl down gently, wiped her palms on her apron, and whispered,

"May no evil cross this threshold. Not by mouth, not by spirit, not by thought. This is holy ground. This is truth ground. This is womb-safe ground."

As the final word settled into the floorboards, the skeleton key on Lucille's altar upstairs pulsed faintly, a gray-red shimmer leaking across the wall, not warning, not invitation, but recognition.

Lucille and Dalton had just left, their laughter still echoing faintly from the walk down the block. Fresh peaches in a bag, sunflowers peeking from her tote.

Mama June stood tall, unbothered.

And in that quiet moment, Mama June heard it. A single heartbeat. Not Claudine's.

Fainter.

New.

But alive.

The bell jingled.

Claudine stepped in, a pale green blouse buttoned too tightly, eyes darting like a rabbit unsure of the field. "Howdy, ma'am."

Mama June didn't blink. She looked her dead in the eyes and said, voice clear and heavy with weight: "State your business, child."

But she wasn't speaking to Claudine. She was speaking to the spirit of shame clinging to her shoulders. The one with its claws gripping her lower back.

The one whispering, *You're too late.*

Claudine froze.

Her lip trembled for a second. "I... I'm in need of mother roots."

Mama June's face softened, but only slightly. She walked slowly to the back, the wooden floor creaking in rhythm.

She didn't ask questions.

She didn't offer pity.

She just began to pull down jars. Dandelion root. Nettle leaf. Raspberry leaf. Burdock. Yellow dock. "Body needs iron," she muttered. "Spirit needs grounding, and the soul, that needs honesty."

She blended them all with the care of someone who had seen women unravel and still knew how to sew them back up again.

Claudine waiting, staying by the door. She didn't dare touch anything.

The incense curled around her like a reckoning.

She pressed her palm against her lower belly. Still tender. Still quiet.

But a child was in there.

And this, this space, was the only place that felt safe enough to admit:

"I don't know how to be a mother."

Mama June returned with a small cloth bag, tied with gold thread. She handed it over silently. Then placed her hand lightly on Claudine's shoulder. "It's not the baby that's lost, child. It's you."

Sophie shifted in the rocking chair, feathers glowing faintly, as though repeating the message in her own tongue.

Claudine stood there, clutching the small cloth bag Mama June had given her. Fingers tight on the gold thread like it might come undone if she blinked too hard.

The room itself seemed to hum the same frequency she'd felt as a child when Mary Lou's presence brushed the corners of her dreams.

Mama June returned behind the counter, slow and deliberate, not speaking. She knew not to fill the silence.

That kind of silence?

It was labor. Not of body. But of spirit. The Three Mothers are watching, waiting to see which one you'll become, the one who repeats, the one who resists, or the one who reclaims.

Something was trying to be born in that girl, and too many words would only make it breech.

Claudine cleared her throat. "I'm just... tired. That's all."

Mama June didn't look up. "Tired don't make your shoulders fold like that. Tired don't make your voice crack when you ask for help."

Claudine stiffened. "I didn't say I needed help."

"You said *mother roots*, baby," Mama June replied, still stirring her tea. "Not peppermint. Not hibiscus. Not no damn tea for indigestion. You said mother."

Claudine sat on the edge of the chair closest to the door, one hand still resting over her stomach. She tried to speak again, but her lip quivered. She sniffed sharply and turned her head away like the shame was now a person in the room, laughing at her.

"I didn't want it to be like this." Her voice was quieter now. "I did everything right. Got the ring. The house. The man. The image. But it still don't... feel like it's enough."

Mama June's eyes lifted. Calm. Knowing. "Cause you ain't in the picture you painted, baby. You painted your mama instead."

That broke something.

Claudine jerked up from the chair, pacing now.

"Don't you dare bring her into this."

"Why not?" June said, not unkindly. "She in *everything* you do."

"I didn't come here to be judged."

"Ain't judging you. Just naming the shadow before it eats you whole."

Claudine turned away, jaw tight, tears clinging to the edge of her lashes but never falling. "I'm not weak."

"Nobody said you was," Mama June said softly. "But you sure ain't strong if you can't even cry."

That did it. The tears spilled. Two. Then five. Then a flood.

As the tears hit the floor, the skeleton key flickered from the altar lighting up Lucille's entire room. The bright light holding witness to a bloodline standing at its own threshold.

Claudine sat down hard in the chair again, hand pressed to her chest like something inside was breaking loose.

"I don't know how to be loved without pretending. I don't know how to need somebody without feeling like I failed. I never witnessed reality in a sense. Mama performed, and Daddy retreated. And I... I copied both."

Mama June walked over. Not rushed. Not dramatic. Just *present*.

She kneeled in front of Claudine and placed both hands gently over her knees.

"Baby, all that pain you carry don't make you evil. But if you don't deal with it, you'll pass it down. And that little heartbeat I felt on the porch? That child gon' drink from you. So you best get clear on what's in the well."

Claudine sobbed. "Is it too late?"

Mama June looked her dead in the eyes.

"It's too late to pretend. But it ain't too late to heal."

Claudine's sobs grew louder, rising like thunder in her chest.

She wiped her face with the sleeve of her blouse, smearing her foundation, her composure, her carefully curated image. "I didn't ask for this," she cried. "I was just doing what I thought I was supposed to do. I got married, I built a life, I did it right. Everybody said I was doing good!"

Her voice cracked.

"I didn't ask to be unhappy. I didn't ask for a baby I'm not ready for. This ain't fair, none of it is fair!"

Mama June didn't flinch.

She stood slowly, her joints popping just slightly as she rose. "You done?"

Claudine looked up, startled. Eyes red, chest heaving. "I just... I don't deserve this kind of pain."

Mama June narrowed her eyes. "Child, life ain't a punishment. It's a mirror. What you see right now? It's what you built, either by choice, or by silence."

She walked slowly to the shelf, pulled down a jar of honey and another of dried hibiscus. "You wanted your mama's life. The parties. The husband. The image. But baby, you forgot, your mama's life ain't never been sweet. She's just a damn good actress."

Claudine looked away, ashamed.

Mama June turned back to face her. "You wanted applause, not alignment. And now you carrying a child, not a prop. Not an accessory. Not a photo op. A person. And that little soul ain't ask to be part of your performance."

Claudine choked on another sob. "I didn't know..."

"You did know," June cut in, voice firm. "You just didn't want to believe it mattered."

The room fell quiet. Even the wind outside paused. Sophie wings spread on the tree branch.

Claudine stared at the cloth bag on her lap her "mother roots" and felt the weight of it shift.

Not heavy with herbs. Heavy with truth.

"So what do I do now?"

Mama June walked back over, her voice gentler now, but still anchored.

"Now, you stop performing. You stop pretending. You go home and sit with yourself, not your makeup mirror, not your social calendar, but your soul. Ask her what she really wants. And if she cries again, let her. But this time, listen."

Claudine wiped her face again, but this time it was slower. Still crying, but the edge of denial was gone.

"I'm scared," she whispered.

Mama June nodded. "Good. Means you close to being real for once in your life."

Chapter Fifty-One

Where Gods Lay Down
Their Armor

The sun hung low and golden as Lucille stepped onto Dalton's back porch.

The scent of fried catfish and hush puppies swirled in the air, chased by the sound of Muddy Waters drifting through the open kitchen window.

Dalton stood by the grill, shirt unbuttoned halfway, muscles relaxed, smile wide. His military friends were scattered in lawn chairs, holding red cups and telling stories that made them throw their heads back in laughter.

Lucille felt the warmth of it all, not just from the food or the music, but from being welcome, without performance. She wore a linen wrap dress and no shoes. Her hair was pinned loosely, curls kissing her shoulders.

"Got the blues, the grease, and the goddess," Dalton said as she approached, offering her a plate.

"Can't ask for more than that."

As the sun went down they danced to Bobby "Blue" Bland, to BB King, and Johnnie Taylor.

Slow.

Close.

Laughing between songs.

Dalton's hands never left her back. No clutching, just guiding.

When his boys said their goodnights, full and grateful, Lucille helped him clear plates and douse candles. The night quieted. The moon leaned in.

Dalton ran a bath in his deep clawfoot tub. He dropped in a few of Lucille's oils, lavender, vanilla, and just a touch of rosemary.

They undressed each other slowly, like unwrapping something sacred.

Not rushed.

Not driven by heat but drawn by reverence.

They soaked, legs intertwined, letting the smoke of Mary Jane curl around their thoughts. Dalton rubbed her feet, her thighs, and her scalp.

"You know," he whispered, "you move like your body used to be worshipped in temples."

Lucille smiled, high and holy. "Maybe it still is."

Sophie began cawing and circling the house covering it with protection and warding off evil eyes from known and unknown entities.

Later, in his bedroom, with nothing but moonlight and a fan spinning overhead, Dalton kissed her as if he'd studied her breath pattern in past lives.

He didn't just touch her, he read her. Her hips moved with rhythm born from generations of women who knew what it meant to birth life from pleasure, not pain. Dalton kissed her womb, her throat, the space behind her knees.

"You feel like a prayer," he whispered against her skin. And then he devoured her. Not out of hunger. Out of offering to a new plane.

They made love again.

And again.

And again.

Each time deeper, each time slower, each time more aligned.

Lucille's spirit left the room more than once and each time the skeleton key lit up and began emitting steam.

She saw stars.

Rivers.

Women dancing in velvet.

She saw her ancestors smiling and nodding in approval.

She felt her womb open not for a child, but for divinity. When it was over, they lay entangled in sheets and sweat, fingers still searching for each other.

Dalton looked over, eyes heavy with awe. "Lucille…"

She turned toward him. "Yeah?"

He cupped her cheek, kissed her once more gently this time. "I love you."

Lucille closed her eyes, resting her forehead against his chest. "I know. I felt it before you said it."

Lucille pressed her lips softly against Dalton's chest, her fingers tracing idle circles across his ribs. His heart beat steady beneath her touch, like a quiet drum that had always known her rhythm. She whispered it so softly it might've gotten lost between heartbeats.

"I love you too, Dalton. I've never told a man that before."

He didn't flinch. He didn't tease or hesitate. He placed his hand behind her head, pulled her closer, and kissed the top of her crown.

"Then let me honor that."

Lucille looked up, eyes wide with the weight of her own words. Dalton's voice was low, sure, and warm as earth.

"Would you do me the honor of being my woman, Lucille? Not my fling. Not my secret. Not my sometime. My woman. 'Cause you sholl ain't no girl."

For a moment, Lucille's body melted into his. But then she heard it, her own breath quickening. The room shifted. The heat of the moment gave way to a sudden chill, not from him, but from somewhere inside her chest.

Dalton saw it in her eyes. "What is it?"

Lucille sat up slowly, pulling the sheet around her, her back to him now. "It's just..." She couldn't find the words. She wrapped her arms around herself.

"You live in a world with uniforms and orders and structure. You move from base to base. Your life is wrapped in somebody else's schedule."

Dalton sat up too, watching her carefully. "You scared of that?"

Lucille nodded, not looking at him. "I'm scared of... disappearing. Of becoming someone's wife and getting swallowed up in their world. I've worked too hard to know who I am... what I carry."

Dalton reached for her hand. "Lucille, if we ever get married, you wouldn't be swallowed. You'd be honored. I want a woman beside me who knows how to see spirits and boil rosewater and bless doorways. You think I'm tryna erase you?"

Lucille's eyes welled up. "I've never been loved like this before. And now that I have...it scares me more than being alone ever did."

Dalton pulled her hand to his lips. "Then let's move slow. But not scared because I'm not asking you to be my property. I asked you to be my partner."

She leaned her head against his shoulder, tears slipping down silently. This was not Hattie's marriage.

This was not control, image, or legacy.

This was choice.

And choice, even when it's good, can still be terrifying.

Chapter Fifty-Two

The Sweet Return

The day was warm, with just enough breeze to make the sunlight dance across Dalton's windshield as he drove down the road toward Mama June's shop. Lucille sat in the passenger seat, her legs curled beneath her, still humming the blues songs from the night before. She looked over at him, broad shoulders, clean fade, eyes sharp and soft at the same time and smiled.

Dalton glanced her way. "You feelin' alright?"

Lucille nodded. "Still floatin'. Still sore. Still... grateful."

Dalton smirked. "Good. You're supposed to feel seen and stretched." She burst out laughing, and he reached over to squeeze her thigh.

Before they reached the shop, Dalton pulled off the road. Lucille frowned. "Where you goin'?"

"I got one errand to run."

She stayed in the car, eyes narrowed but curious.

Ten minutes later, he returned with: A bottle of Cola, sweating from ice, a small brown pouch of sunflower seeds, and a bundle of sunflowers and wild herbs, wrapped in butcher paper with twine. He handed her each item like a ceremony. "Cola to cool you, seeds to keep your mind sharp, and sunflowers 'cause you light up any room like one."

Lucille melted in the seat. "You tryna make me marry you today?"

"No rush," he said, winking. "Just planting seeds."

They pulled up to Mama June's shop as the sun tilted toward early afternoon. Sophie was sitting in a tree branch like she was waiting on her return.

Lucille stepped out barefoot, holding her flowers.

Dalton circled around the car, opened the shop door for her, and as she walked through the threshold, he grabbed her wrist gently, pulled her back into his arms, and kissed her.

Long.

Slow.

Deep.

The kind of kiss that tells a woman you're safe here, and that you can be all woman without apology. That says I'm not afraid of your power, I want to stand beside it.

Inside, Mama June sat in her chair, arms folded, sipping her tea. The two neighborhood sisters who always came in for hair tonics stared with mouths open. Lucille didn't care. She kissed him like the world wasn't watching. Like it didn't matter who was behind that window.

Dalton finally pulled back, breath steady but heavy. He leaned in again and kissed her forehead, sealing it like a prayer.

Then he turned to Mama June, voice clear as a bell. "I'm returnin' your girl. But really... I'm just droppin' off my future wife."

Mama June didn't smile. She just blinked slowly and said: "We'll see."

Dalton tipped his head like a man who wasn't scared of earning approval and turned to walk away. Lucille stood in the doorway, face flushed, holding her flowers like armor and invitation all in one.

Chapter Fifty-Three

The Tea After the Fire

The shop door closed with a soft jingle behind Lucille.

Dalton's scent still lingered in the doorway. That kiss had left her lips warm, her womb humming, her knees slightly uncertain.

Mama June didn't say a word. She turned her back, walked to the stove, and began boiling water. Lucille hovered near the counter like a schoolgirl just caught daydreaming in church.

"You gon' scold me?"

Mama June raised an eyebrow but didn't turn around. "You grown, ain't you?"

"Yes, ma'am."

"Then I don't scold grown women. I brew tea for 'em."

Mama June pulled down jars like she was choosing scripture. Chamomile for softening emotion. Motherwort for calming the heart. Ginger for courage. Damiana for sacred feminine strength. She dropped each into the pot with quiet reverence, stirring slowly.

"That man's got something ancient on him," she finally said. "Not dark. Not heavy. But... steady. Rare kind of root." Sophies' cawing echoed in the shop, as if she confirmed the root on Dalton as ancient.

Lucille slid onto the stool. "He makes me feel like I don't have to dim anything."

Mama June glanced over. "That's what real masculine energy do. It don't cage you. It covers you."

She poured the tea into two clay cups and handed one to Lucille.

"But let me ask you this, chile... You ready to be seen every day by somebody?"

Lucille sipped the tea slowly. "I think so."

"It ain't about feelin' sexy and chosen when the sun's out and your dress is blowin' just right," Mama June said, "It's about what you gon' do when your mood swingin', your faith low, and he still want access to your spirit. You ready to let a man watch your soul grow?"

Lucille sat quiet. The tea warmed her, but so did the question. "I don't wanna lose myself."

"Then don't," June said. "But just know, marriage ain't a hiding place. It's a mirror. A magnifier. It'll show you what you still ain't healed. And what you really believe about yourself."

Lucille looked up, eyes glinting with both joy and hesitation. "So what do I do?"

Mama June smiled gently. "You stay awake. You remember who you were before his kiss. And you build who you wanna be while he's still learnin' your rhythm. Don't stop growing to keep him comfortable."

She reached across and took Lucille's hand. "And if it's real? You won't have to choose between being loved and being free. He'll make sure you can be both."

Lucille nodded slowly, sipping the last of the tea. The fire in her hadn't dimmed.

But now it had direction.

Chapter Fifty-Four

The Petition

That night, Lucille prepared the space like an offering. She opened every window in the shop, letting in moonlight and the hum of cicadas. She laid white linen across the floor, dressed in a sheer gown soaked in rosewater and crushed bay leaves.

The skeleton key sat on her altar, gleaming from Lucille polishing it earlier. Sophie watched silently from the rafters, her eyes gleaming with knowing. Lucille lit seven candles, each one a doorway.

She whispered the names of the women in her line:

"Mary Lou.

Sister Alma.

Miz Claudine the First.

Aunt Zora.

Beatrice Anya

Annie Mae

Ethel Murphy

And the ones unnamed but never forgotten."

She sat in the center of the circle, bones loose, breathing steadily. "I'm not asking for permission," she said aloud. I'm asking for precision."

The Veil Opens

The room shifted, the air grew heavy, the way it does right before rain touches earth. Lucille's eyes fluttered closed, and then, she was no longer sitting on the floor. She stood barefoot in a long corridor made of bone and wind. In front of her were mirrors, each reflecting a version of her:

1. One with a child on her hip and eyes tired but kind

2. One dressed in black, walking alone into a forest

3. One laughing in a candlelit kitchen with Dalton by her side

The corridor pulled like a living thing, and from the far end, they came.

The three hooded women, who trained her in the elements, stepped forward.

One held a book. One held a stone. One held a flame cupped in her palm.

They spoke together, not aloud, but into her bones.

You called us to ask about a man. But first, do you know who you are?

Lucille nodded. "Yes. A woman of root and rhythm. Of fire and flow. A mirror, not a shadow."

The mothers stepped aside, as in giving Lucille the floor.

Lucille swallowed hard. "Is Dalton...Is he part of my purpose? Can I bind myself to him without losing myself?"

The mirror to her left shimmered and a scene emerged:

Lucille standing in a kitchen year from now, hair wrapped, stirring something fragrant in a pot. Dalton entered from behind, kissed her neck, whispered into her ear. There were children laughing in another room.

But then, the mirror cracked, just slightly, and the vision shifted:

Lucille standing at a crossroads, her body strong, older, powerful, alone, but not lonely.

A fire burned to the left.

A temple stood to the right.

She understood.

Either path could be divine.

The mother with the flame stepped forward and placed it in Lucille's hands.

He is not your test. He is your mirror.

The one with the book spoke next.

Marriage is not the prize. Alignment is.

The one with the stone said last

If he remains true, and you remain true, then your paths will not compete. They will converge.

Lucille's breath caught. "And if I falter?"

Then you forget. But only until you remember again.

The Return

Lucille opened her eyes, and the candles were still burning. Sophie cawed once, softly welcoming her back.

Lucille picked up and pressed the skeleton key to her lips. "I'm not afraid of love anymore. But I won't be blind." She rose from the floor like a priestess anointed. She had her answer.

He's not her permission. He's her reflection.

And reflections must be kept clean.

Chapter Fifty-Five

Mr. Charlie's Visit

It was a slow, sticky morning.

Lucille was sweeping bay leaves out the front of the shop, the sun already bold in the sky, when the screen door creaked open behind her.

A man stepped inside. Tall, older, with a slight limp and a hat too fine for the sweat on his brow. He held his posture like he used to command a room, but now he moved like time had caught him.

"Mornin', young lady," he said, tipping his hat. "I'm lookin' for Mama June. Got... a private matter."

Lucille studied him. He had that Southern gentleness wrapped in pride. The kind of man who was once sharp with his tongue and smooth with his hands.

"She's in the back," Lucille said, not moving. "Can I tell her who's asking?" The man took a deep breath.

"Tell her Charlie's here. Mr. Charlie."

Mama June stepped into the doorway like the veil had parted. She took one look at the man on the other side of the counter and stopped cold. Her lips tightened. Her hand gripped the edge of the shelf just a little too long.

"Well," she said finally, "I'll be damned."

Mr. Charlie took off his hat and placed it gently on the counter. "Didn't come to haunt you, June. I just need some help. My prostate... actin' up somethin' fierce. Doctors don't do nothin' but poke and guess."

Lucille felt the air thicken. This wasn't just about herbs. This was unfinished business.

A Tense Silence spewed.

Mama June's voice was calm, but sharp as flint. She cleared her throat. "You ain't walked through this door in over twenty-five years. And now you come limping in, asking for a brew?"

Mr. Charlie bowed his head a little. "I know how it sounds and looks. But I didn't come for drama. I came for what only you know how to fix."

Lucille started to step out, but Mama June raised her hand. "Stay put, Lucille. You stay and watch. You gon' need to know what to do when your past show up in a weakened body but still full of pride."

Mama June moved slowly, measuring saw palmetto berries, nettle root, and corn silk like her hands were on autopilot, but her eyes? Her eyes didn't leave Charlie.

"You still drink too much coffee?" she asked, flat.

"Cut back," he murmured. "Since the second wife left."

Lucille blinked. June didn't react.

"You still stubborn as a mule? That ain't changed." "Shame," she said. "That might be why your prostate's swollen. Too much pride lodged in your root chakra."

As she stirred the blend, her voice softened, just a hair.

"You hurt me, Charlie. Not just back then. You hurt me by never sayin' it out loud. By never acknowledgin' what you took."

Mr. Charlie lowered his gaze. "I ain't have the tools, June."

"And I didn't have the time to wait."

Lucille stood still, watching her elder not just make medicine, but reclaim her narrative.

Mama June handed him the jar, her hands steady. "Steep it three times a day. Don't add no sugar. Let the bitterness work."

Mr. Charlie nodded, quiet. He reached for his hat. "Thank you."

"Don't thank me," she said, voice low. "Just... don't die with a closed mouth. Speak to your children. Make peace with your body."

He paused at the door. "You were the best thing I never held right."

Mama June didn't answer. She just watched him walk away, slow and tired. And when he was gone, she turned to Lucille.

"Love ain't the lesson, baby. Closure is. Sometimes, spirit sends 'em back sick...so we can finally let it go."

From her perch outside, Sophie spread her wings wide, circled once over the shop, then settled again.

Not in warning this time, but in release.

Chapter Fifty-Six

The Steam and the Story

It was late evening when Mama June pulled out the cedar-wood stools with the carved openings at the center and motioned for Lucille to follow her to the back.

The moon was full. The air was still. And something in June's spirit said it was time.

"Tonight, we steam," she said. "Every woman needs to clean the temple every now and then, physically, spiritually, emotionally."

Lucille grabbed the bundles of dried herbs from the shelf without question. She knew the practice, but she'd never done it with someone like June.

This wasn't a self-care Sunday. This was ancestral maintenance.

June laid out the herbs like a recipe for soul work. "For cleansing after sex or spiritual heaviness: mugwort, rose, calendula, and lemon balm." She passed Lucille a bundle. "For emotional release or grief in the womb: damiana, lavender, red clover, and blue vervain."

Lucille added hers to the pot. "For new beginnings or manifestation: basil, yarrow, motherwort, and spearmint."

Mama June smiled faintly. "That's what I'm steamin' with tonight."

The room was dim. Steam rose thick and fragrant as the two women undressed, draped their long cotton smocks, and settled over their stools. The joints were already rolled. The candles are already lit. The mirror is already covered.

"We don't stare at ourselves in these moments," Mama June said. "We stare into ourselves."

The steam curled up from beneath, gentle and pulsing. It warmed their centers, loosened their hips, made their spines stretch and breathe.

They smoked in silence for a while. Until Lucille whispered:

"I love you, Mama June."

The old woman exhaled slow. The kind of exhale that'd been building for decades. "I know, baby. That's why I'm gonna tell you somethin' I ain't never said out loud."

Lucille sat up straighter, heart slowing.

Mama June's eyes glistened but no tears fell yet. "Mr. Charlie...He was the only man I've ever been with."

Lucille froze. The steam between them thickened.

"Nobody knows that. Not him. Not family. Not even the spirits. I ain't ever spoke it."

Mama June lit her joint again, hands shaking just slightly.

"I was a virgin. Young. Curious. He love-bombed me till I thought it was heaven, drives, dinners, gifts I didn't ask for. Put money in my pocket when I didn't ask. Made me feel like I had been chosen."

She paused, pulling a long draw. "Then we moved away. And the mask dropped."

Her voice didn't tremble, but the words cut the air like blades. "He beat me when I spoke too loud. Told me my dreams weren't holy. Said my gift of seeing was demonic. Told me no man would want me if I kept talkin' to shadows."

Lucille covered her mouth.

Mama June's eyes stayed forward, unfocused, like watching a film only she could see. "He took from me. My money. My voice. My light. And when he cheated and had kids outside, he blamed me for not giving him any."

Lucille whispered: "You never told anyone?"

"What was there to say? People thought he was a good man. And I was just the strange woman who read herbs and smelled like dirt."

There was a sacred silence in the air and Sophie bowed her head in the windowsill. The skeleton key started pulsating, matching Lucille's heartbeat, because anger was consuming her.

The steam rose. So did the pain.

But it didn't destroy June. It purified her.

She finally turned her head to Lucille, eyes raw. "I stayed single because I had to rebuild my goddamn soul from ashes. Piece by piece. And now I teach. Not because I'm wise. But because I survived."

Lucille began to cry, not just from empathy, but from reverence. In the steam she thought she heard a faint whisper, one of the Three Mothers, just one word: *Witness.*

The skeleton key began pouring droplets of water onto the altar.

She reached over and held Mama June's hand. "You didn't just survive. You transformed."

They sat there in the steam, smoke curling around them, bodies warm, wombs humming with legacy.

That night, Lucille didn't learn root work. She inherited womb-truth, the kind carved into bone, carried in the spine, and passed only through fire.

Chapter Fifty-Seven

The Pine and the Proposal

The sun hadn't fully stretched across the sky yet, but Lucille was already awake. Mama June was still resting in her back room, wrapped in a dream she'd earned.

Lucille moved barefoot through the shop like a priestess in morning prayer. She lit a stick of frankincense and laid it beside a bowl of water.

Then she poured a full basin of pine water, its scent crisp and commanding. With each dip of the mop, she whispered Psalm 51:10:

"Create in me a clean heart, O God; and renew a right spirit within me."

She moved from back to front, from corner to threshold, occasionally ringing a golden bell that chimed like wind in a crystal garden.

The air shifted. Light poured in stronger. The room felt awake.

She guided the last of the energy toward the front door, where the twin horseshoes hung above the frame like silent guards.

"Out you go," she said softly. "Ain't no vacancy for anything unclean." With the floor still drying, Lucille washed her hands, turned on Mahalia Jackson, and brewed a strong pot of chicory coffee.

She stepped onto the porch in a simple cotton robe, curls tied up, body still damp from sweat and prayer. The morning air kissed her.

And then she heard it, Dalton's truck rumbling up the gravel road, moving like it had been summoned. He parked, stepped out in a soft linen shirt and dark slacks, and walked up the porch like he'd been doing it for years.

He smiled wide. "Happy day, gorgeous."

Lucille smirked but couldn't help the blush blooming across her cheeks. Dalton leaned in and kissed her not rushed, not teasing. A kiss that tasted like home, blessing, and desire. Without a word, Dalton walked back to his truck and returned with a metal pail he proceeded to fill with warm water, a bar of black soap, and a clean towel.

Lucille stared. "What you doing?"

"Smelled that pine soon as I stepped out the truck," he said, kneeling before her. "You did holy work this morning. And I want to honor the feet that walked through it."

Lucille watched, breath caught. Dalton removed her slippers and gently dipped her feet into the pail. He washed each foot like a prayer. Then kissed the tops, the arches, the space just beneath her ankle bone.

"You protect everything," he said quietly. "The shop, the people, the air around you. But I want to protect you, Lucille. Even though I know you don't need it."

He looked up at her now, hands still wet, heart bare. "Marry me."

Lucille's eyes widened. "Dalton..."

"I ain't talkin' about ownership. I'm talkin' about partnership. You... me... the spirits, the land, the work. Let's build a life where nothing sacred gets lost."

Lucille reached for his cheek, caressing it gently. She didn't answer. Not yet. But this time, she didn't pull away.

Dalton emptied the basin down by the garden, pouring it slow like libation. He stood for a moment, hands still wet, letting the pine-scented water soak into the earth. Then he turned back toward the porch and walked up slow. Lucille watched him, legs tucked under her, coffee in one hand.

Dalton sat beside her again, took both of her hands, and bowed his head. "Lord," he said, voice smooth and low, "Bless the ground she walks on. Bless the work of her hands, the weight she carries, the peace she's created. Let no weapon formed against her womb, her word, or her rest prosper. And let me... let me love her in a way that honors You."

Lucille stared at him, caught between breath and spirit. After a long silence, she finally spoke.

"What about my life here, Dalton?" Her voice wasn't angry. Just honest. "This shop...This porch...The women I help, the spirits I speak to, the girl I used to be...I built all of this with my own fire. I make a living here. I live here."

Dalton nodded, listening.

"I finally found freedom. Freedom from my bloodline's shadows. From mama's bitterness, from Claudine's performance...and now you want to uproot me. To cage me in a uniform schedule. Military moves every few years, always packing, always adapting." She placed her hand over her heart. "I'd have no home base. No roots. No ground to bury my herbs in or lay my head on."

Dalton didn't flinch.

Didn't argue.

Didn't raise his voice.

He reached over, slid her coffee out of her hand, and grinned. "Damn, woman," he said with a chuckle, "I'll just move into your room."

Lucille burst out laughing, slapping his shoulder. "You'd have to sage every corner before steppin' in and pray daily for protection. Protection over our love"

"Done. I'll even light the frankincense myself."

They were both laughing now, truly laughing. Not to deflect. But because they knew...This was the way forward: with truth, compromise, and joy braided like strands of blessed rope.

Lucille leaned into him, kissed the side of his face. "You know I'm not easy."

"Good," he said, pulling her closer. "Easy ain't sacred."

Sophie landed on Daltons pick up truck to confirm their union.

"There's your bird friend security" Daltons said jokingly but in a jealous tone.

Chapter Fifty-Eight

Porchlight Communion

The breeze was soft as cornbread.

Lucille leaned her head on Dalton's shoulder, still chuckling from their jokes, the scent of pine and coffee dancing between them.

The front door creaked open behind them. And out stepped Mama June. Wrapped in a deep blue house robe, hair pinned back in silver curls, eyes clear like she had just woken up reborn. She walked slowly, barefoot, her ankles whispering against the wood as she moved across the porch with a grace only time could give.

"Mornin' my love birds," she said, voice still raspy with sleep but sweetened with peace. Dalton immediately stood up, straight-backed, respectful.

"Mama June." She tilted her head, amused. "That's my name."

Lucille smiled up at her, quietly glowing.

Dalton held out her chair before she could sit. "Got your favorite spot waitin' on you."

She looked at him sideways, then, for the first time, smiled.

Not the tight, polite kind. A real one. Soft. Surrendered. Safe.

"Well," Dalton said, grinning wide, "God must be on his way back if I got Mama June to smile at me." June rolled her eyes, blushing as she settled down.

"Hush now, child. Ain't nobody askin' for all that holy commentary."

Lucille laughed. "He's just excited you didn't hit him with a proverb or a broom."

Mama June waved them both off. "Y'all out here flirtin' and blessin' the air like I can't feel it from my pillow."

They sat there, the three of them.

No rush.

No need to speak.

Just sun, soft music playing from the window, the scent of healing herbs drying behind the screen, and the faint taste of joy lingering on everyone's tongue.

Mama June sipped the coffee Lucille handed her and looked over at her like she was seeing her fully for the first time.

"You didn't just save me tea, chile," she said quietly" "You helped me lay down what I thought I had to carry forever."

Lucille's throat tightened. "I didn't even know."

June nodded. "That's how you know it was spirit-led."

They all sat in silence again. The kind of silence that heals your grandmother's ghost. The kind of silence that says: This is what it feels like when the war finally ends.

Chapter Fifty-Nine

The Rooted Womb

The bell above the door jingled softly. Lucille looked up from her workstation, expecting someone asking for teas or a reading.

But what entered was not a request, it was a cry from the veil.

A young girl, barely grown, stumbled into the shop wrapped in a heavy wool blanket. Her skin was pale, lips cracked, eyes glazed like she hadn't slept in days.

Then, without a word, she collapsed. Lucille dropped her mug, coffee splashing across the floor. "Mama June!" she screamed, already running.

Lucille knelt beside the girl, her breath shallow. She pulled the blanket back, and what she saw nearly knocked her soul sideways.

There was blood, thick, black, red, clinging to the girl's thighs and pooled beneath her skirt.

And then, a baby.

Half emerged.

Skin turning blue, lifeless.

Lucille's heart pounded. But that wasn't the worst of it. Hovering just above the girl's open womb was an entity, thin, shadowy, sharp-toothed, chewing on the umbilical cord like it was rope candy. Lucille froze.

The Spirit of the Womb

The creature hissed without sound. Its eyes glowed faint purple. Its claws were sunk deep into the girl's belly. Lucille could see the energy draining from the child's spirit; see it being pulled into something dark.

"Oh God… someone rooted this child…" This wasn't labor. This was a spiritual attack. "MAMA JUNE!!"

June burst from the back room in her house shoes and robe, staff in hand like Moses on judgment day. She took one look and cursed under her breath.

"Hold her hips, Lucille. Don't let that baby fall between worlds."

Lucille obeyed, hands already glowing faintly from her own energy. June grabbed a bowl of cedar water, a satchel of herbs, and lit a flame that seemed to hiss at the spirit.

"Somebody didn't want this child to be born.

But we ain't letting no soul get swallowed today."

Lucille stared down the spirit, rage and discernment mixing in her chest.

"This shop is holy ground," she whispered. She reached for the bay leaves and pressed one to the girl's forehead. "You don't belong here," she told the entity.

"You weren't summoned by God. You were purchased with bitterness and bone dust. I cancel the contract. I sever the tie."

The spirit shrieked, but Lucille didn't flinch.

Mama June whispered over the baby's crown, "Come now, child. Choose life. Come through."

She anointed the girl's womb with pine oil and blew cinnamon into the air.

"Lucille, speak Psalms. Out loud."

Lucille didn't hesitate.

"Deliver me from blood guiltiness, O God, thou God of my salvation..."

"And my tongue shall sing aloud of thy righteousness..."

The girl let out a low groan.

The baby's shoulders shifted.

The entity began to unravel, smoke peeling off it like burnt cloth.

"One more push," Mama June ordered.

Lucille whispered to the baby, "Come on, little one. Come on. You've been claimed. You've been protected."

With one final cry, the girl arched her back, and the baby slid free, covered in blood, cord still twitching.

Mama June moved fast, lifting the baby, clearing the mouth, smacking the soles.

A sharp wail pierced the shop. The spirit let out a final hiss and dissolved into ash, sucked into the floorboards and trapped by the horseshoes at the door.

The baby screamed.

So did the girl.

Lucille collapsed onto her knees, sobbing.

Mama June rocked the newborn, her hands shaking now that it was over.

"She's here," June whispered. "She's here."

Lucille looked at the girl, whose eyes had fluttered open. "Who rooted you?" Lucille asked softly.

The girl cried harder. "My aunt. Said I'd ruin our bloodline if I birthed a bastard child. Said the baby didn't deserve to live."

Lucille clenched her jaw. "Well, she was wrong. And we just proved it." The skeleton key lit up in an angry fiery red to match Lucille's rage.

A tear dropped from Sophies eye, and she flew over to sit at the side by Mama June and the baby.

Chapter Sixty

The Hood and the
Warning

The shop had been cleaned.

Blood mopped, herbs gathered, and candles relit. The baby was safe. The girl was resting.

But Lucille, Lucille was burning. She moved through the space like a storm dressed in linen, hands shaking, eyes glowing faintly under her lashes.

Mama June watched her from the kitchen doorway. "You need to sit, baby. Let it settle."

Lucille didn't speak. She pulled her hair up into a tight bun, tied it off with red thread. She grabbed a clove from the altar bowl and began chewing hard. It burned, but she welcomed it.

The scent of pine still lingered, but something darker began to rise.

"I'm goin' in," Lucille said simply. And before Mama June could reach for her, Lucille was gone.

The Spiritual World

Lucille stood in an open plain made of wind and smoke, the ground cracked with veins of fire. She followed the trail like a hound eyes locked, senses sharp.

"Where are you, wicked thing," she whispered. Then she saw her.

A woman floating above a creek in a black veil, not walking, not rooted. The aunt.

Astral traveling.

Lucille stepped into her line of sight and the veil between them snapped like glass. "You thought you'd hide here?" Lucille growled.

"You don't belong in this realm, girl," the aunt hissed. "You not old enough to know what you're stirring."

Lucille's voice came deep from her chest:

"I'm old enough to know that you tried to kill a child before she took her first breath."

She stepped forward, fire rising from her footprints.

"If you ever put work on another womb again, if you so much as mix rosemary in vinegar with evil in your heart, I will come for you myself. And I won't leave your soul whole when I'm done."

The aunt shrieked and tried to vanish.

But Lucille reached out, grabbed the black hood from her head, and yanked it free, binding her essence. The spirit around the aunt cracked, and she was flung backward into the void.

Lucille stood alone, clove on her tongue, heart thudding.

Back in the Living World

The house was shaking. The windows rattled like they were afraid to break. All the candles blew out at once, snuffed like breath had left the room.

Dalton's truck pulled into the driveway just as a gust of wind slammed the porch swing against the siding. Mama June met him on the porch, eyes wide.

"Don't go in yet!"

Dalton stepped out fast.

"Where is she?!"

"She's in the spirit realm. Too angry. Too deep. If we pull her out now, she might bring the whole veil down with her."

Dalton's hands shook. He wrapped Mama June in a strong, trembling hug. "Lord protect her," he whispered. Cover her. Don't let her stay lost in that fire."

He closed his eyes and began to pray harder than he ever had, palms raised, voice deep and urgent.

The Return

Then, everything stopped.

The wind died.

The house stilled.

And from the back room, Sophie the raven began to scream, circling the ceiling like a mad omen, wings slapping the walls.

Lucille emerged. Covered in sweat.

Holding a black hood in her right hand like a trophy.

Her eyes flickered briefly with shadow, then cleared. And then,

She fell to her knees.

Dalton ran in, catching her before her head hit the floor. "I got you," he whispered. "I got you."

Mama June stood by the door, tears forming but unshed. "That girl just walked through the underworld and brought back justice. She's not just a root worker anymore. she's becoming a legend."

Chapter Sixty-One

The Milk and the Moon

Dalton carried Lucille up the narrow stairs like she weighed nothing. Her body was hot, her breath shallow. Her hands were still clutching the black hood.

He whispered to her the whole way, words soaked in prayer and reverence: "You did what you had to do, baby. You made sure that child could breathe. Now you breathe."

He sat her down gently on the bed and slipped the hood from her hands. Then he ran a bath.

He filled it with rose petals, chamomile, and lavender from Lucille's own apothecary jars. He poured in a scoop of Epsom salt and set a candle at the corner of the tub.

When she stepped in, her body trembled. Dalton didn't try to speak anymore.

He just sat on the floor beside her, one hand resting near hers, anchoring her to earth.

Downstairs: The Young Mother

Meanwhile, Mama June sat in the back room, rocking the baby in a soft cloth sling against her chest. Julian, the girl, was awake now.

Her eyes fluttered open, and she blinked slowly like the world had just returned to her.

"Where am I?"

"Safe," Mama June answered. "You're safe now."

She passed the girl a warm mug of tea, lightly sweetened with honey and fennel. Julian's hands were shaky, but she held the cup.

"What happened?"

Mama June smiled gently. "You and your baby were attacked. But the spirits brought you to the right place. Lucille brought you back."

The baby whimpered.

Mama June shifted and gently passed the tiny girl to Julian. "She's hungry, chile. You ready?"

Julian nodded slowly. Mama June helped her adjust her robe and showed her how to guide the baby's mouth.

"There. Just like that. See how she's workin'? You just needed to be seen." Julian watched her baby begin to latch, tears falling silently. "I thought I was gonna die."

"You almost did," Mama June said. "But you didn't. And now you get to raise that child with a different story than what you came from."

The Backstory

They sat quietly for a while, the sound of the baby suckling and a clock ticking on the wall. Then Mama June spoke again.

"What's your name, baby?"

"Julian."

"Pretty. Where you from?"

"Two towns over. Little place called Glades. Ain't much there."

"And who you livin' with?"

Julian's face darkened. "My aunt. She's been my guardian since Mama died two years ago. She hated me. She called me fast. Said I was gonna ruin her name. When I found out I was pregnant, she told me I wouldn't live to deliver."

Mama June's jaw clenched. "And she tried to make sure of that, didn't she?"

Julian nodded slowly, looking down at her baby. "She almost succeeded."

"But she didn't," Mama June said, brushing Julian's hair gently behind her ear.

"Because you're a warrior. Just like Lucille."

Mama June stood slowly and reached for the phone. "You got anybody who can come get you?" Julian shook her head. "No one but her. And I ain't goin' back."

"Then I suppose you can stay right here for now. We'll figure out the rest."

She kissed Julian's forehead and whispered something about boo hags in a tongue older than English, a blessing only the spirits could fully understand.

Upstairs, Lucille was drying off. Dalton was waiting with warm clothes, a blanket, and quiet eyes. And in the back room, a baby fell asleep on her mother's chest... safe for the first time in her short, blessed life.

Chapter Sixty-Two

The Council of Blood and Spirit

That night, Julians aunt, tossed and turned in her bed. Her room was dark, heavy with the scent of mothballs and old wood.

Outside, the wind whispered through the cracks in her window like it had a message to deliver.

She woke up sweating, heart pounding. Then, everything went still.

Before she could rise from bed, her eyes rolled back, and she was snatched from her body.

The Spirit Realm

She landed hard on the floor of a vast room made of obsidian and moonlight.

The walls were endless.

The air was thick. In the center stood twelve hooded figures, each with golden thread woven through their robes, faces hidden but presence undeniable.

They stood around a shallow pool of water that glowed like it held time itself.

The aunt scrambled to her feet. "Where am I?!"

A voice boomed, not angry, but final. *You are in counsel. You have been summoned to answer for attempted spiritual erasure.*

Another voice spoke, feminine, ancient.

You tried to sacrifice an anointed womb. Not once. Twice.

The pool in the center rippled and showed two scenes:

Julian at six years old, sitting in a closet, crying as her aunt screamed spells over her mother's coffin.

Julian on the shop floor, bleeding out, a dark spirit chewing at her child's cord.

The aunt stepped back. "She was a mistake," she hissed. "A curse. She came through my sister like a crack in the family name. She needed to be erased. Why the fuck aren't they here, they are the sin, not me. I've lived my life right, all my life. They get blessed and not me. Why the fuck not me?"

She began to cry uncontrollably.

Another voice rose, trembling with power:

She was born sacred. And so was her daughter. You attempted to extinguish a divine bloodline.

Another voice rose with the spirit of the Almighty:

Who made you a judge of the counsel, Gretta! You had no right to attempt to eradicate a soul from this terrain short of reasoning in self-defense. Has it ever traversed your tenacious mind that you are not consecrated and preferred because of your heart teeming of jealousy and detestation?

Gretta fell to her knees in embarrassment and shame, tears flowing to hell. Her body began to shake uncontrollably, and she let out a huge scream of terror.

The Judgment

One of the hooded women stepped forward.

Her voice was like water hitting stone.

You have been warned before. You have cursed children, twisted herbs into poison, and performed blood rites from pride, not prayer. You did not act from fear. You acted from ego.

The pool showed Julian's baby wailing into life.

And yet she lived. And yet both survived.

The hooded figure raised her hand and Gretta stopped shaking and instantly rendered to no bodily movement forcibly.

You are now marked. Not for death. But for consequence.

The pool flashed.

Your gifts will wither. Your tongue will tangle when you speak curses. Your sleep will be thin, and your ancestors will turn their backs to you. Until you seek repentance. Gifts aren't to be abused, which is why you were never accepted in the heavens.

The aunt screamed "Nooooo, please don't turn your back on me, I did this for you all, to help keep earth sin free."

But no one moved.

You will remember this counsel. You will wake with its weight.

The Return

She gasped awake, flung upright in her bed. Sweating. Trembling. Her tongue swollen.

Her voice stuck. Her altar?

All the candles had melted flat and the water in her bowl had turned black.

The mirror on her wall cracked straight through the center. She touched her throat, unable to say a word. She tried to chant, but all that came out was silence.

The spirits had turned their backs.

She had been seen.

And she had been stripped.

Chapter Sixty-Three

The Flame and the Flesh

The room was dim, lit only by the moon spilling through the window and a single beeswax candle on the dresser. The skeleton appearing frozen on the altar to represent Lucille now.

Frozen in the spirit world.

The air smelled of eucalyptus and Mama June's cornbread still warm on the tray.

Lucille sat propped up in bed, a velvet blanket pulled over her lap. Her curls were wrapped. Her face, though flushed, still carried the fire of the battle-born.

Sophie rushed out the window as to alert Mama June that Lucille was awake.

Dalton sat beside her, feeding her spoonful's of greens and bits of roasted sweet potato from a wooden bowl.

"Mama June said if you didn't eat, she'd drag you out the spirit world by your ankles next time." Lucille gave a tired smirk, but her eyes were still dangerous. "I wanted that woman's blood," she muttered. "Julian's aunt. I wanted to take her teeth out with my bare hands. I ain't never felt rage like that, not even with Claudine."

Dalton stilled, then placed the bowl down on the tray. "You got a soft spot for folks who've been hurt."

"I was that girl, Dalton," she said, her voice thick with memory. "I know what it's like to be dismissed, silenced, cursed. But to do it to a baby?" She shook her head. "That kind of cruelty... it deserves reckoning."

He took her hand gently, tracing his thumb along her wrist.

"You cooling off now?"

She leaned her head against his shoulder, eyes closing briefly. "Yes. With you here."

Dalton smiled, his breath catching. He turned toward her and pulled her close, wrapping her in his arms like she was fragile glass and molten lava all at once.

"I thought I lost you, pretty lady," he whispered against her forehead. "You were moving like a giant.

I ain't never seen a woman so strong... and so mad."

He paused, then added with a crooked grin: "I know better now. I ain't ever gonna hurt you."

Lucille chuckled softly, tears finally threatening to rise.

He kissed her, deeply.

A kiss that told her she was home, not just held.

Dalton leaned back and reached into his jacket pocket. He pulled out a hand-rolled joint and lit it with the flick of his lighter.

He took one slow drag, then held it out to her.

"Here. This'll help bring back the soft and delicate woman I know lives under all that fire."

Lucille took it, inhaled slow, exhaled like she was finally surrendering. They passed it back and forth in silence, smoke curling between them like spirit threads.

When it burned down to the last inch, Lucille rose.

She moved to the dresser, lit a small stick of rose incense, and turned on the old radio. A down-home blues tune began to hum low and slow.

Lucille turned to face Dalton, hips already swaying. Her eyes shimmered, not with seduction, but with invitation.

"I love you so much," she said. "And I want you to make love to me tonight. Not fast. Not rushed.

I want to feel like I'm being carried back to earth."

Dalton stood up slow, eyes darkening with reverence. "I'll do whatever you want. Whenever you want." He stepped toward her.

She met him halfway.

And he devoured her, not with hunger, but with holy intention.

Every inch of her body was touched like scripture. He kissed her until she forgot the spirit realm.

He worshiped her curves like altars. Her legs wrapped around him, her nails raked down his back, not in pain, but in prayer.

The blues played on.

And Lucille, once again, was remade in love.

Chapter Sixty-Four

The Steam Between Us

T he morning was soft.

Light streamed through the shop's wide windows, warming the wooden floors and glinting off glass jars lined with roots, salts, and petals.

Lucille stepped downstairs slowly, her robe tied at the waist, her spirit finally settled after the storm.

In the back room, she heard quiet coos and soft conversation.

Julian was seated in the rocking chair, her baby cradled against her chest, both wrapped in a soft cotton blanket Mama June had laid out.

Lucille knocked gently against the doorframe. "Hey, sweet girl."

Julian looked up, eyes wide. She held the baby a little tighter but relaxed when she saw Lucille's smile.

"Hi," Julian said shyly. "You're the one who... helped me?"

Lucille walked in slowly, barefoot, her aura heavy with light. "I'm Lucille."

She sat on the stool across from her. "And yes, I helped. But it was the spirits who made sure you got here. You were meant to live."

Julian blinked back tears. "My name's Julian. And this here..." she glanced down, "this is Rosalie."

Lucille's chest swelled. "She's beautiful. And strong, just like her mama."

Lucille stood and motioned toward the side room. "When you're ready, I want to help you do something.

We call it a steam. It's a way to clean the body and soul after childbirth. Not just from blood, but from fear.

From everything that touched you without your permission.

Julian looked unsure but nodded. "Okay."

A little later, Lucille prepared the room.

She laid a towel across the bench and pulled down a small, deep pot from the back shelf.

She filled it with:

Red raspberry leaf – to tone the womb

Yarrow – for healing tears

Calendula and rose – for softness and heart restoration

Motherwort – for courage

And a touch of mugwort – for clearing the spiritual residue of trauma

She poured steaming water over the blend and watched it come alive. The scent filled the room sweet, earthy, protective.

From the windowsill, Sophie watched, feathers puffed, her eye reflecting the rising steam like fire contained in water.

Julian entered slowly, a fresh robe wrapped around her body. Mama June held Rosalie just outside the room. Lucille gestured to the bench.

"This is just for you, baby. Sit down. Let the steam rise. Let it carry out everything your body's been holding."

Julian sat, legs parted over the steam, her breath shallow. Then it deepened. Then it slowed. Then, it broke.

Tears slid down her cheeks. Lucille sat on the floor beside her and held her hand.

On the altar, the skeleton key glowed faint silver, not fierce this time, but tender, as if blessing the womb's return to itself.

Neither spoke.

Because they didn't have to. This was a moment between women, between survivors, between anointed ones.

Lucille thought she heard a whisper in the steam; three voices braided as one: *She has been reclaimed.*

When Julian finished, she looked lighter, glowing, even. She turned to Lucille and said softly:

"I feel like... I'm mine again."

Lucille squeezed her hand.

"That's the whole point."

Chapter Sixty-Five

The Daughters of Her Spirit

Mama June sat in her favorite chair by the front window, sipping a tall glass of lemon balm and honey tea.

Sophie perched on the sill beside her, wings calm, eyes sharp as ever.

Lucille was at the herb table, refilling jars and writing notes in her big brown leather journal.

Julian was rocking Rosalie in the back, humming an old melody her mother used to sing to her when she was small.

The shop didn't just smell like roots and pine anymore; it smelled like rebirth.

Mama June leaned her head back against the window and let out a long, quiet sigh.

Not of exhaustion.

Of peace.

A Family Built by Spirit

Lucille glanced up and caught the look on Mama June's face. "What you thinkin' about over there?"

Mama June smirked without opening her eyes. "I'm thinkin' the Lord done played a trick on me."

"What kind of trick?"

"The kind where you say you don't want children," she said, sipping again, "And then one day you wake up with three grown ones, full of fire and secrets and spirit."

Lucille laughed softly.

"Julian's not grown yet."

"That girl birthed a child into a curse and lived to hum about it," Mama June said. "She's grown enough."

Julian stepped into the room then, Rosalie wrapped snug across her chest. Her face was softer now, her eyes no longer hollow.

She paused in the doorway. "Mama June?"

"Yes, baby?"

"I'd like to stay. Not just for a few days. I want to stay here. Help around the shop, learn what y'all do. Raise my baby around love, not bitterness."

Mama June blinked. Her eyes misted over, but no tears fell. She stood and walked over, brushing Julian's curls behind her ear like a mother might.

"Then this your home now."

"You mean it?"

"I don't speak what I don't mean. You and that baby belong to the light. And this is a house of light."

That night, Mama June sat on the porch, Lucille at one side, Julian at the other, Rosalie cooing gently in her lap.

The stars were bright.

No wind.

No spirits stirring.

Just the deep, content hum of three women who had walked through fire and made it to the garden.

Lucille rested her head on June's shoulder. "You raised yourself. And now you're raising us."

Mama June smiled. "I ain't raisin' y'all. I'm just loving you through it. That's what real mothering is."

Julian nodded, rocking slowly. "Feels like I can finally breathe."

Rosalie let out a soft sigh and curled closer.

"You're all mine now," Mama June said softly, her voice full of truth and tremble.

"And I'm all yours."

Chapter Sixty-Six

The Smoke They Didn't
Want

The afternoon had been peaceful.

Lucille had just brewed a pot of rosemary tea. Julian was folding baby blankets on the reading couch. Mama June had her feet up, sorting dried hibiscus petals.

And then, the bell rang.

But the energy that blew in wasn't just off, it was rank.

Lucille froze mid-step.

She turned toward the front door and saw three men, all leather boots, crusted denim, and rotten grins.

The air dampened.

Not just cold.

Heavy.

Foul.

Tainted.

Lucille's spirit squinted before her eyes did. "Darkness," she whispered.

"Every one of them touched by filth," Mama June muttered."I feel it in the floorboards."

Julian's skin crawled. She didn't say a word.

She just scooped Rosalie into her arms and climbed the stairs, heart pounding, mouth dry. She didn't have sight like Lucille. But she had knowing. And what she felt slither into the shop was not just bad, it was evil disguised in swagger.

Downstairs, the tallest of the three strolled toward the counter.

"Howdy, ladies," he said, voice slick as grease. "Any menfolk workin' back there? Or is it just y'all sweet things?"

Lucille narrowed her eyes.

Mama June didn't move.

She simply said: "State your business, all of you."

The men exchanged looks.

The filthiest one stepped closer, breath thick with tobacco and sweat.

"Calm down, old lady. We just lookin' for some smoke. Heard y'all keep the good stuff. Herbs and whatnot."

Lucille's voice dropped a tone, "This is a healing shop. Not a trap house. And you've got three seconds before we stop being polite."

The energy in the room shrank and the skeleton lit up purple for protection.

Mama June reached slowly under the counter and gripped the old iron shotgun she kept wrapped in a purple shawl.

She didn't raise it.

She didn't have to. Her spirit spoke louder than steel ever could.

Sophies croak was no ordinary sound, it was a summons. A signal to the other side to man their battle posts.

"Last man to speak sideways in my space got carried out foamin' at the mouth," she said calmly.

"And he didn't even mean no harm. Y'all came in here lookin' to take."

Lucille stepped beside her, holding a smudge stick already lit.

The smoke curled black. That was all she needed to see.

"Y'all got rape on your hands," she said, voice shaking with disgust. "And your auras look like tar. You came in here for smoke...But you about to get FIRE."

The men shifted uncomfortably. The smallest one turned toward the door, already unsettled.

But the dirtiest one grinned wider. "You women always so dramatic. All that voodoo talk don't scare me."

Mama June cocked the shotgun with one smooth movement.

Click-clack.

"Ain't nobody said nothin' about scarin' you," she said. "We said we'd end ya."

Lucille raised her other hand, fingers glowing faint with energy she wasn't even trying to hide.

"You feel that? That buzz in your throat? That's your body realizing you walked into a temple, not a storefront. Your spirit ain't safe here."

The third man grabbed his friend's shoulder.

"We need to go. I don't like this. Feels... wrong."

The leader snarled. "You'll regret this, witches."

Mama June leaned in, eyes blazing. "And you'll regret ever thinkin' God ain't watchin'.

Now get out. All of you."

The bell rang again, this time with relief, as the men stormed out, shadows trailing behind them like tails tucked between their legs.

The shop's air trembled. Lucille threw open the windows. Mama June poured salt at the threshold.

Julian peeked from the stairs, holding her baby tight.

"Y'all good?" she called down.

Mama June nodded. "We always good, baby. This house is watched."

Lucille lit fresh white candles. Mama June locked the door and whispered:

"Let that be the last time these fools mistake softness for submission."

Chapter Sixty-Seven

Smoke, Salt, and Story

The windows were wide open, letting the last of the foul energy drift away on the night air.

Lucille was grinding herbs in the stone mortar, whispering as she worked.

Mama June and Julian stood beside her, each woman holding a piece of protection work, a charm bag, a salt bowl, a key dipped in rue oil.

The baby was asleep upstairs, wrapped in soft cloth and guarded by a silver bell in the window.

This was a warding night. A night to seal the house and raise the veil.

Mama June laid down lines of salt and crushed black tourmaline at each window.

Then she began to speak, not just to instruct, but to witness.

"You think men like that only show up once you're grown," she said. "But some of us see them too early. And sometimes... they don't look like men at all."

Lucille and Julian looked up.

Mama June didn't stop. "I had a woman once. Family friend. Real pretty, dressed in pastels, smelled like gardenia. She used to braid my hair and whisper things I didn't understand.

Told me I had 'the light' and needed to be trained. Said I was lucky she loved me first."

She scoffed softly, eyes far away now. "She didn't love me. She was grooming me. Touching my spirit without permission. Using sweetness to hide sickness."

Lucille stopped grinding, her hands going still. Julian sat on the floor, wide-eyed.

"They never talk about women predators," Mama June continued. "But they exist. The jealous aunt. The 'cool' older cousin. The best friend who don't like to see you rise."

She sprinkled rue in a spiral on the floor. "Some women don't want to raise you. They want to drink from you. Use your softness. Twist your gift. Make you small so they feel big."

Julian swallowed hard. "Like my aunt."

Mama June looked at her, eyes sharp but soft. "Exactly like your aunt."

The Protection Work

They moved together in rhythm.

Lucille lit a new bundle of rosemary and lavender, walking it through every doorway.

Julian followed behind her with the salt dish, whispering:

"May no harm enter. May no mask remain. Let every spirit show its true face."

Mama June added three braids of red thread to the doorframe. "You're not just protecting a shop anymore," she said. "You're protecting each other. And Julian, if you gon' walk with spirit, you need to know this..."

She turned to face her fully. "Your gift is strong. And it makes you a ligh and lights attract insects and seekers. You better learn the difference."

Julian nodded, hand over her heart. "I don't know what my gift is yet."

Lucille stepped forward, holding a small pot of warm herbs. "We'll help you find it. But first, we protect it."

She sat Julian down and handed her a dish of oil to anoint her wrists and throat.

Mama June handed her a silver coin wrapped in string. "Keep this in your pocket until you dream something new. When you do, we'll start your training."

Julian's eyes misted. "Y'all make me feel like I'm somebody."

Mama June leaned down, placed both hands on her head. "You're not just somebody. You're a survivor, a mother, and a rising root worker. And any spirit, or person, who tries to harm you now,"

She looked toward the door, where a soft wind had just stirred the salt.

"They'll be met by three women. Sweet when we want to be... but mean when we have to be."

Sophie flew around the room three times and cawing for the induction of Julian into the spiritual roots of protection.

Chapter Sixty-Eight

What Was Stolen, What Remains

Julian sat in the back room, sunlight warming her shoulders as Rosalie nursed quietly. Her skin glowed with the faintest shimmer, not magic, but awakening.

The rituals, the protection, the steams, they had started to stir memory.

Mama June noticed the shift first. Lucille said the air around her moved differently. And that morning, while Rosalie slept in her sling, Julian whispered,

"Can I tell y'all somethin'? Something I ain't never said out loud?"

Mama June paused from sifting dried rosemary.

Lucille closed her book gently.

They nodded.

Julian took a long breath, looked down at her child.

"My granddaddy was a wealthy man. Land, cattle, stocks, all that. He left it to my mama. She was good. Sweet. A singer in church. Didn't know nothing about manipulation. Didn't see it coming. She met this man, he was charming, and older. Said he'd protect her. Within six months, he had her married, drugged, and locked away."

Mama June clenched her jaw. Lucille whispered, "Psych house?"

Julian nodded. "They pumped her full of psychotropic meds till she couldn't remember her own name. She came out walking slow. Mouth dry. Eyes empty. Then he shot her and said it was an accident. Skipped town with her bank accounts and all the land in his name."

Julian's voice dropped to almost nothing. "I don't know who my real daddy is. Mama never said. Just that he was 'a good man who died too early.'"

She looked at Rosalie now, who stirred in her sleep. "But I know who her daddy is. Same man who destroyed my mama. He came into my room at night. Told me I reminded him of her. Said if I screamed, I'd end up like she did."

Lucille's eyes flooded with tears.

Mama June grabbed a candle and whispered a protection prayer under her breath.

Julian placed her palm over Rosalie's head. "And my aunt... she knew. She knew. Said it was my fault. Said I tempted him."

Her voice broke then. "I was fifteen."

The skeleton key again began to drop droplets of water in reference to how Lucille was feeling on the inside. Julian doesn't know it yet but Lucille looks at her like a little sister now and an Aunt to Rosalie. Their traumatic entrance to the shop forever bonded them.

Lucille reached over and held her hand, firm and sacred. "Rosalie ain't a curse. She's not his child in spirit. She came through him, not from him."

Mama June stepped forward with a string of prayer beads and placed them around Julian's wrist. "You and this baby carry the strength of three generations trying to survive wicked men. But that stops here at your tender age of seventeen."

She walked to the altar and retrieved an old box wrapped in deep plum cloth. "Your granddaddy's name?" "David Ezekiel Carter."

June's eyes flickered with recognition.

"I knew his sister. She came through here once, twenty years ago. Said there was blood money on the wind and that her niece might need protection one day."

She placed the box in Julian's lap. "This was hers. She said to give it to the girl with moonlight in her eyes and rage in her bones."

Julian opened it.

Inside was a small deed, a corner of land in her mother's maiden name, still untouched. A gold ring with an opal stone. And a folded letter:

"To the one who comes after. Your name will be dragged. Your womb will be war. But your child will be blessed. You are the one who breaks what tried to become tradition. Bury nothing. Speak all. And rise."

Julian sobbed into Lucille's shoulder. Mama June stood over them both.

"Your mama's story ain't lost. And yours is just beginning. Seventeen, and already walked through more shadows than most in a lifetime. But the spirits picked you because of that, not in spite of it."

Mama June glances over at Rosalie sleeping in her basket, "But look at her, sleeping like light itself. That's how I know both of you been chosen, one to survive, one to guide."

She tells Julian and Lucille "this is what can cause a mother to be jealous of their daughter. They had a hard time and want their daughter to experience pain as well. So always remember to check and reflect on your own soul so that doesn't happen to you ladies."

Chapter Sixty-Nine

The Voices at the Market

F<u>lashback: Lucille, age 9. Claudine, age 11.</u>

The sun was already high when Hattie packed up her two daughters and headed into town.

Their father, Dr. Green, had left earlier that morning, starched coat crisp and eyes full of urgency, he was going to check on a patient who had taken a turn during the night.

"We'll meet him at the market once he's done," Hattie said, adjusting her earrings in the rearview mirror.

Lucille sat in the backseat, face pressed against the glass. "Mama," she whispered from the back seat,

"I don't think I want to go to the market today."

"And why not?" Hattie asked, barely glancing back.

"The air feel wrong."

Claudine rolled her eyes dramatically. "She always talkin' nonsense."

Lucille ignored her. "Mama, I really got a bad feelin'. Like something's watching me that ain't there."

Hattie sighed as she pulled into the crowded gravel lot outside the market. "Cut out that devil talk," she snapped. "Ain't nothing wrong with this place. Now get out and stop embarrassin' me."

Lucille stepped out of the car slowly, stomach turning, her fingers tingling like they were brushing against cold water. The moment they stepped through the market doors, everything changed. The bad feeling in her stomach was coming to the light. It was packed, voices, carts, shoes on tile, but for Lucille, the noise behind the noise was louder.

She could hear whispers. Not from mouths, but from air. From walls. From shadows.

She has it...

Watch the younger one...

Close your eyes, child, you'll see me better...

She blinked hard. Looked around. No one spoke to her. Yet the voices were clear as day.

Her fingers tightened around the small skeleton key in her pocket. It grew icy in her hand, colder than bone, as if it were echoing the fear rising in her chest. As they passed the vegetable section, Lucille saw something tall and gray flicker behind the tomatoes. In the frozen food aisle, a hunched, translucent figure traced its hand along the glass door, whispering ancient words in tongues she didn't recognize.

"Mama..." she whispered again. "There's people here but they ain't... alive."

Hattie didn't stop walking. "Don't say another word," she said coldly. "You are not gon' grow up strange like your grandmother. You're gonna be normal. Do you hear me?"

Lucille nodded but inside, something settled. She had realized that public places are like crossing through a portal. And once you see spirits in the mundane, you never unsee them. Even though Lucille was used to seeing spirits she realized that she was getting stronger because she could hear them more clearly now.

That day, Lucille didn't touch anything. Didn't speak. Didn't even eat the apple Claudine offered her in the car.

She had learned something powerful:

Spirits don't just haunt graveyards. They haunt places where souls move in and out.

Grocery stores.

Airports.

Train stations.

Hospitals.

Hotels.

And yes... markets.

She whispered into her palm:

"I see you. But I don't invite you."

Chapter Seventy

Smoke, Blues, and
Belonging

The coals crackled sweet under the grill pit as Dalton flipped the ribs with one hand and sipped a cold cola in the other. Incent and BBQ smoke curled into the late afternoon air like a prayer being answered slowly.

Lucille stood nearby, barefoot, wearing a tied-up gingham blouse and high-waisted denim shorts, hips swaying softly to a down-home blues record playing from the back room. Light bounced off her skin like butter on cornbread.

Mama June was stretched out in her favorite porch chair with a plate of deviled eggs on her lap, one foot tapping to the beat, eyes half-closed in contentment earned.

Julian sat cross-legged on a quilt; baby Rosalie curled in her arms like a flower in bloom. She had the faintest smile on her lips, the kind that only comes after a storm has passed.

"These ribs," Mama June called out between bites, "taste like they been blessed by Moses and Mahalia."

Dalton grinned. "I aim to please, Mama June."

"You aim right. I ain't had ribs like this since the 50's."

Lucille laughed and passed around sweet tea with mint and lemon. "You say that every time you eat ribs."

"That's because every time I eat good ribs, the Holy Ghost shows up. And chile, He here today."

Julian took a sip of her tea and leaned her head against the porch beam.

"I ain't never had a cookout without tension," she said softly. "Somebody always mad. Somebody always fighting. This here... this feels like a life I ain't never known."

Lucille knelt beside her and placed a hand on her knee. "That's because you're writing a new life now. Rosalie gonna grow up remembering music, not yelling. Smoke from the grill, not from a house burning down behind her."

Dalton sat down beside them with his plate and added, "We don't just heal wounds here. We build memories. The kind that feeds your soul ten years from now when you smell hickory wood or hear a guitar wail just right."

The record changed and slid into a slower tune, "Love and Happiness" rolling through the speakers like syrup over flapjacks. Lucille stood and pulled Dalton to his feet.

"Dance with me."

"Always," he said, setting his plate down.

They swayed slow and close in the grass, her head on his chest, his arms around her like they'd been carved for that moment. Mama June smiled wide, her heart quiet for once.

"Look at my babies," she whispered. "All of 'em. Covered in grace."

Julian closed her eyes and let the music fill her chest. Rosalie cooed once in her sleep, like she too knew something beautiful was unfolding.

The sky turned pink. The ribs disappeared. The music kept playing.

Sophie flexing her beautiful wings, opening and closing, creating herself a smooth spiritual breeze.

And for the first time in a long, long time...No one looked over their shoulder. Because they were home.

Chapter Seventy-One

Perfume and Permission

The morning was soft, kissed by dew, with the faint hum of cicadas stirring in the distance. Dalton stood by the front steps of the shop, wrapping his arms around Lucille, who wore her softest cotton dress and a sleepy smile.

"You sure you don't want me to stay longer?" he asked, kissing her forehead.

"You've spoiled me enough this week," Lucille replied, tracing his collarbone.

"Go build something so I can brag about you later."

He grinned. They kissed one last time, slow and tender. And just as he stepped down the last stair toward his truck, the shop bell rang.

Lucille turned.

A tall, lean figure entered the threshold like a storm wrapped in satin. He wore a long black dress, the hem brushing his worn sneakers.

His lips were painted red like roses in mourning, and his perfume clung to the air like a memory that refused to fade. His skin was deep and radiant, but his eyes were tired.

So tired.

Lucille blinked. Dalton paused on the path.

"Mornin'," the figure said, voice low but soft. "I'm lookin' for Mama June."

Lucille stepped forward with a warm smile. "You found her."

Mama June, already walking from the back, stopped in her tracks when she saw him. Her eyes narrowed, not in judgment, but in recognition.

"John John," she said.

"Yes, ma'am," he replied, lips trembling.

"It's been a long time."

John John stepped into the light, the perfume curling behind him like incense.

"I don't want to lie no more, Mama June," he said, barely louder than breath. "I'm tired.

I don't want to pretend I'm a man. I want to be a woman. I am a woman." He looked around, nervous. "I know folks talk. I know how it looks. But I came here because... I know this is the only place left where I might not be damned for sayin' it."

Mama June walked to the counter, pulled down a jar of hyssop and another of frankincense. She didn't rush. She didn't flinch.

"Sit down, child," she said, motioning to the chair in front of the altar. "You came to the right place. Ain't nobody here in the business of policing souls."

John John sat slowly, legs shaking. Lucille brought him water with a sprig of mint, watching him closely.

"When did you know?" she asked gently.

"Always," he said.

"Even when I played football and cut my hair short and wore them damn suits. I was always... her underneath. But my daddy said if I didn't change, I'd be buried like a sinner."

Mama June laid out three white candles, a bowl of anointing oil, and a strip of soft cloth.

"This ain't about gender, baby. This about truth. And truth got a sound. It echoes different when you finally speak it."

She motioned for Lucille to assist. As Lucille walked over, the skeleton key lit up a bright rainbow color to represent acceptance and love.

Together, they lit the candles, each one for a stage of transition. The great mothers shook the room:

What was

What hurt

What is to come

Mama June took the cloth and wiped the tears from John John's cheeks. "Do you have a name you want to be called?" John John paused.

Then, with the faintest smile, "Joan. Like Joan of Arc."

Mama June nodded. "A warrior name. Fitting."

Dalton stood outside by the truck, watching quietly. Lucille stepped out to meet him, placing a hand on his chest.

"You good?" she asked.

"I am now," he said.

"You sure do keep a holy house, Lucille. Ain't no place like this anywhere else."

She kissed him again for what felt like a day.

Sophie flew around them as if she was wrapping them in gold twine.

As they separated Dalton got into his pickup truck, he said "I stuck around to make sure yall was safe my lady. "Tipping his hat.

Lucille blushed, watching as he drove off. And inside… Mama June poured rosewater into Joan's hands and whispered:

"You're not too late. You're right on time. Now let's help you remember who you've always been."

Chapter Seventy-Two

The War in the Womb

The screen door slammed open so hard it knocked one of the hanging wind chimes clean off the hook. A tall man stumbled in, carrying a heavy-set pregnant woman in his arms. Sweat rolled down both their faces.

"Mama June!" he shouted.

"Please, please help us!"

Lucille and Julian came rushing from the back. Mama June was already moving, staff in one hand, her spirit buzzing.

"Put her down here," she instructed, pointing to the long bench lined with quilts. "Tell me what's going on."

Nathaniel's voice shook as he laid his wife down. "Her name's Tally. She's eight months with twins. She says it feels like they're tryin' to rip each other apart in there."

Tally cried out and clutched her belly. "It's like they hate each other," she wept. "My whole stomach's been twisting. I can't eat, I can't sleep. It's like... there's a war goin' on inside me."

Mama June moved her hands across Tally's belly slowly, feeling the vibration beneath the skin. She inhaled sharply. "Somebody rooted you."

Tally nodded. "His mama, I know it's her! She said I stole her son. Said I was takin' what belonged to her. She's hated me since the weddin'. And now she wants to ruin my babies."

Lucille stepped forward, already unwrapping the red binding cord and grabbing her black salt. "We're not lettin' that happen," she said, voice like iron.

Mama June pointed to Julian. "Get me the hot water basin and the jar of rue and valerian from the bottom shelf. You're gonna learn midwifery the right way, through spirit and instinct."

Julian moved fast, hands trembling but determined. "Y-yes ma'am."

Mama June placed one hand on Tally's forehead and whispered an old Gullah prayer of womb peace and divine separation. Lucille circled the room, burning sage and wild garlic root to flush the curse energy.

"Julian, rub the rue oil on her feet," Mama June instructed. "The feet are gatekeepers. We closing up her spiritual gates so nothin' else enters."

Lucille stood behind Tally, eyes closed, holding the red cord. She saw it in her mind's eye: a dark thread connecting Tally's belly to an old woman rocking on a porch somewhere, her mouth full of bitter words and old rage.

"I see it," Lucille whispered. She tried to braid hatred into the womb. Made each child think the other was the enemy."

Mama June nodded without turning. "Then unbraid it, chile."

Lucille lifted her hands and moved them through the air like a weaver undoing knots. Sophie flew outside to monitor the evil spirits and make sure they depart.

Lucille spoke firmly: "You will not divide what was created in harmony. You will not pit soul against soul. I return you to the heart that cast you. And may you face what you sent."

She tied the cord three times and snapped it, tossing the ends into the flame. The candle sparked violently. Then stilled.

Tally gasped, clutching her belly. Julian moved to her side. "What is it?"

"They stopped fighting," she whispered. "I can feel it... they're... they're hugging."

Mama June smiled and wiped her brow. "That's the womb's natural memory. Harmony. Your babies knew peace before the curse. Now they remember again."

Nathaniel dropped to his knees, sobbing.

Lucille placed her hand on his shoulder. "This ain't just about breaking spells. It's about protecting love from the people who fear it."

Mama June looked at Julian. "You did good. You watched. You moved. You listened. That's how midwives are born."

Julian wiped her hands, her eyes wide with wonder. "I didn't know helping birth could feel like breaking chains."

"That's exactly what it is, baby," Mama June said. "Every time we bring life into this world right...We undo a little bit of the poison that tried to run it."

Sophie cawing hysterically outside, but it grew fainter. Mama June and Lucille looked at each other.

They said in unison, "Sophies watching the spirit move."

Chapter Seventy-Three

She Who Catches Life

The shop was quiet the morning after Tally Brewer's cleansing and the air still smelled of bay leaves and lavender ash.

Julian stood barefoot in the back room, watching Rosalie sleep peacefully in the sling tied to her chest. Her fingers absentmindedly stroked her daughter's hairline.

Mama June walked in with two cups of tea and passed one to her, saying nothing at first.

Julian took it and whispered, "I think... I know what my gift is."

Mama June raised a brow, eyes soft. "You ready to say it out loud?"

Julian nodded. She held the warm cup in both hands like it was a prayer bowl.

"I've always had these dreams," Julian said, voice low. "Of babies. Always babies. Sometimes I'm catching them in water. Sometimes I'm in a field and a woman is screaming, and I'm whisperin' to her, 'Push now, just like that.' Sometimes I'm just rocking them and singing old songs I didn't even know I knew."

She paused, eyes glassy. "Even when I was pregnant with Rosalie...I had a dream I was walking down a dirt road, and my baby was ready to come. But something told me... clench your body, baby, tighten your core. So, I did. I woke up sweating. And the next morning, my water broke."

She looked up at Mama June, voice trembling. "I walked here... with her pushing down like she was already halfway through. And somehow, she didn't fall out. I didn't know why then. But I know now."

Mama June didn't blink. She just reached out, took Julian's hand, and placed it on her own heart.

"You've got a midwife's heart," she said, voice velvet and fire. "It beats steady in the face of chaos.

You don't just birth babies, you birth peace. Your womb remembers things your mouth don't even know how to say yet."

Julian's throat tightened. "Every time I see a child, I feel like I need to hold them. Even when they cry, they stop when I get near. Rosalie... she don't even cry when I'm close. She knows I'm hers. And I feel like I belong to her too."

Mama June smiled wide. "You're a mama to the world now. And your gift ain't loud, but baby... it's holy."

Mama June walked to the altar, grabbed the oil mixed with calendula, sage, and hibiscus, and returned.

She placed a single drop on Julian's forehead. "I name your gift now," she said. "You are She Who Catches Life. Not just with your hands, but with your presence. The spirit chose you to be a guardian of birth. A protector of the passage between realms. You are a Womb Tender."

Julian fell forward into Mama June's arms, sobbing softly. Rosalie stirred, then settled again.

Mama June rocked them both, whispering,

"Your mama would be proud. And so are we."

Chapter Seventy-Four

Turn the Child, Turn the Fear

The storm hit just after sunset.

The sky cracked open with thunder, and rain slammed against the porch like urgent fists. The candles in the shop flickered but never died.

Julian stood in the back room beside a woman laboring on the birthing bench, her name was Eunice, a young farm girl from the outskirts who'd heard about "the women with holy hands." She was screaming now.

"It hurts bad, worse than it should!"

Lucille was pacing the perimeter, burning mugwort and sprinkling vinegar water around the room. Mama June sat nearby, watching with eyes sharp as blades.

Julian leaned down and placed her hand on the woman's belly. Then her eyes widened.

"Oh God. The baby's feet... they're what's coming." Breech

Mama June didn't move. "Say it louder," she said calmly.

Julian stood frozen. "The baby's breech."

The room shrank. Sophie flew over to the door to watch for spirits.

Eunice wailed again, grabbing the sheets with fists like roots. Julian backed up one step.

"I don't know what to do, what if I hurt the baby?"

Lucille moved to her side fast. She grabbed Julian's hand and locked eyes with her.

"Don't you dare start doubting now."

Julian's breath hitched. "What if I mess up?"

"What if you don't?" Lucille snapped, her voice steady as a drumbeat. "You were born for this. That baby is waiting on you. Now get in position. I'll keep the space clean."

The skeleton key shined brightly, since it was tied to Lucille's inner being. She was internally proud of Julian in this sacred moment where the portals are opening.

Mama June finally stood, slow and rooted. "Julian."

"Yes, ma'am."

"I'm gonna walk you through this. You will do it. You hear me?"

Julian nodded, trembling.

"First thing you do...Don't panic. Second thing...Turn that child."

Julian knelt back down and gently placed her hands on Eunice's belly.

She closed her eyes and remembered every dream, every tug, every whisper she ever felt through her own womb.

She pressed slowly, softly, not just guiding the baby, but inviting it to shift.

"Baby girl," she whispered to the unborn child, "I know it's dark in there. I know you scared. But it's time to come through. Turn to the light, little one. I'm right here."

She moved with rhythm, using the breath Mama June taught her.

In... press.

Out... shift.

In... hold.

Out... turn.

Then, movement.

A ripple passed under her fingers.

Lucille gasped. "She's turning her!"

Mama June nodded once. "Just like I knew she would."

Minutes later, the baby crowned. Julian caught her first breech-turned birth like a woman who had done it a thousand times.

She held the slick, wriggling body against her chest and burst into tears.

Eunice sobbed with relief. The baby wailed.

Lucille clapped once, tears streaking down her cheeks. Of course, the skeleton key started to perspire just like its proprietor.

"You did it. You turned more than the baby. You turned your-self."

Sophie flew around the new baby and Julian to bless them and initiate the first round of protection from wicked spirits on the physical pane.

Mama June walked forward, her voice a low hum.

"You didn't just catch a child tonight, baby. You caught your power."

Chapter Seventy-Five

The Right to Choose the Spirit

The shop was quiet. because Rosalie was napping. The day felt slow and holy with calm energy.

Julian was rearranging jars on the apothecary shelves, and Lucille was outside sweeping salt along the porch. Mama June was finishing a tincture blend when the bell above the door gave a sharp chime.

The woman who stepped in was striking in her silence.

She wore a long black dress, gloves, and large dark sunglasses. Her hat veiled her face, but the tightness in her jaw and the tremor in her hands gave her away.

The air shifted and the candles on the altar guttered low, as though dimming in grief.

The skeleton key on Lucille's altar turned icy, a cold bite spreading through the wood around it. From the rafters, Sophie gave one slow, uneasy shuffle of her wings, her black eye fixed on the woman like she already knew her story.

Lucille caught sight of her through the window and narrowed her eyes. Julian turned to greet her but froze slightly at the woman's presence. She was white and not from their town. And she smelled of fear and wealth with the essence of Elizabeth Taylor.

"May I help you?" Julian asked.

The woman removed her glasses, but not her hat. "I don't want to give my name child, but I was told Mama June could help women... with certain kinds of... situations."

Mama June stepped forward, voice calm. "Depends on the situation, baby. Why don't you tell me plainly."

The woman hesitated. Then she took a breath so deep it shook.

"I'm pregnant. And I can't have this child. I've already got four, and my husband, he's a god-fearing man who don't believe in... in this." She swallowed.

"But I can't do it again. My body can't. My mind can't." She twisted her gloves in her hands. "You don't understand," she whispered.

The candles flickered harder now, bending toward her words like they were testifying to truth.

"I never even had time to heal. After my last baby, I still had stitches in me when he came home from work. I begged him, 'please, I can't yet.' He put his hand over my mouth and said, 'The Bible told me not to withhold from my husband.' I laid there bleeding, praying it would be over quick." Her voice cracked.

"Every time I birthed, every time my body was torn, he came back before I was ready. I told myself that was love. That was marriage. But it wasn't. It was ownership."

A tear dropped from her tired, but beautiful eyes. "I came from three towns over because someone told me... you don't judge."

Mama June nodded. "That's correct. I don't."

Julian stood to the side, arms crossed unconsciously.

Lucille caught the shift.

Mama June did too.

"Julian," she said without turning,

"I need the red clover, mugwort, and motherwort blend. It's on the top shelf. Go ahead and make a pot."

Julian moved, quiet but conflicted. She set the herbs down too hard and whispered, "But Mama June... isn't this murder? Won't it come back on her? On us, even, for helping?

Mama June looked her square in the eye.

"No, child. Murder is when you snuff out life already walking its path. This here is different. A spirit ain't the same as a body. Some come knocking before their time. Some come through the wrong gate. You think God cruel enough to damn a woman for closing the gate to save her own soul? No. The only curse comes from forcing a womb to carry what it cannot."

The skeleton key pulsed faintly, as if echoing the violation described. Its glow wasn't rage-red this time, but pale blue, trembling like water, reflecting Lucille's empathy and the memory of pain carried by every woman in the room.

Lucille took a deep breath, steadying her spirit.

As Julian poured hot water over the herbs, Mama June began her work, preparing tinctures, drawing a sigil of protection on the woman's wrist with bay leaf oil, and speaking softly to her about how to rest after the ritual.

"You'll have to be alone when the time comes," Mama June said. "But you won't be unguarded. Spirits are watching. And the child's soul... it already knows."

The woman's eyes welled up. "Will it hate me?"

Mama June shook her head slowly.

"A child's spirit don't hold grudges. But they do know when they're not wanted. And some... stay behind anyway. Wreak havoc. Create chaos. Not because they're evil, but because they came through the wrong door."

Sophie let out a sharp croak, her wings spreading wide in the shadows, then softened her call, cutting through shame. The sound seemed to braid with Mama June's words, a promise that this soul would be guided safely across.

Mama June told the lady, "This little birdy right here will ensure that spirit crosses back over. You just make sure you follow the directions I give ya' and recite the petition word for word. Put your soul in it so the baby can be at peace with you."

After the woman left, silent, grateful, clutching her paper bag of herbs like a lifeline, Julian sat on the back steps, shaken.

Lucille joined her but said nothing.

Mama June followed, sat beside her, and handed her a cold drink.

Julian finally spoke. "I don't know if I could've done that. It felt... wrong. But also, right. I don't know what to believe."

Mama June nodded. "That's how you know it's real work. Real work don't feel simple. You help people at the crossroad, not after the path is clear."

Julian blinked back tears.

"She was white. From one of those towns that hates us. Why help her?"

Mama June looked to the trees as Sophie was perched on a branch.

"Because spirit ain't got a race. And neither do ancestors. You don't know what's in her blood. Might be one of yours in there trying to break a cycle. You help people based on their soul, not their skin."

Mama June leaned forward, her voice heavy as scripture,

"The world tells women their bodies are for men, their wombs are for children, their pain is for silence. But I say a womb is a holy gate, and gates got locks for a reason Every gatekeeper got the right to say no. And no spirit, no man, no scripture can undo that right."

Mama June stood, dusted off her apron. "Let me tell you something else."

Julian looked up.

"A woman has to want to mother a child, or else that child comes through un-held. And un-held children often grow into fire. That don't mean abortion is right or wrong. It means it's sacred. It's a decision that rearranges the spirit world. So when she came in here...I didn't see a sinner. I saw a woman brave enough to say no before bringing in a spirit she couldn't carry right."

Julian was quiet. "Thank you, Mama June."

"No need to thank me, baby," she said, walking inside. "Just remember to listen with more than your ears."

Julian reflected,

"I thought catching life was the holiest thing. But today I learned... sometimes guarding death can be holy too."

Chapter Seventy-Six

The Rope and the Return

Dalton returned on a Thursday.

The wind carried the scent of dust, rain, and distant gunpowder, things he brought back with him from the field.

Lucille stood at the porch, her heart racing.

The moment he stepped out of the truck, her eyes filled with tears, but not just from joy. There was something else.

Something attached.

He held her tight, buried his face in her neck, and said, "I missed you like breath, baby."

But even as he kissed her, Lucille's vision flickered in unison with the skeleton key on her altar. Behind him... wrapped around his chest, his heart...a black rope. And coiled into that rope was the letter L, spelled in salt, thorns, and grief.

The Vision

Lucille blinked, trying not to show it. "Come inside, baby. Let me fix you something warm."

Mama June watched from the window, already sensing the offbeat rhythm in the air. Julian held Rosalie tighter.

Sophie landed on the rail to ward spirits and said, *he didn't come back alone.*

Lucille locked eyes with Sophie and nodded. She knew just like they all knew.

Dalton laughed and followed Lucille inside and she could still see it, sense it. The rope twisting tighter the closer he got to her. Every time he looked at her with love, the rope coiled in defiance.

Julian and Mama June kept glancing at each other as they prepared some salt and grabbed bay leaves to crush and leave around the house. They knew Dalton didn't come back alone so they got to work immediately when Dalton and Lucille retreated upstairs.

Later that night, after Dalton was asleep, Lucille sat on the floor in front of the altar.

She took out her silver mirror, lit a flame beneath it, and whispered:

"Show me the hands that tied the cord."

The mirror fogged, then cleared.

And in it:

Claudine.

Sitting on her back porch, whispering into a red thread soaked in used bath water and rose stems.

"He needs to be free," she murmured. "She don't deserve everything."

Lucille clenched her jaw.

Mama June was coming to check on Lucille before bed and as she stepped into the room, saw the mirror, and hissed through her teeth.

"That girl been eatin' envy for breakfast since y'all were children. Now she throwin' roots over your joy?"

Lucille nodded, tears burning her eyes. "She tried to separate us." Lucille was extremely hurt and her soul was aching. She didn't know what she had done so badly to deserve a sister who hates her so much.

Mama June said, "Lets prepare to get this up off of him." She then instructed Lucille to go bathe and add drops of pine oil in the water. She woke up Julian to go mop the shop doors with pine and cinnamon told her to prepare protection for the thresholds.

Julian was tired but she popped right on up because she could feel the energy being choked in the air. She put rice around Rosalie and got right to work with a silent psalm prayer.

The Ritual

They woke Dalton gently. Lucille explained everything with a calm fire.

"Someone tried to turn your soul away from mine."

Dalton nodded slowly. "I felt it. Feel it. Like I loved you but couldn't reach you."

Mama June led them outside to the back garden. Under the moon, they built a fire circle of bay leaves, rue, and red brick dust.

Dalton stood shirtless, rope still visible in Lucille's sight. She lit a candle and whispered:

"I call back what was stolen. I break what was falsely bound. I restore what was born in light."

She wrapped her fingers around the black rope in spirit and pulled.

Mama June said softly while waving praying hands, "Pull steady, chile. Don't fight the rope's scream, just claim the truth louder than it."

It fought her.

Twisted.

Lucille's hands were burning as if all of skin was being pulled off with tweezers, but she held on. She was fighting for her lover.

It screamed like wind through broken glass. But Lucille's voice did not waver.

"I love him in truth. I claim him with honor. And I free him with all my power."

Lucille fell to the ground and the gravel skinned her knees causing blood to drop onto the pavement.

The rope snapped, and the wind died. The L on the rope was lifted up in smoke and dissolved to serve as a cease and desist.

They all watched as the last of the rope burned in the fire like it was being accepted back into hell.

Dalton collapsed into her arms, chest on fire, "Lucy don't let me go."

Sophie flew around them three times with sparks flying. That sealed their love circle within them again, like renewal.

Mama June blew cigar smoke in the air to aid its disappearance. The smoke curled eastward, toward the resting ground of their kin, as if carrying proof of love defended.

The skeleton key started pulsating a light so bright they could see it up in the window slightly lighting up the darkness. This time it was pulsating to the beat of Daltons heart as if Lucille and his love was being mended back together in the heavens of passion.

The Aftermath

Later, as they lay in bed, Dalton held her tighter than ever before. "She tried to kill what we have."

Lucille nodded. "But she didn't know what I am." Sophie sitting in the windowsill and said, *envy kills the soul.*

He kissed her shoulder. "She gon' learn. Oh she gon' learn"

The fire pit still smoldered behind the house, smoke lifting slow like incense rising toward ancestors.

Inside, the bedroom was dim, lit only by the flicker of one beeswax candle on the windowsill.

Dalton lay with his head on Lucille's stomach, arms wrapped around her waist like she was the only steady ground in the world.

Neither of them spoke for a long while.

Then, Dalton exhaled deep and said: "It started three weeks ago. Before I even got orders to come back."

Lucille brushed her fingers through his curls. "Tell me what you felt."

"At first it was little things. Couldn't sleep without seeing your face... but it made me angry. Not soft. Not warm. Just angry, like the memory of you was taunting me."

He paused.

"Then came the pull. Like somethin' was turnin' my chest away from you. I still loved you… but it was like the love didn't know where to land."

Lucille's jaw clenched. She was pissed, livid at her sister.

"That's how roots work. They don't erase love. They confuse it. They twist it until it feels like a weapon in your own chest."

Dalton nodded, eyes wet.

"I was having dreams where I was walking through a hallway tryin' to find your door. But every time I touched it, it would vanish. Sometimes I'd open it and it was Claudine standing inside."

Lucille's breath caught. "She was trying to replace me in spirit."

Dalton nodded.

"It didn't feel sexual. It felt… territorial. Like she wanted me to belong to her version of me."

Lucille placed her hand over his heart.

"She ain't never wanted me to have anything good. Not since we were little girls and I saw the spirit sittin' on her shoulders. She got an addiction to attention and control. And she hates that you love me without her permission."

Dalton kissed her palm, voice low.

"I love you because my spirit remembers you. Even when my body couldn't feel it. Even when my mind was cloudy. My soul still knew your name."

Lucille closed her eyes, tears sliding silently down her temples.

"They'll come again, you know. Maybe not her. But someone. Some spirit. Some test."

Dalton nodded. "Then let's get stronger. Let's learn how to protect this."

Chapter Seventy-Seven

The Snap of the Cord

Claudine sat at her vanity, slowly twisting a silver bobby pin through the base of a thick braid. Her mirror reflected a woman perfectly put together, but her eyes... her eyes twitched.

Then the mirror glitched, showing her reflection with the rope tied around her neck like a noose. Blood was coming from her eyes as the rope tightened. She immediately knew something was wrong.

Her fingers trembled slightly as she reached for the red thread she kept hidden in her drawer. The one she'd tied and sealed with spit, hair, and candle flame, a cord meant to bend Dalton's path away from Lucille.

She'd tied it tight. Said the prayer over it three times. Burned the tip in a saucer that once held holy water. It should have worked. But it didn't. She felt it first the night before.

A sharp ringing in her right ear.

A gust of wind through a sealed window.

A flicker in the flame of her candle that twisted into Lucille's face before vanishing. Then an image of Dalton drifting farther and farther away in the candle smoke.

She tried to hold the cord, but it crumbled in her hands like dried blood and ash.

"Noooooooooooo…" Her voice cracked as she opened her palm. The cord had rotted. The charm was gone.

She rushed to her back porch, barefoot, hair unraveling from its careful shell. The rose bush she planted with her intentions had wilted overnight. Thorns black. Roots dry.

"She broke it," Claudine whispered. "Lucille broke it."

Her stomach turned. Not because the spell had failed, but because she knew… something had been returned.

When a spell is unraveled with power, some of its energy always returns to the sender. Not the part cast in anger, but the part that came from the deepest truth of the one who cast it.

"I didn't want Dalton. I just didn't want Lucille to have something I didn't feel worthy of!"

She sat on the edge of her porch, staring at the dead vine curling around her wind chime. A faint buzz began in her head. The same voice she used to ignore was louder now.

You are not owed what you envy. You are not owed what you cannot carry in peace.

She held her temples. "I didn't mean to hurt her..." But even she didn't believe that. Because deep down, Claudine didn't want Lucille to be happy.

She wanted her humbled.

She wanted her reachable.

She wanted her to need.

Claudine stood suddenly and locked every window in the house, sweating and trembling. She didn't know what Lucille had done. She didn't know what Mama June might've seen. But she felt eyes on her now. Old eyes. Hooded eyes.

She'd stirred a nest of spirit women by trying to strangle a union sealed in light.

Now all she could do was wait, and hope Lucille never came knocking with her own rope in hand.

Chapter Seventy-Eight

What You Send, You Marry

Claudine fell asleep with her robe still tied tight around her waist and a cup of mint tea untouched on the nightstand. She had tried to pray, tried to call on a protection she hadn't earned, but the moment her head hit the pillow, the air thickened. Her lamp flickered once. Then twice.

Then darkness swallowed the room. She stood barefoot in her childhood home, but the walls were pulsing. The wood grain moved like breathing skin. She turned toward the hallway, but it was endless. At the far end, the door glowed red and as she stepped toward it, she could hear voices behind it.

Familiar.

Ancient.

Whispering in sync: *What you send, you marry. What you curse, you carry.*

She reached for the doorknob, and it burned her palm. She jerked away, but the room began folding inward. The pictures on the walls, her and Lucille as little girls, melted. The floor turned into water. She stumbled and landed in a mirror room. She looked up and saw herself, but not the version she showed the world. This version had cracked lipstick, wild hair, and green eyes glowing with envy.

You don't want love, it said. *You want to win.*

Claudine shook her head. "That's not true. I...I..." She stuttered.

The mirror spirit circled her slowly.

You rooted a man who never belonged to you. Just like your mama rooted a husband with silence and eggshell smiles. But you...You meddle.

The Ancestral Council

The mirror shattered, and Claudine dropped to her knees in a circle of hooded women. Their faces were obscured. But their voices thundered.

You do not touch what was not spoken over you, you call yourself powerful, but you do not know humility. Your actions echoed, and now you will feel the return.

A burning rope dropped into her lap, black, twisted, charred at one end. The same rope she'd used on Dalton.

What you send, you marry.

It wrapped around her waist, tightening. She screamed! But no one moved to help.

The Awakening

She woke in a sweat, gasping. The tea on her nightstand had spilled over and the mirror across the room had cracked diagonally. Around her waist, she found the red thread she thought she had burned. Wrapped there like a snake. Lucille's name written in ash. She ran to her window, opened it, and screamed into the night:

"I'm sorry!"

But wind answered her instead. Cool and unforgiving. Claudine stumbled to the bathroom mirror, gripping the sink with shaking hands. Her reflection was pale, lips dry, eyes frantic. She lifted her robe, what she saw made her scream.

The red cord was no longer around her waist. It was coiled around her belly, tight and pulsing like a serpent. alive and feeding. Black veins spidered out from her navel. Her once-round womb now looked sunken, bruised. She reached to pull the cord off but it wouldn't move. She felt a sharp pain, deep and low.

And then...Warmth.

Something was running down her thighs. She looked down and saw blood and water, rushing and sliding down her legs. It was all pooling at her feet.

"No. No. Nooooooo, not my baby!"

She fell backward, hands slipping on the tile. Her husband, hearing her scream, ran in.

"Claudine?!"

When he saw the blood, he froze.

"Call, um call someone please! Get me to the hospital!" she shrieked. "Now!" The drive was a blur of streetlights and sobs, Claudine clutched her belly, whispering,

"Please stay with me, baby. I didn't mean it. Mama didn't mean it. I just wanted to feel... important." But the pain didn't let up. The cord, still there in spirit, tightened with every mile.

By the time they arrived at the hospital, the child was already gone. The emergency room nurse called her father Dr. Green to come to her bedside.

He entered the room pale as a ghost. "Claudine?" He looked at the blood-soaked sheets. At the silent monitor. At the way her body shook, but no sound came out anymore. He knew. And still, he asked no questions. He just put on his gloves, turned to the nurse, and said:

"Prepare for D&C."

The Spirit World Watches

Somewhere between sedation and grief, Claudine entered the veil again. The hooded women stood before her in a circle, and in the center, wrapped in light,

A child.

Not crying.

Just watching her.

A girl. Full of knowing.

One of the elders spoke:

This blessing has been returned. The womb is sacred ground. You poisoned yours with another woman's pain. So now you must sit with yours.

The girl turned slowly, smiled and faded.

Claudine woke up to the sterile cold of the recovery room. Her father sat beside her, face unreadable. She opened her mouth to speak, but he raised his hand.

"You don't have to explain," he said softly. "But just know, some pain don't come from God. Some pain we plant ourselves."

He stood.

And left her alone.

Dr. Green may have come off coldhearted, but he knew deep down inside his own daughter caused this due to her lack of self-control and humility. She was essentially just like a her mother but without charm and charisma.

Chapter Seventy-Nine

No One is Above the
Energy They Create

The shop was quiet, wrapped in the warm scent of clove and cedar, when the bell jingled sharp and fast. Lucille looked up from bottling new oils, already knowing who it was by the shift in the air.

Hattie.

Hair wrapped in a silk turban. Face beat like she was attending a revival. Lips red. Purse tight. Posture high and cold. She stepped inside like she owned the floorboards.

Mama June was sitting in her chair near the window, stringing dried flowers together. Julian paused from behind the counter.

"Lucille," Hattie said, voice tight as piano wire. "Your sister's in the hospital. She lost the baby."

Lucille put down her bottle calmly, even though her spirit bristled. "I know."

Hattie blinked. "You knew?"

Lucille turned fully toward her mother. "I felt it the moment the cord snapped in spirit. I saw what Claudine did. She tried to bind Dalton with a separation root and I returned it to sender with prayer."

Hattie's face cracked. "You did that?" she hissed. "You're telling me you caused your own niece's death?"

Lucille stepped forward and threw down the towel she had in her hand to the ground forcefully. "No, Mama. Claudine did that. She killed her own blessing with envy. I just removed what never should've been placed on the man I love."

Hattie stepped back, shaking her head. "You think you're holy, but you're hateful. You've always had a jealous streak."

Lucille looked like she wanted to strike her lying mother but kept her composure. The skeleton key pulsating profusely shining raging red again.

"That's enough," Mama June's voice rang out like thunder.

The shop shifted. Even the herbs on the wall seemed to still. Mama June rose, slow and sure.

"No one is above their own energy, Hattie. Not you. Not Claudine. Not anybody."

Hattie's mouth opened, then closed.

"That baby was tied up in a curse Claudine designed herself. She fed it with obsession. She weaved it with lies. And what she created took something from her that was never yours to protect."

"You want to be mad? Be mad at the monster you raised when you taught her to covet what looked like love instead of building her own."

Hattie's chest rose and fell rapidly. She turned toward the door but paused.

"I didn't teach her that."

Mama June's eyes narrowed. "No. You taught her to perform while hiding the work. You've been lucky your husband never sent back what you been feeding him in silence."

The shop went still. Even Rosalie stopped cooing.

Nobody has ever had the guts to speak to her that way to her face, but oh they whispered it behind her back. Hattie's lipstick didn't move, but her eyes flickered. She straightened her dress, clicked her purse shut, and said with a soft smile,

"Well. I suppose everyone's entitled to their version of events."

She turned, put on her signature sway, the one that said everything's fine when it wasn't.

And walked out.

Sophie flew right behind her and everyone in the shop saw her almost fall down the stairs swinging her purse at her.

Chapter Eighty

The Cost of Her Crown

Flashback ~ 1962, St. Augustine, Florida

The scent of lemon polish filled the campus library, where a young Hattie Jackson stood behind the desk, pretending to rearrange books as she watched a tall, soft-eyed medical student in a pressed button-down shirt take notes under the lamplight.

Eli Green.

He was quiet. Brilliant. Confident. And he laughed with his eyes. Hattie's lips curled when he smiled. She knew men like him didn't look her way often, not because she wasn't beautiful, but because she didn't come from anything.

But that didn't matter. Because Hattie had already decided. "He gon' be mine," she whispered one evening to the wind, "Even if it costs me."

Her only problem had a name. Sandra Merryweather. Poised. Gentle. And legacy-bred.

The Merryweather's and the Greens had dined together since before Eli and Sandra could write their names. They were expected to marry and merge brilliance, two Black dynasties of intellect and grace.

Sandra was already halfway through her second year of medical school. She and Eli would've changed history together. And Hattie couldn't stomach it.

"You got the grades," Hattie said bitterly to her reflection. "But you ain't got the roots."

Hattie didn't go to church. But she did know a woman named Miss Lorrie, who sold bundles of grave dirt and spoke in riddles at night. Hattie went to her with a bottle of Eli's cologne, a piece of his writing, and a single strand of Sandra's pressed hair, stolen from a library chair cushion.

Miss Lorrie looked her up and down. "You tryin' to bind a man? Or bury a girl?"

Hattie didn't blink. "Both."

Miss Lorrie said nothing.

She just pulled out a black candle and a rusted railroad spike. And three nights later, Hattie buried the hair and dirt at the fork of a two-lane highway, whispering:

"Take her out the way. Leave him lookin' for comfort. Let my arms be the only place he finds it."

<u>The Sacrifice</u>

The car crash was blamed on faulty brakes. Sandra was thrown from the vehicle and pronounced dead on arrival. No drugs. No alcohol. No scandal. Just tragedy.

Eli went silent for months. Hattie wrote him letters. Stood near him at services. Brought him books she claimed he'd left behind.

Until one night, broken and grieving, he let her in. She never left.

They were married six months later.

The Legacy of That Night

What no one knew, was that when Sandra died, Hattie felt something change inside her.

Her womb pulsed for the first time in months. The next morning, she bled for seven days straight, not from a cycle, but from the price.

A sacrifice had been accepted. And the spirit realm had marked her.

You wanted to be a doctor's wife, the wind whispered. *Now you wear a crown made of bone.*

Chapter Eighty-One

Keep Your Power Clean

The rain tapped softly against the windows of the shop, and the candles burned low and steadily. Mama June sat in her old chair wrapped in a crocheted shawl, her knees folded under her, a mug of steeped lemon balm and rose petals in her lap.

Lucille was perched on a stool near the herb wall, grinding dried cloves into powder. Julian sat cross-legged on the floor beside Rosalie's basket, her hands resting in her lap like she knew something serious was about to be said.

Mama June looked at both girls. Her tone wasn't harsh. It was sacred, like a priestess in temple robes speaking over the daughters of a divine bloodline.

"Let me tell y'all something," she said, voice smooth as oil but laced with weight. "Y'all walk with power. You know it. You feel it when your palms tingle or your dreams come in colors. But power don't make you special. What you do with it does."

Lucille stopped grinding.

Julian sat up straighter.

Mama June sipped her tea and continued. "This work we do? It ain't for material things. It ain't to win lovers, or curses, or prove nothin'. It's for protection. It's for healing. It's for order."

She pointed her finger slowly in the air. "If you ever use your gift to force something that ain't aligned with God's will, money, attention, a man, even a baby, God will take your favor. Quick."

The room stilled. Only the sound of water dripping outside.

"Y'all better hear me on this part real good, love is not promised to you by anyone on this earth. Not your mama. Not your daddy. Not your children. And sure as hell not your man."

She stared at both of them. "The only guaranteed love is the one from the Creator. Everything else is a gift, not a right."

Lucille swallowed hard.

Julian looked down at her hands.

"So when you give your body to a man, don't do it for validation. Don't do it 'cause he asked nice or paid a bill. Only do it when you feel that burn."

Mama June leaned forward, eyes sharp. "You know what I mean. That holy fire in your lower belly. That heat behind your knees. That ache that's not about lust, but recognition. If your body don't call his name in silence, don't open your altar to him."

Julian gasped softly.

Lucille closed her eyes and nodded.

Mama June softened then.

"Your body is sacred. You a gateway between spirit and flesh. You don't owe your fire to nobody. But you can explore it for yourself."

She smiled faintly now. "Masturbation is not dirty. It's not shameful. It's exploration. How else you gon' know what makes you rise? Touch yourself with love. Pray while you do it if you want. Let the fire start at your root and travel up your spine, through your heart, and all the way to your crown. That's not just sex. That's alchemy."

Lucille whispered, "You turnin' us into temples."

Mama June nodded. "You always been temples. I'm just reminding you to light your own damn candles."

The shop was still, except for the low hiss of cedar smoke curling in the air.

Julian's voice was quiet but firm now. Not shaky. Not frightened. Just ready. "I need to say it out loud. All of it."

Mama June and Lucille both nodded, giving her the space. The air shifted.

"He was supposed to protect me. My mama married him when I was ten. And by eleven... he started visiting my room."

She looked down at her hands. "He made me feel like it was my fault. Like I made him weak. He'd say, 'You got that fire on you early, girl.' And I started believing my body was the problem."

Sophie couldn't take hearing about that type of sin, so she flew outside to scan the perimeter while they went in deep touching unseen emotions.

Lucille closed her eyes, holding back tears, but the skeleton key cried for her. Mama June just listened, steady as a mountain.

"I walked around like I was contagious. Afraid to wear anything that made me feel good. Afraid to be seen by anyone. Because all I saw when I looked in the mirror was filth he put on me."

Mama June leaned forward, her voice low and deliberate. "That man was a thief. He broke a sacred law. He didn't just touch your body, he tried to stamp out your spirit."

She placed her palm over Julian's chest. "But look here. Your soul survived. Even under all that dirt, your spirit never died. And now it's time to wash it clean."

Julian swallowed. "How?"

Lucille moved beside her and took her hand. "We speak it off you, that's how. We name the lie, and then we bury it."

Mama June nodded and lit a fresh white candle. "Repeat after me, baby. Say, I was touched by filth. But I am not filthy."

Julian, softly, "I was touched by filth. But I am not filthy."

"Say, He confused my body. But my body is not confused."

"He confused my body. But my body is not confused."

Lucille added, "Say, my fire is holy. My curiosity is divine."

Julian closed her eyes as tears fell. "My fire is holy. My curiosity is divine."

Mama June dipped her fingers in cedar oil and touched Julian's forehead.

"We cast out the spirit of shame. We release the shadow of guilt. We return the filth to the sender. We call back your name, baby. You are not what he did. You are what you choose to remember. And I want you to remember this."

She pressed her hand to Julian's heart. "You were never the sin. You were the light he couldn't handle."

Julian burst into quiet sobs. And for the first time in years... she cried without hiding her face.

The candle flame flickered high, then steadied. Lucille wrapped her arms around Julian.

Mama June whispered over them both,

"What was done ends here. You are not what he did. You are what you do next. And baby... you got the power now."

Chapter Eighty-Two

The Ring and the Roots

The late afternoon sun stretched long over the porch steps as Lucille swept the doorway with cinnamon water and rosemary, humming low to herself.

She didn't hear the truck at first, just felt the shift in the wind. Then she heard the door shut, the boots on gravel. And her heart already knew.

"Dalton."

He stood there in uniform, sun-dusted and smiling. A little leaner. A little wearier. But the same eyes that always found her in a crowded room.

She dropped her broom and ran into his arms. They held each other for what felt like years.

That night, under the stars, Dalton led her to the back garden where Mama June had planted lavender and moonflower.

He pulled a small ring box from his pocket, nothing flashy, just elegant and heartfelt.

Lucille's breath caught.

"I know you ain't the kind of woman who needs a ring to feel chosen," he said. "But I'd like to offer it anyway. Not to trap you. Not to tame you. Just to say, I want to walk this life with you.

On your terms."

He opened the box. A simple gold ring, etched faintly with a sun and a skeleton key.

Lucille smiled as tears filled her eyes. She took the ring...But didn't put it on.

"Dalton," she said gently, "I love you. You know I do."

He nodded, waiting.

"But I need to sit with this in spirit. I can't say yes until I know my soul agrees. Not just my heart."

"What's holdin' you?" he asked.

Lucille exhaled slowly. "I want to belong to myself. I don't want to follow orders or hop from base to base. I don't want a marriage that uproots me."

She looked up at him.

"This shop, this town... Mama June...I belong here. With my herbs, my books, my work. I'm not a city girl. I ain't trying to chase anything big. This is my big."

Dalton nodded again, slowly. He stepped forward and kissed her forehead.

"Then keep the ring. Not as a promise, but as a possibility."

He placed it gently in her hand and closed her fingers around it. "I won't pressure you. I love our rhythm. Our fire. And truth is, I like having someone to come home to."

Lucille felt a tear slip down her cheek. Then his face grew serious.

"But I need to tell you something else, She looked up.

"What is it?"

He swallowed. "There's talk I might be sent to Korea. For a year."

The garden went still. The wind stopped playing in the flowers. Lucille blinked slowly, heart dropping into her belly.

"A year?"

He nodded. "Could be longer. Could be shorter. But if it happens, I leave in two months."

Lucille gripped the ring tighter. Not because she was angry. But because the weight of love and the weight of freedom never felt so close.

Chapter Eighty-Three

A Ring, A Reflection, A Name

Lucille leaned back in the warm Epsom salt water, the scent of rose oil and lemon balm curling in the steam that floated around the clawfoot tub. The window beside her was cracked, letting in the low hum of cicadas and the sweet breath of Southern air. Sophie let out a soft croak and landed on the windowsill. She wanted to guard Lucille's spirit because she sensed the escape that was coming.

Lucille held her left hand up slowly, letting the candlelight catch on the gold band wrapped around her finger.

Dalton's ring.

It felt both light and heavy. A promise and a pause. A what-if and a maybe.

She didn't know if she was saying yes to Dalton or just imagining what yes might feel like.

She closed her eyes. And let herself dream.

<u>Visions in the Steam</u>

In the silence, Lucille saw flashes of a life not yet lived:

A porch swing with two cups of coffee. A man in uniform rocking a brown-skinned baby. Laughter around dinner plates.

An ache in her chest began to pulse and then the house fell silent again.

But there were other visions that came on display:

A quiet apothecary.

Books stacked beside an altar. Spirits visiting in the middle of the night. A woman free to speak and pray and move in her own time.

Her heartbeat fast beneath the still water.

She could see both futures. She just didn't know which one belonged to her.

A soft knock broke the stillness.

"Baby, you want a sandwich?" Mama June's voice called through the door, muffled but warm.

Lucille smiled. "Come in."

Mama June opened the door, Rosalie resting on her hip, swaddled and half asleep.

Julian soon followed, tying a scarf around her curls.

Lucille shifted to cover herself modestly with a towel across her chest.

"Well ain't this a full moon gathering," Lucille laughed gently.

Julian walked over, lifted Rosalie with practiced ease, and sat in the rocking chair to breastfeed.

Mama June sat beside the tub, dipped a cloth in warm water, and began washing Lucille's back the way only a mother-figure could, with love, with intention.

She glanced at the gold on Lucille's finger. Silent at first and just smiling.

"So...Did you say yes?"

Lucille looked down at her hand, then at Mama June. "Not yet."

Mama June nodded slowly, her eyes understanding more than her mouth said.

"You don't want to be no base wife," she whispered with a little smile. "Ain't nothin' wrong with that."

Lucille exhaled.

"I love him. I really do."

"But you love your peace more," Mama June said, finishing the sentence for her.

They both laughed softly.

Then Mama June said what needed saying: "Seek God in all that you do. Not fear. Not pressure. Not time. Not love. But God. Let Him show you what your 'yes' is for, then you won't regret it."

Julian, rocking gently with Rosalie on her chest, looked up suddenly and said without thinking, "That's right, Mama Lucy."

The room went still. Lucille's eyes lifted slowly, and Mama June turned her head.

Julian blinked, startled. "I..........I meant to say Mama June," she said quickly. "I don't know why I said.......that......wow"

Mama June just chuckled, her voice low and knowing. "No mistake, baby. Just spirit speaking and sometimes spirit tells the future." She winked at Julian.

Lucille looked down at her hand again. Not at the ring, but at the fingers that had anointed foreheads, mixed herbs, prayed over wounds written in journals, and stirred the sacred.

She smiled softly. "Maybe it's time I say yes to myself first."

The skeleton key made the altar rattle in that moment of truth.

Chapter Eighty-Four

The Induction of the Mother

Lucille lay in bed that night, the candle at her altar burning low. Sophie on her nightstand as if she's watching over her. The room was quiet except for the hum of crickets and the creak of old wood settling into the rhythm of night. The gold ring on her finger glinted in the firelight, and her hand rested over her womb as if instinctively protecting something not yet there. She had not fallen asleep. She had been summoned.

The Three Return

Her eyes closed, but her spirit opened wide. She was back in the sacred realm, the place of dream but not a dream. There stood the Three Hooded Mothers, wrapped in deep violet robes trimmed in gold and black. They stood in a perfect circle beneath the night sky lit with moons she'd never seen before. They carried bowls filled with water, earth, fire, and air.

Lucille stood barefoot in a long, white gown that swayed as if underwater.

One of the mothers stepped forward and placed a black veil over Lucille's head. Not to cover her, but to anoint her.

You are no longer a maiden, the center Mother spoke. *You are now Mother.*

Lucille's lips trembled, but she did not speak. She simply felt.

Not only to child…But to healing, to wisdom, to spirit. You carry more than a womb, you carry remembrance.

The second Mother dipped her fingers in the bowl of fire and touched Lucille's womb. A warm heat spread through her.

The third Mother blew into Lucille's face and said:

The child that will come from you…is not only yours. It is ours. It is the covenant.

As the mothers began to chant a prayer in the tongue of the grandmothers, Lucille felt the ring on her finger tighten, not painfully, but firmly, like a rope pulling her into alignment with destiny.

Suddenly, a vision exploded behind her eyes:

Dalton's arms around her, his mouth on her shoulder. Their sweat, their breath, their rhythm was everything. The sacred fire between them no longer a burn, but a spark. Dalton, crying., weeping as he entered her. Their love was so pure and sacred, he whispered: "You are my home, my heaven, my healer."

Lucille gasped in the dream world. Her body arched back and a small moan escaped her lips. She could feel life pass through her. Not conceived yet in flesh but declared in spirit.

It is done, the mothers said in unison.

Then they were gone.

The Dance of Flesh and Spirit

Dalton picked Lucille up later that night. He didn't know why he had the urge to hold her tighter than usual, to breathe her in like he was afraid she might slip away. They danced all night to a live blues set, her body soft and surrendered against him.

Back at his place, there was no rush, only rhythm. No talking, only breath. Dalton made love to Lucille with reverence. His tears fell on her cheek as he whispered: "I've never loved anything this way before."

Lucille held him like water in a sacred vessel, wrapping her legs around his waist and letting the fire take over. And in the stillness after, as their foreheads pressed together, Lucille knew... Her spirit had already said yes. Dalton was her spiritual husband and their love was ancient. The child had already heard the call.

The skeleton key had a faint red pulse, not for Lucille or Dalton.

Chapter Eighty-Five

The Gatekeeper's Dream

Julian was deep in sleep, Rosalie curled at her chest, both wrapped in a velvet throw near the hearth. The air in Mama June's shop was still, but Julian's soul was moving. The dream came quietly, like warm water.

The Sacred Birth

Julian stood barefoot on a riverbank.

The stars above were bright and pulsing, and the trees swayed like ancient witnesses. In the distance, she saw Lucille, round with child, breathing through labor, her body swaying like a willow. Dalton was behind her, arms around her belly, whispering sweet encouragements in her ear. Lucille was radiant, divine.

Julian stepped forward to catch the baby, and the moment she did, the sky cracked open in golden light. The baby emerged slowly and peacefully, wrapped in a golden caul.

A baby girl. Eyes wide open. A mark glowing on her chest in the shape of a spiral sun. Julian looked down at the child and began to weep.

The Whisper of the Hooded Mothers

From behind the trees, the Three Hooded Mothers emerged in their deep purple and gold cloaks, holding candles that didn't flicker despite the wind. They approached Julian silently, their eyes glowing white.

Julian, they whispered in unison. *You are the Gatekeeper of Souls.*

Julian knelt before them, the baby still warm in her hands.

Lucille carries an ancient one. A matriarch from long ago. She will be multi-talented, a healer, a singer, a dream walker, and a judge among spirits.

Julian's body trembled.

She will usher a new cycle to your town. You must never tell Lucille what you know. You may not disclose what souls walk the Earth again. Only that they are known in the Book of Mothers.

A book appeared in Julian's hands, golden and glowing. Every page turned with wind only she could feel. *The Book of Mothers...* passed down to each midwife, each gatekeeper...In every lifetime.

And now it belonged to her.

Julian clutched the book to her chest and nodded; she would protect the sacred lineage. Her skin began glowing with gold words of all the special women who birthed and would birth sacred women.

Morning at the Shop

Morning came with the sweet smell of chicory coffee and cinnamon from the back kitchen. Dalton pulled up to the shop with a bouquet of yellow sunflowers, Lucille in the passenger seat looking like she had just walked out of Heaven.

Her cheeks glowed. Her skin glistened. She looked like honey warmed in the sun.

Dalton opened her door and kissed her hand before she stepped out.

"I'll write you every week, Mama Lucy," he whispered with a grin. "And when I get back, we're gonna create a ritual to protect our sacred love. The way you make love to me is out of this universe and I want to keep learning and creating with you."

Lucille blushed and a bit teary eyed reminiscing on the orgasms she had last night.

Mama June opened the shop door just in time to hear it and yelled out to them.

"Come back in one piece and remember to protect your heart from wicked works now son, I ain't tryna' get in the field again about y'all's precious love" waving at Dalton.

As he drove away, Lucille floated inside like she was walking on air. Mama June and Julian were sitting at the counter sipping tea, snickering and blushing like hens in a henhouse.

Lucille tilted her head. "What's y'all gigglin' about?"

Mama June sipped slow. "Just admirin' the glow on your skin, chile," she said with a wink. "You smell like life."

Julian raised an eyebrow. "And honey," she whispered under her breath.

Lucille rolled her eyes, but deep down, she felt it too.

Something was beginning. Something ancient. Something divine.

Chapter Eighty-Six

Spells for Sacred Love

It was a cloudy afternoon when the bell above the shop door chimed gently. Lucille glanced up from her workstation, Julian rocked Rosalie with her foot, and Mama June was lighting mugwort and lemongrass near the window.

Two women walked in, hand in hand.

One was pale with auburn hair tucked into a scarf, dressed in worn denim and a cotton blouse. The other was a brown-skinned woman with short, coily hair, a nose ring, and the kind of posture that showed she'd fought for herself more than once.

Their love was wrapped in tension. Not for lack of connection, but because the world around them hadn't learned how to see it yet.

Lucille smiled warmly. Julian gave a respectful nod. Mama June didn't miss a beat.

"You came to the right place, babies. Now tell me what you need."

The auburn-haired woman spoke first.

"I'm Claire. This is Essie. We... love each other," she said, voice trembling. "But, but our families, mine especially, say it's a sin. Her mama calls me a mistake."

Essie's jaw tightened.

"We've been spit at. Called filth. I've even been followed home," she said, eyes watering.

"We didn't come for sympathy. We came for power. Protection. Maybe even revenge. I heard about you conjure women and I would really love your help"

Lucille stood slowly and walked closer to them. "You don't need to hex them," she said, calmly rubbing Claires shoulder. "They're already hexed, by their own hatred."

Julian nodded, holding Rosalie tighter.

"We offer protection, not poison, and everyone deserves their dignity and respect" she added. "What y'all got is sacred. Don't invite low spirits into something so divine."

Mama June pulled out a velvet cloth and began laying down items:

Black tourmaline for deflection

Rose quartz for love

White chalk for boundary lines

Bay leaves and rue for protection

A golden key wrapped in red thread

"You gon' write both your full names on this paper," she told them. "And then burn it while you pray for peace, not punishment. Ask for your union to be shielded. Not hidden but covered."

Lucille handed them each a small bottle of oil she'd just prepared with mugwort, rosemary, and dried lilac.

"Anoint each other with this before you leave the house," she said. "Behind the ears. The heart. The heels. Speak love aloud as you do it."

Julian passed them a satchel with protective roots, blessed salt, and black thread.

"This will ward off bad stares and gossip," she said gently. "But your love has to do the rest."

Claire's lips trembled. Essie's eyes filled.

"No one's ever... made us feel like this was okay before," Claire whispered.

"That's 'cause most folk don't know how to mind they business," Mama June quipped.

Before they left, Mama June lit a white candle and said a prayer, "Let no evil thought, law, nor spirit tear what love has made whole. Cover them like clouds cover the moon on a too-bright night. Let their joy be loud, their bond be strong, and their path be clear. Amen."

Essie squeezed Claire's hand tightly. "Thank you. From both of us," she said.

Claire turned to Julian and Lucille. "You ever need two loud lesbians to fight beside y'all in a storm, you know where to find us." They laughed together, genuine and full.

As the women walked out, the sun broke through the clouds just enough to shine a beam right through the shop window. Sophie followed them out to their car and circled it three times to warn the spirits of the prayer of protection over them.

Mama June turned to Lucille. "Even in this world," she said softly, "Love still chooses brave hearts."

Chapter Eighty-Seven

The Women Who Came
with Smoke

The bell above the door jingled sharply, cutting through the soft hum of blues playing on the record player. The door swung open and in stepped Hattie Green and her oldest daughter, Claudine.

Hattie's posture was pristine as ever, chin high, pearls in place, hands folded in front like she was entering a white-gloved tea party instead of a root shop thick with spirit and healing.

Claudine slouched behind her, lips pressed tight, face pale with shadows under the eyes. Her skin was dull, hair frizzy and unkept. She didn't carry herself like the show pony she used to be. Her aura was frayed, dark, brittle, breaking down from the inside out.

She was unraveling.

Lucille remained behind the counter, eyes calm, hands resting atop a bundle of lavender and dried hibiscus. "Didn't think you'd remember where this place was," she said plainly.

Hattie ignored the comment, walking in like she owned the space. "We came because you hadn't called. Your sister has been through trauma, and you didn't bother to check on her."

Claudine's eyes darted away. She couldn't hold her sister's gaze. She knew the truth, and so did Lucille.

Claudine hadn't just lost a child; he'd lost her mask.

Her husband, once wrapped tight in charms and roots, had come home from a long shift and found every spell she ever cast laid bare on their bed. Sheets of parchment stained with oils, his underwear tied with her hair, his initials carved into a lemon now rotting on the windowsill.

He packed and left in the night. No goodbye.

Just a note that said: "Whatever you thought you had on me, it's broken. And so are we."

Claudine hadn't spoken since. Hattie came to Mama June's shop not out of belief, but desperation.

Mama June stepped out from the back room slowly, apron dusted with powdered rosehips and eucalyptus. She wiped her hands on her skirt and looked both women over like she could see every lie and every inch of pride clinging to them.

"You don't bark orders in my house, Hattie. This is sacred ground. I'll ask you once to leave that high-society voice outside."

Hattie bristled but didn't respond.

Mama June turned to Julian, who had Rosalie in her sling. "Julian, baby, get to makin' a tea for grief and broken spirit. Something soft but honest. Make it for two."

Julian looked Claudine over, her eyes cold. "I'll make it," she muttered. "But not because she deserves it." She walked away without a second glance.

As Julian worked, Rosalie began to fuss.

Julian gently bounced her, but Rosalie wailed louder, her cries shrill and unsettled. It was like she could feel the negativity coming off Hattie and Claudine.

Claudine's face broke.

She covered her mouth and began to cry, loud and deep like a woman mourning something she knew she'd never hold. "I just wanted to be loved by something!" she shouted.

Julian stared at her and couldn't keep quiet any longer. "You wanted something to love you, but not something to love. That's the difference," she said sharply. "Children aren't dolls. They're spirits. And yours felt your energy long before you even bled. You cursed your own womb. May God forgive you!!!" Tears began to drop from Julians eyes onto Rosalie.

The shop went still. Lucille and Mama June exchanged looks as if their child just took their first steps.

Mama June wrapped the herbs, tying them tight in red string. She handed it to Julian, who passed it coldly to Hattie.

Lucille, quiet through it all, bowed her head. In her heart she whispered a prayer for Claudine, not out of love, but pity. "May she someday know peace, if not joy."

Hattie turned to Lucille, eyes sharp. "She deserved the life you're living," she hissed. "She was made for it."

Julian stepped forward before Lucille could speak. "No. She was made for performance. Lucille was made for purpose, and I don't know her but can feel the wickedness in her bones." she spat. "And Mama Lucy will be a better mother than you two could ever dream of being. By the power of the God within me you better pray I never get a hold of either of you in spirit that I can justify!!!!"

The name hung in the air like incense.

Lucille gasped, clutching her belly as a ripple passed through her. In that moment Lucille confirmed with spirit that she was with child.

Before she could steady herself, the door opened again, and Dalton walked in. He rushed to her, kneeling to meet her.

"What's wrong? You, okay?"

Lucille nodded slowly, wiping a tear from her cheek.

With Hattie and Claudine there to witness the care and love Dalton has for Lucille sent them both in a torment of spiraling into a frenzy of jealousy that quickly wrapped around their bones and soul. They couldn't take it, couldn't stomach it. How could Lucille get a man to love her like that without the work of binding?

Hattie, ever the actress, straightened her posture and grabbed Claudine's limp hand. "We've overstayed our welcome," she said tightly. "Come on, Claudine."

Without another word, they exited, heels clicking over the floor that would never be theirs. Outside Sophie was perched on their car and literally didn't move until they got inside and Hattie put it in reverse. She then flew off and hovered in front of the driver's side glass looking Hattie straight in the eye. Instant fear fell over them, Hattie turned towards Claudine and said, " Aint' nothing but the devil around these parts."

Hattie knew Mama June loved Lucille and would protect her like she was her own daughter. It was eating her up inside because she knew she never loved Lucille in that way and hell, not even Claudine.

Chapter Eighty-Eight

A Covenant of Flesh and Spirit

The shop had settled again. Smoke from the earlier storm of energy had cleared, but the residue still lingered like ash behind the eyes.

Dalton stood on the back porch, arms crossed over his chest, jaw tight. The sun was starting to dip behind the trees, casting streaks of gold across the sky.

Mama June stepped out with a fresh brew of nettle and raspberry leaf tea in hand, earthy and grounding. "Sit down, son," she said softly, but it wasn't a request.

Dalton obeyed.

She handed him the tea and he sipped without question and didn't even think to ask what was in it.

"You love her?" she asked.

"With everything I got," he answered, no hesitation.

Mama June nodded slowly. "Then know this, you ain't just layin' beside a woman. You layin' beside a bloodline, a legacy, and a force that draws spirits and envy alike."

Dalton furrowed his brow. "You sayin' folks gon' keep tryin' to come for us?"

"No, baby," Mama June corrected. "I'm sayin' folks gon' try to come for you. You just got marked. Not by her ring, but by spirit. You made a covenant the minute you touched Lucille with love and created life."

She leaned forward, voice low and thick with warning. "You carryin' her light now and that light's expensive. You got to protect it. With more than fists and good intentions. You got to learn the work, the prayers, the knowing. Playtime is over, Dalton. You a soldier, yes. But now you a spiritual warrior. And your fight starts right here. You see some women you bed and not have to worry, but some women like us you have to be serious and constantly think about yalls soul. Messing over a woman like Lucille will have grave spiritual consequences, especially since she knows who she is and accepts her calling. She ain't on to be toyed with ya hear me?"

Dalton swallowed hard. "What do I need to do? I already fight wars, why do I need to fight unseen ones too?""

Mama June smiled. "First, humble yourself to the spirit world. Ain't no rank here, no stripes. Just obedience, protection, and truth. You gon' have to learn how to cleanse, how to cover, how to pray without words. And you gon' have to stop thinkin' you're in control. You ain't. She ain't either, Gods in control and your angels and your demons, cuz we all got em."

Dalton started to cry, Mama June got up and hugged him and rubbed his back like he was her son. She knew he had just had a revelation and break through thinking about what he has gotten himself into.

Mama June said, "I know you're feeling overwhelmed at the reality of which you've gotten yourself in son, but if you keep the faith in God and learn to fight like we do, you'll be covered and protected. But if you go out here in this world unaware of the dangers of sacred love and what will always come after it, yall gone fall. Don't let the other peoples devils, demons, and opinion attack yall you hear?"

Dalton cried like a baby holding on to Mama Junes apron.

As she prayed over him, the smoke from her cigar curled upward and faint outlines of ancestors began to appear, watching silently. Old eyes, tired hands, faces half-shadow and half-light, all witnesses to the covenant being sealed.

They sat in silence and she prayed over their union.

Inside, Julian was rubbing Lucille's back with a gentle but firm hand, working rosehip oil into her skin while humming an old Negro lullaby she learned in a dream.

Sophie perched in the window lightly making low croaks and admiring the beauty of this sisterly connection. She said, *Sometimes you find your sister in the world instead of your mothers' womb.*

Lucille lay on her side, belly glistening, wrapped in serenity.

"How's the baby feelin'?" Julian asked.

Lucille exhaled deeply. "Peaceful. Tired. Like she's stretchin' her arms into the world already."

Julian smiled, placed both hands over Lucille's womb, and gasped softly. In her spirit, she heard a faint hum, a psalm whispered by the unborn child. The sound wrapped around her like a lullaby from heaven itself.

She whispered, trembling, "This one gon' speak to God in her sleep."

Lucille's eyes welled with tears, not from fear, but gratitude. "I ain't never felt this safe," she whispered.

Julian looked up at her. "That's because you're finally surrounded by people who understand your light."

Dalton re-entered the shop, face changed, energy grounded. Mama June had lit a blessing candle and tucked a small satchel of protection herbs into his pocket.

As he stepped through the threshold, Sophie swooped from the porch, circling him once before returning to her perch. And when he placed his hand on Lucille's belly, Sophie circled him again, slow and deliberate, approving his initiation.

He didn't say much. Just walked to Lucille, kissed her forehead, and placed his hand over her belly. "I promise to protect both of y'all," he whispered. "Even from myself."

The skeleton key on the altar began pulsating three different heartbeats now, Lucille, Dalton, and the child, woven together like a holy trinity.

Chapter Eighty-Nine

Bones Don't Lie

The moonlight draped over the shop like a silk veil, soft and shimmering. Everyone had gone to bed, Lucille was resting with her oils and prayers, Julian humming lullabies upstairs with Rosalie.

Dalton, for once, was still, breathing heavy in sleep after the long emotional day.

But Mama June? She was just getting started.

The Secret Room

There was a room behind the herb wall. Only Mama June had ever walked inside. Not even Lucille. She entered barefoot, her gray braids wrapped in a violet scarf. Candles lined the floor. Lavender and ash hung in the air like breath. At the center sat a small purple velvet bag with gold stitching, threaded with strands from her own wedding veil.

She knelt, kissed the bag, and whispered,

"Grant me sight that sees beyond feeling. Let the bones speak what lips cannot."

Her hands trembled slightly, not from fear, but reverence. She untied the golden knot and poured the bones slowly onto the floor.

Click.

Crack.

Clatter.

No one ever knew what happened after her husband beat her nearly to death behind closed doors all those years ago. While her body was broken, her soul had crossed over. The hooded Ancestors came to her, stood around her bed like a crown of thorns and told her,

We cannot stop what's happened to you. But we will give you what he tried to take: your sight.

From that day forward, Mama June could read bones.

She circled her fingers around the spread, chicken wishbone. A deer tooth. A tarnished brass thimble. A small smooth stone with a single black dot in the center. Each had meaning. Each was Spirit's whisper. There was a rectangle of basilisk skin to throw the bones on for appraisal.

She narrowed her eyes at what lay before her.

"They'll last," she murmured, brushing over the deer tooth. "They'll last long and strong. Ain't nothin' gone break them two, unless she turns away from who she is."

She touched the thimble, steady hand. Teamwork. Patience. Purpose. They'd work together as a mortar and pestle. But her hand paused at the ring bone, flat, flipped over. "Mmm…"

Mama June whispered, "She won't marry him." Not because she didn't love him. But because Lucille belonged to Spirit. Not to man. Not to ring. Not to law.

Mama June swept the bones and snakeskin gently back into the pouch. She smiled, not in sadness, but in awe.

"She gon' love him like a wife. Bear his child like a wife. Honor him like a wife. But she'll always belong to herself. That's the agreement."

She kissed the bag once more and tucked it away behind the herb wall, right where it always sat. Then she whispered a final word, "Let no one question what the bones declare. So be it."

Chapter Ninety

Her Freedom Papers

The shop was quiet that evening. Julian had just finished sweeping. Dalton had brought in fresh wood and made sure the porch lanterns were lit. Lucille sat folding herb packets; her fingers scented with chamomile and lemongrass.

Mama June brewed tea, not for healing, but for speaking.

She had been carrying something. Heavy. Ancient. And tonight, the Spirit told her it was time to let it breathe.

"Mama June," Dalton said, noticing the weight behind her silence, "you alright?"

She looked up at him, then at Lucille and Julian. Her daughters. Her truth-keepers. "Y'all sit," she said gently.

Lucille took the rocking chair beside her. Julian curled into the floor cushion with Rosalie on her lap. Dalton stood respectfully near the door, hat in hand.

The kettle screamed. Mama June silenced it with one hand and poured four cups, peppermint and rosehip.

"Let me tell y'all how I earned this peace," she said.

The Night Joy Left Her Body

"Charles wasn't always a monster," she began. "That's how they get you. He courted me sweet. Took care of me. Made me laugh. Gave me the stars."

"But stars can burn too," she whispered, her voice growing soft. "One night, he lost a gambling bet. Money, we didn't even have. He came home drunk, eyes black with rage. I had cooked, cleaned, polished every floor, lit candles. He walked in, looked at me, and beat the joy right outta me."

Julian gasped. Dalton lowered his head and kneeled on the floor. Lucille's hands curled into fists making the skeleton key vibrate thunder so red. Sophie had to fly outside to keep watch of the watchers.

"He left me in that kitchen. Bleeding. Curled. He stepped over me like trash and went to bed."

"I don't remember nothin' after that... not physically. But my spirit?" Her voice trembled.

"The three hooded mothers came.

They lifted me from my body. I saw myself on the floor. I saw the sadness in my own face. I saw every time I said 'yes' when I shoulda said 'get gone.' They gave my soul a chance to rest while my body healed. That's how I survived." She sipped her tea.

"I woke up at sunrise. Could barely move. Charles was hungover and scared. Tried to act like he cared. He helped me to bathe. Said maybe I should go to the hospital."

"I said no. I healed myself and that day was the time I agreed to be a weak and broken woman with low self esteem."

"For a month, I said not a word. Just healed. Drank broth. Rocked on that porch. Watched the crows gather. Watched the bees come and go. One morning, I stood up, walked into that kitchen, took the same knife I used to slice okra with and pressed it to Charles's neck. He froze. The weather clouds outside turned black and it started to thunder and rain something fierce."

She leaned forward, her voice low and thunderous,

"'Hell will freeze over before you ever lay a hand on me again. I drew a thin line under his chin and his blood dripped slowly on his coat jacket and tie.'"

Dalton's grip tightened around his cup pissed at this point.

Lucille stared in awe.

Julian whispered, "Damn..."

"He saw what he woke up in me. I wasn't his little sweet girl no more. I was fire. I was bone. I was me. He signed the divorce papers like a ghost. Didn't say a word. Gave me a stack of cash and walked outta my life. That money? That was my freedom papers. That's how this shop was born." She smiled faintly.

"I did so many protection spells on him, he couldn't hit another woman if he tried. Now look at him, prostate cancer eatin' him from the inside. His little young wife don't know a single root or brew. She just waitin' for his will to be read."

Mama June stood up, stronger than the wall behind her. "I vowed never to let love turn me into a slave again. Never gave myself to another man. My body is mine. My power is mine. My soul is mine."

She looked at Lucille. "And you got a good man, baby. But don't let love make you forget who you are."

Lucille nodded slowly, tears catching at the corners of her eyes.

Mama June raised her cup. "To freedom," she said.

The others raised theirs.

And the bones behind the herb wall vibrated in silent agreement.

Chapter Ninety-One

Sacred Union

Dalton and Lucille sat quietly on the porch swing at his house, the warm breeze blowing through the screen door, carrying the scent of pine and honeysuckle.

Rosalie was napping upstairs after a long morning of giggles and toddling through the garden. Lucille had her head on Dalton's shoulder; his arm wrapped firmly around her waist.

"I don't want a courthouse. I don't want a white dress," Lucille whispered, staring out at the trees swaying under the sun. "I just want something real... something that's mine, not the government's."

Dalton nodded slowly. "So, no legal marriage?"

Lucille shook her head. "I want a spiritual ceremony. I want Mama June to bless us, to throw rice, to pray over us. I want to jump the broom like our ancestors did. But I don't want to be owned by a piece of paper. I still want to belong to myself." She looked at him defeated and confused.

Dalton turned to her and kissed the top of her head. "Then that's what we'll do. I ain't ever cared about what's on paper. I care about what's in spirit. And if you say yes to me in the eyes of our people and the Most High, that's all I'll ever need."

Lucille smiled, her heart at peace. "Mama June will do it, I know she will. She already sees you as family."

They agreed on a private ceremony at the shop's back garden. Just a few chairs, wildflowers picked by hand, a pot of tea for the ancestors, and one long broom with red and gold ribbons tied to the handle.

Julian would hold Rosalie's hand, helping her toss flower petals along the path.

The day arrived under a velvet sky.

Mama June wore her best shawl and blessed the space with smoke and salt. She whispered ancient words only the spirits could translate. As the smoke curled, faint outlines of ancestors appeared at the edges of the garden, their silhouettes swaying with the trees, unseen witnesses to what was about to be bound.

Rosalie, barefoot in a white lace dress, toddled down the garden path throwing petals, her laughter sounding like chimes.

Dalton stood proud in a crisp white shirt, Lucille glowing in a flowing earth-toned dress with her curls pulled back with a golden pin Mama June had passed down to her.

With no witnesses but their closest family and the trees, Mama June declared over them,

"You are joined not by contract, but by covenant. Not by man's law, but by the laws of the spirit.

As the broom sweeps away the past, may your footsteps mark a future strong enough to carry generations. May no harm come to what God has blessed. May your love withstand fire and flood. May your union reflect truth and not performance."

Sophie flew around the ceremony, circling three times and cawing with authority, as if confirming the blessing of the Three Mothers. At one point she perched on the broom handle itself, wings spread wide, blessing it before it touched the earth.

Mama June threw rice over them as they jumped the broom hand-in-hand, Rosalie clapping with delight and Julian crying silently behind her. Her sister was a married woman now!

In that moment, Lucille's spirit flickered open, she saw Dalton surrounded by ancestors and heard the faint hum of her unborn child, a psalm rising in her womb. It was confirmation, their covenant was already threefold.

Dalton pressed his hand to her belly, blinking in awe. "I swear I feel somethin' movin' already," he whispered, though he didn't understand what had stirred him.

The skeleton key was full of bright sunlight all day because the spiritual blessings were running deep.

Later at the fire pit, Sophie perched nearby, finally quiet, her wings tucked as if her watch was complete. The broom leaned against the altar now, no longer just a tool but a relic of covenant. The fire crackled, and the whispers of the ancestors faded into the smoke, sealing what had been witnessed.

Afterward, they sat around the fire pit in the garden, sipping tea and listening to old blues records. No papers were signed. No rings exchanged.

But Lucille had never felt more married in her life.

Chapter Ninety-Two

The Breaking of Bonds

The bell above the door jingled gently as Dr. Eli Green stepped into the shop. He carried himself with his usual quiet dignity, but Mama June and Lucille both noticed something different in his eyes, he looked tired, not physically, but soul deep.

Lucille was wiping down the front counter when she saw him. "Daddy?" she said, the word escaping her lips like a question.

He offered her a small smile. "Hey, baby girl. Thought I'd come check on you... and pick up something for this damn prostate pain."

Mama June stepped forward, already nodding. "I'll fix you a tea to ease it. Come on in the back."

As she prepared the blend, Lucille led her father outback behind the shop.

They sat beneath the old pecan tree where Mama June often hung herbs to dry. The breeze carried the scent of sage and wild mint. For a while, neither of them spoke.

Lucille broke the silence. "You shouldn't have come if all you wanted was a cure."

Dr. Green sighed, rubbing his temples. "I did come to see you, Lucille. I miss you. But... I also need help."

Lucille's jaw clenched. "So which is it? You miss me, or you're hoping I'll fix what you let mama destroy?"

He looked down at his hands. "Your mother... she's not right, baby. She knows. She smelled perfume on me. I think she's put something on me. Something heavy, dark. Like she's trying to trap me from the inside."

The skeleton key on Lucille's altar inside the shop rattled violently at that moment, its pulse glowing red as if it heard the truth before Lucille could even answer.

Lucille's eyes welled up. "So I was right. You didn't come for me. You came because you're scared of her. Again."

"No," he whispered, reaching for her hand, but she pulled away. "I came because I want out. I've met someone, Lucille. One of my old patients. I helped her through breast cancer. She... she helped me remember what love feels like."

The weight of his words crushed something in her chest.

"So now you're ready to burn the whole house down after all these years of letting mama silence you? Now you come for my help?"

By then, tears were falling from her eyes, hot and full of pain.

Her father opened his mouth to speak, but before he could, Mama June and Julian came rushing out.

Julian reached her first, cradling her shoulders. "Breathe, Mama Lucy. Breathe for the baby."

Mama June's eyes flicked sharply to Dr. Green, her tone measured but firm.

"What in the spirit did you say to her?"

Dr. Green stood silent, his shame on full display.

Lucille shook her head, still crying. "He wants me to fix him now that he finally wants to be free. But where was he when I needed him? When mama tore us apart?"

Mama June took her hand. "That man's been under her thumb for too long. But you don't owe him your peace, Lucille. You hear me?"

Julian looked at Dr. Green then, her voice like iron. "Don't come here looking for healing if you're still scared of breaking chains. You can't ask her to carry what you never had the courage to cut."

Julian helped Lucille to sit on the porch bench while Mama June turned to Dr. Green.

"Well, how you plan on telling Hattie?" she asked, folding her arms.

His voice was shaky but resolute. "I'm gonna ask her for a divorce. I can't live like this no more. I don't love her. And I won't keep lying."

Mama June nodded slowly. "Then you best prepare yourself. You know she'll try to scorch this whole town with her rage."

"I'm ready for it," he said. "She's losing her grip, June. I can feel it." As his words left his mouth, a hush fell over the pecan tree, and for a brief moment, faint ancestral silhouettes stirred in the shadows of the branches. Silent witnesses. Silent judges.

Mama June stared at him for a long moment before handing him the tea. "Then drink this. And pray you don't wake the serpent in her bones when you break the news."

He looked at Lucille one last time.

She didn't say a word, just closed her eyes and leaned against Julian, the weight of family secrets pressing heavy on her spirit.

Sophie landed on the table by Lucille as to ward any evil off trying to catch her in a weak moment. The balance was shifting. And even Hattie couldn't stop what was coming next.

Chapter Ninety-Three

The Wrath of a Woman
Scorned

It rained for seven straight days.

Not a gentle spring rain, but a relentless downpour that turned dirt roads to rivers and rooftops to drums. Thunder cracked like warning shots from the heavens. Lightning danced across the sky, illuminating a heavy, unmoving cloud that hung over the town like an omen.

It was too dark. Too deliberate. Like someone had pinned it there with spiritual nails.

The townsfolk whispered about it, called it unnatural. Said they'd never seen a storm like this in all their years.

Inside the shop, Dalton wrung out his shirt and dropped a heavy sandbag in front of the back door. His military buddies moved in and out like clockwork, stacking more bags, setting up tarp, checking the generators.

Lucille stood by the window, her hands gently cradling her swollen belly. She watched the sky, her lips moving in silent prayer. The baby inside her kicked like it, too, could feel the tension. She leaned close to her belly and whispered, "Don't you worry, little one. Mama's light will keep you safe."

Mama June stirred a pot of rosemary and sage on the stove, her face set like stone.

"This ain't no regular storm," she muttered. "This is Hattie. She's throwing a tantrum in the heavens and hades."

Julian peeked through the curtains, Rosalie on her hip. "She's trying to call back what's already been freed," she said. "But it's too late. Dr. Green's mind is made up. The tether's been snapped."

Dalton entered from the back, soaked through, his boots caked with mud. He leaned down to kiss Lucille's forehead. "Sandbags are holding for now," he said. "Storm surge is getting stronger, though. I'm staying tonight with my babies."

Mama June didn't argue. Her eyes hadn't left the bubbling pot. "She's mad because her magic ain't working no more. She's losing power."

"She's furious because she's losing control," Lucille added softly. "Over Daddy. Over me. Over the image she worked so hard to protect. Her programs shutting down."

Thunder shook the walls. Julian rocked Rosalie, who had begun to fuss. "It feels like the storm's watching us," she whispered.

Mama June finally turned from the pot, her face grim. "It is. That cloud's been fixed in place like an eye. Like Hattie's spirit hovering overhead trying to drown the land in grief. She's grieving the illusion she built and forced everyone to live in."

The skeleton key on the altar pulsed once, glowing faint gold, as if to remind them that illusions couldn't outshine truth. "This is her last grasp," Lucille thought. "And it won't hold."

Lightning struck so close, it rattled the glass jars on the apothecary shelves. Dalton reached for his rosary and kissed it.

"She's got hell on a leash."

"No," Mama June said firmly. "She's hell without a leash."

Sophie appeared suddenly, wings drenched but eyes fierce, perching on the rafters. She gave a sharp caw, mocking the thunder as if to say, '*We see you, Hattie.*' She shook her wings dry and settled, unbothered by the storm raging outside.

The rain intensified. The roof creaked under the weight of water and wind. In the candles' flames, faint ancestral silhouettes flickered, figures with bowed heads and lifted hands, silently standing guard.

But inside the shop, the women and Dalton stood united, surrounded by walls blessed, floors mopped with pine water, and candles flickering with the strength of generations.

Mama June glanced at Dalton. "Sandbags are good, son. But you gon' need to learn how to stand against storms like this in spirit, not just in flesh. Tonight, consider this your first lesson." Dalton nodded, the weight of her words sinking deeper than the thunder outside.

They were ready.

Let the storm come.

Chapter Ninety-Four

Prayers That Don't Move
Heaven

The rain clapped against the windows like fists.

Inside Hattie Green's house, the air was thick with incense, desperation, and the sound of Claudine sobbing quietly in the corner.

A Bible lay open on the table, pages trembling under the gusts of wind slipping through the cracks in the old windows. Hattie stood over it, candles lit all around her, wearing a long white lace robe, her prayer garment.

Her hands trembled, not from age, but from fury.

Her eyeliner was smeared all around her eyes was added darkness.

Her voice was hoarse from shouting.

"Lord, return my husband!" she shouted into the smoke-filled room. "Return what's mine! He don't belong to that woman, he belongs to me!"

She slapped the Bible shut, then opened it again, flipping furiously to scriptures she had long memorized but now wielded like incantations.

"God, I served you. I stayed in my marriage. I kept up my home. I deserve to be rewarded! Not humiliated!"

Claudine rocked in a nearby chair, her eyes red, a damp cloth in her lap. "Mama, it ain't working," she whispered. "He left. Just like my husband left me. They all leaving."

Hattie turned sharply. "That's your fault!" she spat. "You meddled in what wasn't yours. Playing with roots and tying up that man like he was livestock. You embarrassed me."

"You the one taught me how," Claudine snapped.

Hattie stepped back, her breath catching. For a moment, she saw herself in her daughter, bitter, empty, unraveling.

The rain outside grew louder, angrier.

They both turned to the small altar set up in the corner. Photos of Dr. Eli Green, candles, and hair clippings carefully wrapped in white cloth. Hattie knelt down and placed her hands over the items.

"Lord," she began, "maide him remember the vows. Make him see I'm his helpmate. Let no Jezebel spirit take my place. Let no daughter deceive him into forgetting his wife."

Claudine knelt beside her, her voice shaking. "Bring him home, Lord."

But Hattie's tone shifted, no longer pleading, but commanding. Her voice dropped low, "He is mine. He will not leave me. His soul will not stray." The room itself seemed to recoil at her words.

But as they prayed, the altar candles flickered violently, then blew out all at once. The Bible on the table snapped shut with a clap. The house groaned.

Claudine screamed. "Mama!"

Hattie's face twisted into horror. Her hands began to tremble as she realized something deeper.

Heaven wasn't listening. In fact it felt like something had turned its back on her.

All her sacrifices. All her control. All the image she built of being a godly woman with a pristine family.

Gone.

Dr. Green had chosen peace, and his spirit was rejecting her. Lucille had chosen truth.

The cloud outside grew heavier, not because God had answered her prayers, but because her rage now danced with the elements. On the altar, one candle cracked in half, wax spilling like blood across Eli Green's photo. Claudine swore she saw a shadow lean forward in the corner, faceless, waiting.

Her prayers had become curses, drenched in envy, not faith.

Claudine realized they had gone too far, and fear wasn't just in her mind; it was crawling through her veins like ice. Hattie noticed no ancestors came to their aid.

The silence of heaven was deafening.

Chapter Ninety-Five

Freedom Papers

The clouds loomed heavy, stretching over the town like a bruise that refused to fade.

Dr. Green had been watching from his car, parked across the street beneath the long limbs of an oak tree. He waited until he saw Hattie and Claudine leave the house in their Sunday best, headed into town as they always did, cloaked in pride and perfume. But for the first time, darkness was following them for the town to see.

He slipped the key into the lock and entered the house that had once been his home. Now, it was just a shell, elegant, silent, suffocating. The air was heavy with old rituals and bitter words. Hattie's presence lingered in every corner like a sour perfume.

He moved quickly.

From the study, he collected his medical journals, two pressed suits, and the framed photo of Lucille as a baby, smiling, toothless, and full of light. He grabbed his favorite leather-bound notebook, the one where he recorded herbal remedies and old prayers he hadn't dared to speak in years. He left the wedding portrait. Let her have the illusion.

In the master bedroom, he pulled a suitcase from beneath the bed and packed only what was necessary. The books on prostate health. The scarf the breast cancer patient, his new love, had knitted him. The keys to a brick house he'd quietly purchased under his cousin's name, hidden just beyond the edges of Hattie's long nose and longer reach.

Then he entered his office for the last time.

He opened the bottom drawer and took out the manila envelope marked "Papers." Inside were all the documents for the house, his new business investment, and his personal savings, everything separates from Hattie. Every detail accounted for, every string cut.

He stood for a moment, scanning the space like a man surveying the battlefield after the final war. The spell was broken.

Not just the one Hattie had hexed him but the deeper one. The illusion. The guilt. The shame of staying too long with a woman who had once been his peace and became his prison.

He didn't take the portrait of their wedding day. He didn't take the crystal glasses or the silver flatware passed down from Hattie's grandmother. He left it all.

He left her all of it, all he acquired for them over the years was now Hatties.

When he walked out, the door didn't creak. It closed with a quiet hush, like a sigh of release from the house itself.

And just like that...Dr. Eli Green was free.

Chapter Ninety-Six

The Whirlwind

When Hattie returned home, the air had shifted.

She stepped into the foyer and immediately sensed it, something wasn't right. Claudine, always trailing behind her like a loyal dog, barely had time to shut the door before Hattie let out a piercing scream.

"He's gone!" she howled, eyes scanning the vacant spaces where Eli's presence used to sit like polished furniture.

The study was empty. His suits were gone. The framed photo of Lucille had disappeared from the fireplace mantel. She stormed into the bedroom and flung open the closet. Half-empty. The top drawer of his bureau? Hollow. Even his cologne, the one she had bought him for Christmas was missing.

Claudine stepped in cautiously. "Mama…"

"He left me!" Hattie screeched, fists trembling, mouth foaming with betrayal. "That witch took him!"

But deep down, she knew the truth. She was the witch in this story, but hell would freeze over before she would ever utter those words.

She lost him. Every bitter word. Every hex. Every manipulation. It had all finally come full circle.

Hattie collapsed to the floor, panting, as if an invisible hand was wrapping around her throat. Her eyes rolled back. Her body stiffened. The ancestors had come to collect.

Claudine panicked, she knew what was going on but it still sent chills down her spine to the bottom of her soles.

Torn between fear and hatred, she ran out the door, jumped into her car, and sped to the apothecary shop, nearly knocking over a mailbox on the way. She burst in, tears already wet on her cheeks.

"Mama June... it's Hattie. Something's wrong. She's stuck... like she's not even here."

Lucille and Julian exchanged glances.

Mama June didn't hesitate. She reached under the shop's altar and retrieved her bug-out conjure medicine bag, stitched with red thread, filled with graveyard dirt, dried belladonna, and protective roots blessed in moonlight.

As Lucille reached for her shawl, her eyes flicked briefly to her seer's journal on the altar. She thought of Sophie's warnings and the Three Mothers' charge. This moment had been written long before Hattie ever cast her first curse.

She didn't speak, just nodded to Julian.

"Stay here and watch the shop," Mama June said. "If we don't come back in two hours, start a cleansing burn."

Lucille grabbed her shawl. "Let's go."

When they arrived, the front door creaked open like it had been waiting. The house was alive now charged and humming with energy that made even Mama June pause on the porch. Wind whipped around them, though the trees stood still. Claudine stood trembling at the door, refusing to go back in.

Sophie swooped down, circling the roof once before perching on the porch rail. She cawed three times, her voice sharp, as though announcing: *The judgment has begun.*

Hattie was spinning.

Not physically, but spiritually. In the middle of the parlor, her body stood frozen, but around her spun a violent vortex of wind and memory. Papers flew. Curtains snapped. Glass shattered at her feet, yet she didn't flinch.

"Sweet Jesus," Lucille whispered.

"She's caught in a spiral," Mama June said solemnly. "The ancestors and the Mothers done pulled the veil."

Inside Hattie's mind, a motion picture of her sins played on repeat, every spell, every whispered curse, every jar buried in the dark. The love hex she placed on Eli. The bindings she wrapped around Lucille. The puppet work she did to manipulate Dr. Green's mind. And worse, the vision of Sandra Merryweather's blood and bones, her spirit crying out. Every act of control and power now turned on her like a mirror cracking from the inside.

Sophie flapped her wings against the storm of memory, her croaks sounding like scripture, piercing through the chaos. Lucille felt the echo of the raven's cry inside her womb, the unborn child stirring as though in recognition.

Mama June stepped forward, whispering incantations and shaking the medicine bag with rhythm. She pulled out a black feather, anointed it with holy oil, and brushed it across Hattie's forehead.

"Let her go," she commanded the ancestors. "She's seen what she's done. Let her come back to herself."

Lucille placed her hand on Hattie's shoulder, a flicker of compassion trembling in her fingertips.

Claudine watched from the doorway, weeping silently completely devastated to see her mother in that state.

And then

Boooooooooooooom.

A gust of wind slammed the door shut behind them. Hattie let out a deep groan, like a demon being exorcised from her spine. The winds died instantly. The silence that followed was deafening.

Hattie collapsed to the ground, sobbing.

Lucille crouched beside her, brushing back her hair with caution.

"He's gone, Mama. Daddy's gone. He's not yours to bind anymore."

Hattie clung to her like a child. "I didn't know... I didn't know it would come back like this."

Mama June stared at her with steel in her eyes.

"Everything comes back," she said. "Even the dirt we think we buried."

Chapter Ninety-Seven

The Birth of the
Lightkeeper

The thunder cloud finally passed.

Rain had poured for days, washing away secrets and shadows. The air over the shop was heavy with spirit but light with promise. A strange quiet had settled in, the kind of silence that came before something sacred was about to happen.

Lucille was organizing dried herbs in the apothecary wall when her breath caught. A tightness pulled from deep within her, ancestral and undeniable. She grabbed the edge of the counter and let out a low, throaty moan.

Julian turned instantly, her eyes already glowing with knowing. "It's time," she said, voice calm but urgent.

Lucille nodded, sweat breaking along her brow. "She's ready."

The Sacred Room Prepares

Dalton had just returned from base. Still dressed in military fatigues, he hadn't even taken off his boots when he heard the sound from the back of the shop. His instincts moved faster than thought. He dropped everything and ran to her.

Julian and Mama June were already preparing the sacred birthing space. The front door was locked. The sign was flipped to "CLOSED FOR SPIRITUAL WORK." Incense curled in the air like protective serpents. The blue candle was lit. A bowl of holy water stirred beside a bundle of rosemary and chamomile. Rice sprinkled by all openings.

The wind chimes were blowing signaling peace and the glass blue bottles were warding off energies. A sacred portal was about to be opened!

Rosalie, now toddling and radiant, sat on a cushion nearby. As she rocked her little doll, she hummed something old she hadn't been taught. The sound was almost psalm-like, echoing words far older than her years, a lullaby carried through her bloodline.

The Ancestors Gather

As Lucille lay back on the makeshift birthing cot, Julian pressed her palm to her belly. She whispered low prayers as her fingers traced ancient symbols across Lucille's skin with anointing oil.

"I call the three," she said. "The ones who walk the veil."

And they came, three hooded Ancestors, cloaked in shadow and light, standing silently in the corners of the room. Their presence made the candle flame flicker.

The temperature dropped.

The spirit thickened.

Sophie swooped through the open window then, circling the birthing space three times before perching above Lucille. With every contraction, she cawed, her rhythm syncing with Lucille's breath, guiding her like a midwife of the unseen.

Mama June took her position at Lucille's crown, tying a red cloth around her head and whispering into her ear,

"You are safe. You are seen. You are not alone. The gate is open. Now, walk your child through it."

Lucille cried out, a sound that echoed from her root chakra to the top of her crown. Dalton held her hand, strong but soft, his other hand trembling on her shoulder.

Each contraction brought a wave of energy, rippling through the shop like thunder. The jars on the shelves rattled in time with her body. The skeleton key on the altar glowed brighter with each wave, humming in harmony with her labor, as though unlocking the gate between worlds.

Julian kept time with Lucille's breath, guiding her through the storm with the wisdom of ten thousand wombs before her.

"She's crowning," Julian said, steady and sure. "Let the light through, Mama."

Lucille's body trembled as the final push came, a sound, a scream, a storm, and then…

Stillness.

And then…

A cry.

Julian caught the baby in her arms, bathed in light, wrapped in breath and stars. One of the Ancestors lowered her hand over the newborn's head, blessing her with strength unseen.

Her skin shimmered like honey kissed by moonlight. Her eyes opened wide, holding memories too old for her tiny body.

"She's here," whispered Dalton, tears sliding freely down his cheeks. "Our daughter."

Mama June wrapped the child in a white cloth soaked in rosewater and held her high.

"This child will see through veils and know the names of things not yet spoken. She's not just yours. She's ours. She's the Lightkeeper."

Lucille sobbed, her arms reaching for her baby. She held her against her chest, skin to skin, heart to heart. For a heartbeat, the shop went utterly still. The ancestors leaned in. Sophie spread her wings wide. The skeleton key pulsed like the sun. And Lucille whispered the name that would ripple through bloodlines:

"I name you... Magnolia June-Julian Battiste."

The shop glowed with quiet holiness. Sophie sat by Lucille, Dalton and Magnolia to bless the trinity that is now in the world. Lucille had the skeleton key on the table and it literally shined as bright as the sun.

Mama June and Julian toppled over in tears. That was one of the holiest and purest things that they have ever got to experience. And this experience will always be remembered by Magnolias middle names.

Outside, the last of the rain ceased. Sunlight broke through the clouds for the first time in several days.

The ancestors faded into the candlelight. And Rosalie clapped her hands and said, "Sissy."

Her first words.

<u>The Ritual of Protection</u>

Mama June returned with her Coven Bag, stitched in white thread by the elders. Julian brought out the silver bowl etched with moon and sun phases. Dalton stood barefoot, holding Magnolia while Lucille sat with her legs crossed in the circle.

Mama June began:

"By bone, by blood, by salt, by smoke...

By fire that never dies,

By womb that gives,

By spirit that guides,

By name that cannot be erased..."

She poured black salt in a circle around them all. She burned mugwort and frankincense, letting the smoke rise above the baby's head.

Lucille dipped her thumb into anointing oil made from crushed rose, clove, and motherwort, and touched the baby's third eye.

"Let her be guarded. Let her be known by the light."

Dalton placed a silver key around her neck, a charm made by Julian for protection.

"She is the lock and the door."

Mama June placed blessed rice in Lucille's hands and whispered,

"Throw it in four directions, North, South, East, West. Let no harm find her in this life."

Julian handed Dalton a small broom wrapped in red thread.

"Jump it together, father and daughter. Bind your love outside the law of man, into the realm of spirit."

When Dalton jumped with Magnolia in his arms, the entire shop shook. Jars rattled, the floor hummed, even the wind outside stilled as if creation itself bowed to witness.

The light flickered.

The ancestors whispered.

And outside the shop, where nothing had bloomed in weeks, a single rosebud cracked open. Its petals turned toward the window, as if bending to greet the Lightkeeper by name.

Chapter Ninety-Eight

The Mother's Chain

The rain was soft that afternoon, tapping against the windows like a gentle drummer. Lucille was mixing peppermint and calendula for a new salve when the bell above the shop door chimed. A woman stepped inside, small frame, pale skin dulled by exhaustion, hair pulled back in a limp bun. Her eyes carried the weight of sleepless nights.

She clutched her purse to her chest like it was the only thing holding her together.

"Afternoon," Lucille greeted, offering a warm smile. "You're welcome here."

The woman's voice was barely above a whisper. "My name's Mellie... I......." She stopped herself, tears welling in her eyes. "I don't know what else to do."

Mama June emerged from the back, her apron dusted with dried rue, eyes narrowing as she read Mellie's energy.

"Come sit, baby," Mama June said, motioning to the counter stool. "Let it out."

Mellie sank into the seat, her fingers twisting together.

"My husband, Jacob... he just up and left. Said he was tired. Said he couldn't take two women fighting over him anymore. Said he was depressed."

Lucille and Julian exchanged a glance.

"Two women?" Julian asked carefully.

"Me and his mama," Mellie said bitterly. "She's been against me from the start. Says he spoils me. Says I make him weak. She nags him every time she sees him, tells him he needs to be more stern with me, like his daddy was with her."

Mama June poured Mellie a cup of chamomile to calm her shaking hands.

"Tell me about Jacob's people," she urged.

Mellie sighed. "His daddy was always working. When he did come home, no matter how much his mama cooked, cleaned, dressed herself up, he was never romantic. Never touched her unless he had to. So she leaned on Jacob. Told him she needed him to tell her she was beautiful. That she was special. She trained him to be her little man while his father paid the bills."

Lucille's stomach turned. Mama June's jaw set tight.

"So when he married you," Lucille said slowly, "she felt like she lost her... *companion*."

Mellie's voice cracked. "It's worse than that. I went to see a friend who knows rootwork. She said his mother put a love spell on him. On her own son."

The room went still.

Julian's brows knitted. "That's... dangerous work."

Mama June set down her tea, eyes blazing but calm. "That ain't love, baby. That's ownership. That's a chain made of spirit, and it ain't meant to be there."

Mellie nodded quickly, desperate, "Can you break it?"

Mama June leaned in. "Yes... but understand this, when you break a chain like that, the one who forged it feels the loss. She'll come harder. This ain't a one-and-done. This is war."

Lucille began pulling jars from the shelf, rosemary, angelica root, bay leaf.

Julian fetched the black tourmaline and iron nails.

"We'll start by cutting the cord she tied," Lucille said. "Then we protect you. Then we protect *him*."

Mellie took a deep, shaky breath.

"Whatever it takes. I just want my husband free."

As Mama June mixed the first blend, she looked Mellie in the eye. "When this is done, you need to decide if you want Jacob back for love, or if you just want him back because she tried to take him. Don't fight for him just to spite her. That kind of fight'll eat your spirit."

Mellie nodded slowly. "I understand."

Mama June's hands moved quickly, her voice low as she whispered into the herbs. "Then let's get to work. We got a chain to break." The shop grew heavy with silence as Mama June gathered the work.

She moved with a focus that made Mellie sit perfectly still, her hands clasped tight in her lap.

Julian lit three candles, black for banishing, white for purity, and red for life force and set them in a triangle on the center table.

Lucille laid a strip of black thread across the wood, then placed an iron nail at each end.

Mama June went into the backroom and returned with a small bundle wrapped in purple cloth.

"This is for unbinding," she said softly. "It ain't just the body that can be tied. The mind and spirit can be shackled too. That woman laced her will around your man's soul."

Mama June handed Mellie a length of white cord. "Hold this like you hold your marriage," she instructed.

Mellie gripped it in both hands.

Lucille placed a sprig of rosemary in the center of the cord, then sprinkled crushed angelica root over it. "Rosemary for remembrance of his true self," Lucille murmured. "Angelica to call God's hand in the fight."

Julian brought a small bowl of saltwater and dipped the cord into it, letting it soak for a moment.

Mama June lit the black candle and passed the cord slowly over its flame, careful not to burn it but close enough for the smoke to kiss it.

"This cord is her claim," Mama June said in a low, rhythmic voice. "This cord is her voice in his ear. This cord is her hand on his heart. We call it by name, and we call it out."

Lucille's eyes sharpened as she took the scissors from the altar.

"Mellie," she said, "when I cut this cord, you say his full name out loud and then say, 'You are free.'"

Mellie swallowed hard, tears brimming.

Lucille raised the scissors. "Now."

"Jacob Elias Turner... you are free!" Mellie cried.

The blades closed with a decisive snip. The candles flickered violently, and the air shifted, a low hiss like steam escaping filled the room. They all blew cigar smoke to the heavens and Sophie made sure to guide it out.

Julian quickly swept the cut cord and rosemary into a black cloth and tied it with the same black thread.

Mama June handed Mellie a small pouch of blessed salt, black tourmaline, and a key.

"Bury this far from your home," Mama June instructed. "It'll lock that spirit out. She'll feel the loss, so don't be surprised if she comes calling."

Lucille smudged Mellie with cedar smoke from head to toe, then poured a little protection oil into her palms.

"Rub this on the back of your neck and over your heart every day," she said. "It'll keep her words from settling in your spirit."

The Moment It Broke

As the last of the smoke curled upward, Mellie felt it loosening in her chest, like someone had unclasped invisible hands around her. She gasped, pressing a hand to her heart.

"It's... lighter."

Mama June gave a satisfied nod. "Chains broke. Now it's on him to walk free."

Mellie wiped her tears, thanked them each, and promised to follow every instruction.

As she stepped out into the rain, a flash of lightning lit the sky. Somewhere, miles away, an older woman sat bolt upright in her bed, clutching her chest and gasping for breath.

The cord had been cut.

Chapter Ninety-Nine

Visitors Bearing Light

The air in the apothecary shop was laced with rosemary, rose petals, and warm nutmeg. A small cradle nestled beside the counter, draped in ivory linen stitched by Julian's own hand.

Baby Magnolia slept peacefully inside, her tiny fists balled against her cheeks, lips gently pouting in dreams.

Sophie perched above the cradle on a ceiling beam, her dark feathers glistening in the candlelight, silent as a sentinel. Every so often she blinked slowly, her gaze fixed on the Lightkeeper as though guarding her from unseen shadows.

Lucille rocked gently in the old chair Mama June always sat in, a soft smile on her lips as she greeted another visitor with a warm nod. Since Magnolia's birth, the community had not stopped pouring in. Every day brought more blessings, more gifts, and more words of love.

Nurse Thelma came in with hand-sewn booties and a small jar of goat's milk soap. "She's got your nose," she chuckled as she placed a kiss on Lucille's forehead.

Ezekiel, the gentle woodworker, brought a carved baby rattle made of cedar and elderwood. "To ward off evil spirits and restless dreams," he said softly, placing it beside the cradle.

Mellie, her eyes brighter than the last time she'd come, presented a quilt stitched with star patterns. "To remind her she's from the heavens," she whispered, brushing Magnolias cheek with one finger.

The interracial couple from weeks before, now more vibrant and in harmony, came to lay down a small bouquet of peony and iris, flowers of strength and union. "She's the proof love can grow where the world said it shouldn't."

Even Lucille's father came to visit quietly with a basket of fresh fruit and herbal teas, glancing toward the back room where Mama June was resting. He stayed only a moment, eyes misty, before slipping back into the afternoon sun with his new wife and new life.

Julian kept the shop humming, grinding roots, measuring herbs, and humming softly as Rosalie toddled across the shop floor, grasping the edge of her sister's cradle with wonder. She leaned in and whispered, "You're magic, huh? Mama said so." Rosalies vocabulary was exploding daily.

Lucille watched her daughter with awe and a kind of quiet ache, knowing this was what Mama June had prayed into her bones. She sat quietly taking in all her blessings and thanking

God. Her mind thought briefly about her seer's journal resting on the altar. She promised herself she would write every gift, every blessing, into its pages, so Magnolia would one day read how love had surrounded her from the very beginning.

At sunset, the door chimed one last time, and Claudine entered. She brought nothing in her hands but something rare in her heart, positive words.

"I just came to say you did good," she said, nodding toward the baby. "And… I was wrong about you."

Lucille took her hand, nodded in return, and said nothing. Some healing didn't need words. Claudine turned and walked slowly out of the shop, a full flood of tears forming. She felt remorse but the deep seeded jealously was still consuming her soul. Sophie followed her out to her car and landed on the hood, cawing once, sharp and echoing, like judgment from the unseen. Claudine closed her eyes and said "God, why couldn't this be my life?"

She still failed to understand that her always focusing on other people's blessings caused her own to wither away.

Mama June's Silence

The next morning, Mama June didn't rise.

She had been slowing for weeks, her movements less sure, her appetite gentle. She'd claimed she was simply enjoying her "second stillness."

But when Lucille brought her morning tea and found her still lying quietly, eyes closed in prayer or sleep, something in her chest clenched. On the altar, the skeleton key dimmed faintly, its golden light paling as though it too knew the shift had begun.

Dalton entered behind her, resting a hand on her shoulder. "Let's give her today," he said.

Lucille nodded, and they let the house remain quiet.

Chapter One Hundred

Maiden to Mother

The shop was still blanketed in the warmth of summer's final breath. The trees had begun to whisper secrets through golden leaves, and the scent of cinnamon bark and crushed sage filled the air.

Lucille stood at the apothecary table, baby Magnolia snug in her sling, cooing softly as Lucille labeled fresh jars of golden calendula balm. Her hands moved with purpose now, steady, sure, and maternal.

Dalton entered with a carved wooden box, filled with dried lavender from the backyard garden.

"For the midwives coming tomorrow," he said, setting it down and pressing a kiss to Lucille's temple.

In the corner, Julian sang softly as she swept the floor, her presence gentle and protective. Since Magnolia's birth, she had taken on a quiet but constant watch over the shop. She said she could hear the baby's heartbeat from across the room, like a drum calling the next generation. Julian was becoming more aggressive and possessive with the ones who she loved and as an anointed ancestral mother. She laid a hand briefly on Lucille's shoulder, sealing the bond, three generations of women, one chain of light.

People still came in daily, not just for remedies, but to feel something holy. A vibration in the walls, the scent of new life, the presence of ancestors who seemed more alive now than ever.

Lucille, once a girl with questions, was now a mother with wisdom in her spine.

She had grown beneath Mama June's wing. But wings eventually lower. Elders eventually sit.

Mama June hadn't come out of her room that morning.

Dalton had knocked. No answer. Lucille had sent Rosalie running barefoot across the garden path to check. She returned silent, eyes wide, and whispered:

"She's still in her bed. She won't get up."

Lucille handed Magnolia to Julian and went go see about Mama June herself. A feeling coming over her body of something worrisome. She found Mama June propped against her pillows, pale but calm. Her silver braids were loose around her face, her eyes not panicked, but full of knowledge.

"You alright?" Lucille asked, voice trembling.

Mama June smiled softly. "Baby girl... you know when a tree's done blooming, and the bark starts talking instead?"

"Yeah."

"That's where I am now."

Lucille sat on the edge of the bed, took her hand, and wept silently. She could feel the tiredness in her soul for Mama June. She knew that she had lived a full life of wonders and was a walking historical library that many had visited.

Sophie had been stuck to Mama June's windowsill watching over her since Magnolia's birth. When Lucille entered, Sophie cawed low, as if giving permission for the torch to pass.

Sophie said to Lucille. *She's done being the teacher, it's your turn now to carry the wisdom, Mama Lucy.*

Lucille then cuddled up beside her in bed and Mama June hugged her gently but firmly and said "You're the best apprentice and daughter a woman could ever ask for in this life and for that I have lived."

Lucille sobbed because she was honored to experience a mother's love and warm touch. That night, Julian brewed her strongest healing tea and poured it into Mama June's favorite purple mug. She added honey, rose hips, and a drop of frankincense oil.

They lit candles in every room. Lucille read to her from the Book of prayers, her voice breaking but strong. Magnolia slept on Mama June's chest for hours, swaddled in linen stitched with the names of ancestors.

"You did good, Lucille," Mama June whispered before falling into sleep. "You turned your pain into power. That's how we survive."

Outside, the moon hung low and pregnant in the sky. Inside, Lucille stood over her mentor, protector, and mother-by-spirit. She pressed her forehead to Mama June's and whispered:

"You can rest. I got it from here."

On the altar, the skeleton key pulsed gold one final time, then dimmed, as though it had passed its light into Lucille's bones. In the corner, faint silhouettes of the Three Mothers stirred, bowing their heads as witnesses to the mantle being handed down.

And in the quiet that followed, something in Lucille awakened, clearer than a dream, older than her bones.

She was no longer just the maiden.

She was the mother now, Mama Lucy.

www.ingramcontent.com/pod-product-compliance
Lightning Source LLC
Chambersburg PA
CBHW060817120726
47909CB00006B/1963